DEATH AND THE FANBOY

BY

RANDALL J. FUNK

ALSO BY RANDALL J. FUNK

Death is a Clingy Ex

Death Lives Across the Hall

Death Wears a Big Hat

Death is Sleeping with My Wife

Death Stole My Ride

Death Will Be Brief: Joe Davis Mystery Tales

Published in the United States by Ghost Light Press, LLC

www.randalljfunk.com

ISBN: 978-1-7351016-1-3

Cover design by Ann McMan

First edition

Special Thanks to:

Samantha Papke, for her help in preparing the manuscript.

Ann McMan, for her usual awesome work on the cover.

Everyone who has bought the previous Joe Davis books and helped me along on this adventure.

For Anthony Crep,

and a wonderful friendship that began with the immortal

words,

"Excuse me, was that a comic book I saw you reading?"

CHAPTER ONE

When I was a kid, I loved comic books. I think I treasured them because I figured they wouldn't always be part of my life. There would come a time when I grew to be a man and put away childish things. Surely, once I had a job and a car and bills to pay and kids to raise and afterwork cocktails to consume, I wouldn't worry about The Joker's latest threat to Gotham City. Society, however, threw me a curveball. Everybody *started to embrace superheroes. These days, it seems every movie, book or TV series revolves around a superhero, a vampire or a zombie. Or superheroes fighting zombies. Or zombies teaming with vampires to fight werewolves. Or the affections of witches being torn between vampires and werewolves.*

Now, we could say this sort of rampant escapism is bad for society because it takes us further and further away from real issues. However, my concern is simple: it looks stupid. Grown-ups should not be emotionally invested in the love lives of superheroes. What kind of productivity are we generating when time is spent creating online petitions for the release of the director's cut of the movie because the superhero has a mustache in that version? It feels like the whole world has been sucked into a silly vortex.

My name's Joe Davis. I get paid to write stuff like that.

At this moment, I'm not enamored with my job. Yes, it's nice to be a thrice-weekly columnist for *The Daily Bugle*, a former indie rag that's gone digital. I'm glad my column, *Cup o' Joe* has turned me into a minor league celebrity. But when I find myself going to a comic book convention to get material, even I question my choice of vocation.

My buddy Mike doesn't share my qualms. "This is going to be incredible," he says as we go through the doors of the River Center.

No surprise he's jazzed for this geek fest. His comic book collection fills the entirety of his storage unit at his apartment building. Even Stan Lee would have looked at it and went, "Son of a bitch, get a life, would you?"

It goes without saying Mike's never read *War and Peace.*

Our path takes us through the concourse of the River Center, an event center in the same complex as the Xcel Energy Center and the Roy Wilkins Auditorium in downtown St. Paul. The X is a state-of-the-art arena, the Wilkins has a history going back to the Depression, and the River Center is…kind of there. Functional and antiseptic and totally forgettable. We drop down a flight of stairs and under a large banner reading *Comic Fest!* Tables line the floor, with retailers selling back issues and merchants hawking memorabilia at a disgracefully inflated price. Concession areas circle the floor. There's a large stage in one corner, with a curtain reaching to the ceiling on one side. The curtain bears the logo of the old *The Night Hawk* TV show. Half the population of the Twin Cities seems to be here, and most are in costume. Mike and I, however, are dressed like adults. Or a reasonable facsimile. Jean jacket over a *Flash* long-sleeved tee for me, black leather jacket with an *Avengers* t-shirt for him.

"I told you we should have worn costumes," he says.

I groan, inwardly. Who would have thought a man approaching his middle thirties coming to a public event *not* dressed in spandex and a cape would be an outcast? We slip through the crowd. Mike's big bulldog head gives me a marker to follow. I move delicately, lest I come in contact with these people.

"What's the plan of action here?" I say.

Mike runs a hand through his thatch of black hair. "I want to hit the back-issue tables. See if I can fill out my collection of Eighties *Green Lantern Corps*. Maybe we can look for some memorabilia. But not until I meet James Queen. Lars is getting us in to see him, right?"

Lars is my downstairs neighbor and a self-styled entrepreneur. He and his buddy Chuck have, against all odds, put this shindig together. It affords Mike and me the opportunity to meet one of the VIPs.

"That's what he tells me," I say.

Mike chews his goatee. "I hope I can keep cool. I don't want to embarrass myself."

A five-foot dude dressed like Thor strolls past us. "You'll be fine," I say.

I understand Mike's anxiety. Since all of Lars's ventures eventually go down in flaming defeat, Mike wants to take advantage of all-access before the inevitable disaster occurs. Particularly the opportunity to meet James Queen….

In case you don't remember (or didn't care in the first place), James Queen is known to millions as the star of *The Night Hawk*. It was an uber-cheesy superhero show that had a four-season run back in the Eighties, just before everyone started taking this superhero stuff seriously. Like a lot of people my age, I became a fan of the show in syndication and, later, streaming services. I remember the thrill of The Night Hawk and his sidekick, Wing Red, tearing out of their secret hideout in the Nightmobile. Back then, I took the show seriously because its general campiness escaped me. Now, it's kitschy fun.

Lars has somehow arranged a reunion of *The Night Hawk* cast and its producer. Then again, their IMDB pages don't show a lot of recent work, so it's not exactly like arranging a reunion of The Smiths. Still, they're all in one spot and the people at the convention are willing to overlook the crushing sadness of washed-up actors in costumes answering a series of increasingly stupid questions. And they brought the Nightmobile with them, which is just cool.

Mike slips past an overweight couple dressed as Superman and Wonder Woman. His stride is bouncy; something I haven't seen since college. He holds up the backpack he's carrying.

"I've got all the memorabilia," he says, "The lunchbox, the comic books, the video game. If I get James Queen's autograph on the stuff, you got any idea what that means?"

"No. But I'm guessing getting laid isn't figured into the equation."

Mike gives me a dirty look. We move from table to table, browsing back issues. Someone pops out of the crowd in front of us. It's a tall, skinny dude in a dark off-the-rack suit.

"Glad you both could make it," he says, clasping his hands behind his back, "Everything seems to be going well."

The dude in question is our buddy Lars. While he hasn't dressed in costume, I'm still surprised by his attire. Normally, Lars dresses like The Dude from *The Big Lebowski*, only less dignified. Now, he looks like an undertaker from Target. His quasi-pompadour has been slicked back. He tries to run a hand through it, then withdraws. Must be like dealing with a phantom limb. I give him a slight bow.

"You've got a good turn out," I say.

He does some mental calculating. "It should cover the cost of the hall, the appearance fees and other expenses. And leave me and Chuck a tidy sum in the bargain."

Mike claps Lars on the shoulder. "You're doing God's work, my friend. Now, when do I get to meet James Queen?"

Lars puts a calming hand on Mike's arm. "I deliver on my promises. It's a cornerstone to success. Follow me, gentlemen."

He leads us to the large curtain next to the stage. Lars glides, as if walking on air. Mike follows, trying to control his backpack. Lars's partner, Chuck, guards an opening in the curtain. He allows us to pass. Chuck speaks into his sleeve.

"Stork moving through," he whispers, "Repeat: Stork moving through."

On the other side of the curtain, a long hallway leads away from the stage. I look back toward Chuck. "You have Chuck wired to security?"

"No, he just likes to act that way," Lars says, "It gives him a feeling of, well, security."

Ah. That makes one of us. I get a look at the backstage area. Just behind the big curtain is an apparatus with a large hook hanging from a cord attached to the ceiling. It's a complicated setup, something I wouldn't expect from Lars and Chuck.

"What's going on there?" I ask, staring up.

"It's for The Night Hawk's entrance," Lars says, "There's a harness incorporated into his suit. We attach the hook, hoist him up and fly him in. He detaches the hook by hitting something on his belt."

Mike's eyes light up, like he came downstairs on Christmas morning and found a hooker under the tree. I do some math in my head. James Queen was in his thirties when *The Night Hawk* was on the air. He's got to be pushing seventy (if he hasn't pushed right on through).

"Have you cleared this with James Queen?" I ask.

Lars doesn't break stride. "It was his idea."

Oy. When I get to seventy (although there's no guarantee I'm getting there), I hope I have more regard for my health than to do jackass stunts for adoring geeks.

(Although, since my retirement account is the empty wine jug where I keep my spare change, I shouldn't rule anything out.)

"What about the Nightmobile?" I say, "I thought it was going to be here."

"It is," Lars says, "We have it all planned out. Tim Hefflin's going to drive it in."

Tim Hefflin, in case you don't remember, played Wing Red, the ever-eager teen sidekick to The Night Hawk. I'm impressed he's here. Mr. Hefflin wrote a tell-all autobiography a few years back and his portrayal of James Queen was less-than-flattering. Then again, the book was self-published, meaning only about eight people read it and most of them were Tim Hefflin.

Lars gestures down the corridor. "The Nightmobile is back that way. I need to check on Mr. Hefflin."

The corridor takes us deeper into the bowels of River Center, darkening as it goes. It's easy to imagine I'm walking down the entrance to the Nightplex—the top-secret hideout of The Night Hawk and Wing Red. The fantasy intensifies when we stumble on to the Nightmobile.

Mike stops. I won't be surprised if he starts weeping. "Holy shit. Look at that thing."

The low lighting makes the Nightmobile's appearance more dramatic. It's long and black; sleek and aerodynamic; like a Corvette on steroids (which it most likely is). Black wings extend from the back and curve up, looming over the rest of the vehicle. White stripes come together on the front, giving the impression of a hawk's nose. Gullwing doors extend from the side. A short, middle-aged guy wipes the hood with a rag. He straightens up when he sees Lars.

"I'll leave it to you, chief," the guy says, "I'll come back for it later."

Lars salutes and the guy walks away. I watch him go.

"Who's that?" I ask.

"Manny," Lars says, "He's in charge of the Nightmobile. Hauls it from town to town."

"Is he the owner?"

"No, a private company owns it," Lars says, "They rent it out for events like this."

Mike circles the Nightmobile like an ape around a monolith. "I, uh, I don't suppose I could…"

"Drive it?" Lars asks.

"Yeah," Mike says.

"No," Lars says. Seeing Mike's crestfallen reaction, Lars adds: "Just a liability thing, brother. If it were up to me, you'd be cruising over the Wabasha Street Bridge with it."

Mike gets a faraway look, imagining Lars's exact scenario. The fantasy is interrupted by the approach of yet another costumed figure, this one in a Wing Red outfit. I'll admit this one is a pretty good likeness. A mix of light and dark red on the tunic, the letters *WR* on the chest, a short red cape behind and a red domino mask on the face. Lars offers a hand to the guy.

"Mr. Hefflin," Lars says, "Your chariot awaits."

Holy shit. *This* is Tim Hefflin? The Tim Hefflin I remember was handsome, bright-eyed and athletic (if a tad on the short side). The only thing this guy has in common with that Tim Hefflin is the short side. A significant paunch strains against the Wing Red outfit. His hair is graying and disheveled. Even behind the domino mask, his eyes are bleary. There's a day's growth of beard on his chin and his face is splotchy. You expect someone to look a little battered when they've aged thirty years. But Mr. Hefflin's journey must have been rough even by those standards. He lists to the left and puts a hand on the Nightmobile. It seems to be holding him up.

"When you need me to go?" he asks. The old tinny voice has been replaced by a goodly amount of gravel.

"It depends on when Mr. Queen is ready," Lars says.

"Of course," Hefflin mutters, "Always waiting on *Mr.* Queen. Story of my fucking life."

Mike doesn't seem to notice anything untoward about Hefflin's appearance. He sets his backpack down, dries his sweaty palm on his pant leg and extends his hand. "Mr.

Hefflin," he says, sounding like he might genuflect, "It's a real pleasure. I'm a big fan."

Hefflin takes Mike's hand and struggles to focus his bleary eyes. "You remember me, huh?"

"Are you kidding?" Mike says, "When I was a kid, I wanted to *be* you. I'd run around the house in my Wing Red pajamas. It was great."

Hefflin half-heartedly pats Mike on the shoulder. There's the faint smell of liquor in the air. I wonder if he's safe to drive the fifty feet to the stage, let alone get *on* to the stage. Mike follows Hefflin around the front of the Nightmobile.

"Must be a real honor," Mike says, "Getting to drive the Nightmobile."

"I never got to do it on the show," Hefflin says.

"I know," Mike says, "Wing Red was too young to have a driver's license."

Hefflin blows air through his lips, making a razzberry sound. "*Wing Red* was twenty-fucking-five years old. He just looked young. No reason I couldn't drive the car. Except Mr. Queen thought it would make him look weak to have anyone else driving."

Mike isn't sure what to say. "I, uh…maybe."

"Never cross a star, kid," Hefflin says, feeling his way along the Nightmobile, "Not worth the effort." Hefflin turns away and mumbles, "Fucker thinks he can talk to me like that…"

Mike fumbles with his backpack. Lars helps Hefflin into the Nightmobile. Hefflin lands heavily in the front seat. He settles his hands on the wheel. Lars leans into the driver's window.

"We've got lights lining the route," Lars says, "We'll turn them on when the time comes. Just keep it between the lights and let the volunteers guide you through the curtain. As soon as you're on the stage, the parking place is clearly marked." Hefflin gives that a thumbs up. Lars pats the door. "We'll let you get ready."

Lars leads Mike and I away from the Nightmobile. Hefflin struggles to stay awake. Yeah, this will be a spectacular success. Lars takes a laminated piece of paper from his inside coat pocket and peruses it with his finger.

"I'll check with Mr. Queen," he says, "Make sure he's ready for your visit."

Lars disappears into the shadows. James Queen's dressing room must be nearby. Mike bounces on the balls of his feet, looking not unlike an elementary school kid who has to whiz. Much as I like to mock Mike (on this and other fronts), I admire his enthusiasm. On the comic book front, he's a true believer. Almost makes up for the relative lack of scruples in every other area of his life. Almost. I look in the direction Lars went.

"You notice how calm Lars is lately?" I ask.

"Kind of. It's not like he stresses out much anyway."

"But lately he's been…focused."

You have to understand what Lars is normally like. It's something between a kid with ADD and a small puppy you're trying to potty train. His whole life has been a study in enthusiasm over planning and follow through. Chuck only feeds this particular Frankenstein, providing ideas that are generally bad and follow through that's even worse. When I first heard rumblings about them planning this comic book convention, I dismissed the whole thing as yet another pipe dream. And yet, here I am, smack in the middle of the pipe. Mike, dazzled by the results, doesn't seem concerned about Lars's recent change of personality.

"He said something about having a mentor," Mike says, "Somebody counseling him."

"You know anything about this guy?"

"Nope." Mike wipes his hands on his jeans. "You worry too much. Look at all the shit Lars accomplished. This convention is amazing. Can't you just let him have that?"

I guess. I've gotten used to Lars having an unwarranted rather than a genuine sense of confidence. It's like everything I know is wrong. Black is white, up is down. Cats and dogs living together. Mass hysteria.

Lars emerges from the shadows and glides up to us. "I spoke to Mr. Queen through the door," he says, "I believe he's ready to chat."

We follow Lars through the pools of light. He leads us to a hastily constructed dressing room. The walls look like they've been put together from a kit that was written in Chinese. As we approach, someone is walking away from the dressing room. It's an attractive, dark-haired woman in her fifties. Her dark hair is cut into a bob. She holds a hand over her face, and I hear some sniffling. She blows past us without a look.

Mike, though, has seen enough. He spins toward the woman's fleeing form. "You recognize her? That was Ella Jones."

"Ella Jones?" I say, following Mike's gaze, "Night Girl?"

"You got it," Mike says.

Back in her day, Ella Jones was the face that launched a thousand puberties. But her inclusion in the show was somewhat controversial. When ratings for *The Night Hawk* began to lag, the producers figured a new cast member would be the tonic; something that might bring a female audience to the show. They added Night Girl and gave Ella Jones her fifteen minutes of fame. But it didn't save the series. It was cancelled at the end of her first season on board.

Not that Mike is concerned with that. "You see her? Still *smokin'* hot."

"It looked like she was crying," I say.

Lars slides up to the dressing room door. "I'm sure she was just saying hello to Mr. Queen. They're old friends."

"Right," Mike says, "If you consider being married for five years *old friends.*"

I only vaguely remember that. If I'm correct, the marriage took place after the show was cancelled. I heard something about their divorce, right around the time the disastrous *Night Hawk: The Movie* came out. I wonder what the tears are about. But there's other business at hand.

Lars spins toward the dressing room door. "Ready to go in?"

Mike's visibly sweating. "Let's do it."

Lars gently taps the door. No answer. He tries again. Finally, a voice emerges from inside.

"What?" is all it says.

"Mr. Queen?" Lars says, "It's Lars. You have the meeting we arranged."

"Meeting?"

"With the fan. With my friend."

Another silence, then Queen says: "Fine. Come in."

Lars leads the way into the dressing room. Mike follows (moving sideways to get his backpack inside). The room isn't large, but it's nicely furnished. There's a couch along one wall, and an ornate makeup table along the other. A toy Nightmobile, similar to Mike's, sits on the makeup table. An old-fashioned costume screen sits in the corner. The walls are covered with vintage posters of James Queen as The Night Hawk. There are a few lamps, thus sparing the occupant from harsh fluorescent lighting, and a few rugs on the floor for added comfort. A small table holds a collection of Perrier bottles. For a glorified shotgun shack, it's surprisingly comfortable.

James Queen himself sits in a chair in front of the makeup table, his long legs stretched out and his feet crossed. He wears a blue dressing gown, but his Night Hawk costume is visible. It's mostly purple, with an image of a hawk's beak on the chest. The cape and the cowl hang on the costume screen. The mask has the image of a hawk's beak on the nose. Queen is still lanky and appears to be in terrific shape. His light brown hair is graying at the temples and thinning at the crown. His blue eyes are intense and his smile magnetic. A few wrinkles around the eyes. Not a lot of sagging. (Although the chin is so rounded, I wonder if he's had some work done.) Queen fixes us with a look, as if contemplating our worthiness to be in his presence.

Mike drops the backpack and approaches Queen, his head bowed slightly. "Mr. Queen, it's a real honor—"

Queen looks past Mike to Lars. "Okay, first, I want to know what happened to the bottled water I asked for."

Lars nods toward the bottles of Perrier. "As we discussed earlier, I believe you'll find—"

"I asked for bottled water. Perrier is a sparkling water, you blithering idiot."

Here's the thing: Queen doesn't raise his voice. He uses the same cultured tones as normal. He invests his insults with the same degree of emotion I invest in ordering a pumpkin mocha at Glacier's coffee shop. The effect leaves you chagrined and disoriented.

Lars keeps his hands folded in front of him. "I see the error."

"I need Helm's *Bottled* Water," Queen says, as if Lars hadn't responded, "Do you understand the difference?"

"I do," Lars says.

"Are you certain?"

"Certainly."

"Because if you had understood that in the first place," Queen says, "I'd have the proper water here now."

With that, Queen casually takes a bottle of Perrier and throws it against the wall. Again, he does this with no trace of emotion, no sense that he is, in fact, throwing a temper tantrum. The bottle plops off the wall and bounces around the floor. Lars merely keeps his hands in the fig leaf position and turns to indicate Mike.

"This is my friend, Mike," Lars says, "I believe I mentioned him."

Mike looks at Lars, uncertain. Queen returns to his seat and steeples his long fingers in front of him. Mike again extends his hand toward James Queen.

"Mr. Queen, it's a huge honor," Mike says.

Queen barely opens his mouth, "Of course it is."

"I remember when—"

Again, Queen looks past Mike to Lars. "I also want to talk to you about the shit box hotel you put me in."

Mike freezes in place. Lars calmly slicks a stray hair back into position.

"I can assure you the Ambassador Suites—" Lars begins.

"Is a four-star hotel," Queen says, voice even, "You might as well have stuck me in a Marriot by the airport."

"The only five-star hotel available is—"

"The Kiefer Hotel," Queen says, "I assume you read the rider in my contract. If you want me to perform, you'll get me a room at the Kiefer Hotel. In the next ten minutes."

Lars takes a small pad out of his coat and scribbles a note. "I understand."

"After you get me the bottled water."

"Of course."

I'll hand it to Lars: he's dealing with the situation better than I would. By this point, I'm ready to take James Queen by the scruff of his semi-famous neck and throw him out the door. Or preferably *through* it. Nonetheless, I keep my distance, lest Queen get a look at the stinkface I'm giving him. Lars goes to the door. Mike again turns toward Queen.

"I really wanted to—" Mike says, bowing his head slightly.

That's as far as Mike gets before Queen again addresses Lars. "What about the Nightmobile?" Queen asks, "What's going on there?"

Lars stops, his hand on the doorknob. "Mr. Hefflin is going to drive it in."

"Before my entrance," Queen says. It isn't a question.

"Yes."

"Because my entrance has to be the climax."

"Absolutely."

Queen shifts the steeple of fingers to one side and fixes Lars with a questioning look. He narrows his eyes. "And you keep him away from me. Do you understand?"

"I do," Lars says, reaching up to straighten a pair of glasses he isn't wearing.

"Now get me my water," Queen says, looking in the mirror, "And my hotel room."

Lars practically floats out the door. The sound of the convention crowd briefly filters in. Queen gazes our direction. He opens his hands and flips them toward us.

"And you are?" he asks.

It might be the previous failed attempts. It might be Queen's sour demeanor. It might be delayed stage fright. Whatever the reason, Mike freezes up like Cindy Brady staring at a camera light. I'm waiting for urine to run down his leg. I nudge Mike with my shoulder. He springs to life, returning to full Gush Mode.

"My name's Mike. I'm a, a big fan." Queen doesn't react, as if he hears this sort of thing all the time. (And, his ego aside, he probably does.) "I had all *The Night Hawk* stuff up in my room," Mike continues, "when I was kid."

"When you were a kid," Queen says, his brow furrowing, "How old are you now?"

"I'm thirty-four. I started watching the show in repeats."

"Repeats." Queen looks in the mirror, pawing lightly at his face. "Repeats."

Mike looks to me for direction. I have none. I'm a minor celebrity in a medium-sized city. Queen is (was) a major celebrity all across the country. I can't begin to figure out the protocol. Mike reaches into his backpack and comes out with the toy Nightmobile. He holds it tentatively toward Queen.

"I was hoping you could sign this for me," Mike says.

Queen tears himself away from the mirror. He takes the toy car from Mike and gives him a suspicious look.

"Where did you get this?" Queen asks.

"I got it when I was a kid," Mike says.

Queen turns the car over in his hands. "Have you talked to anyone from the cast?"

Mike's face crinkles with confusion. "Just Mr. Hefflin. Oh, and we saw Ella Jones. But we didn't talk to her."

Queen mutters, "Lucky you."

He grabs a pen from the makeup table and cradles it in his long fingers. Mike rummages through his backpack.

"I've got a few more things," Mike says, "I was hoping you could sign them as well."

Ah, there's our Mike; completely oblivious to when he's pushing his luck. Queen holds up a hand.

"You did pay my signing fee, right?" Queen asks.

Mike stops rummaging. "My friend is in charge of the show. I thought everything had been taken care of."

Queen twirls the pen in his fingers. "Your friend isn't good with details. How can I be sure the fee is covered?"

If I didn't know any better (and I don't), I'd think Mike is about to cry. I can't sit back idly and let this go down. I stand over Mike's shoulder, facing Queen.

"Is the fee really necessary?" I ask.

"Of course, it is," Queen says, "People sell these autographs on eBay or at trade shows all the time. The signing fee protects me. Otherwise, people are selling my autograph and I don't get a dime from it."

Mike holds his hands out, practically begging. "I wouldn't sell this stuff. I wouldn't ever get rid of it."

Queen isn't convinced. I struggle to remain quiet, knowing if I tell James Queen what a complete shit he is, he'll never sign Mike's memorabilia. Then a voice floats in from the doorway.

"Just sign the kid's stuff, Jimmy."

We turn. Standing (for lack of a better term) in the doorway is a gentleman in his seventies, leaning on a cane. He wears a dark suit and his thin gray hair is combed back. His brown eyes are hard and fierce. Even though he's slightly bent, his height gives him a real presence. Queen narrows his eyes. Mike practically leaps across the room to greet him.

"Hal Murdoch!" Mike says, "I'm a huge fan."

Murdoch gives him a wan smile. "You must be, if you know who the hell I am."

Once Mike provides the name, I recognize the man. And his reputation. Hal Murdoch was the executive producer and main creative force behind *The Night Hawk* TV series. His name was in the credits of every episode, frequently more than once. He wrote and directed at least half of them. He also produced the ill-fated *Night Hawk: The Movie*, something I don't think he'll be discussing at the convention (and I hope nobody asks).

Queen looks as if he doesn't want to ask Murdoch anything on any subject. "I thought I made it clear you aren't welcomed here," he says.

Murdoch shakes his cane. "I'm a part of the convention. I go where I please. As for your dressing room, believe me, I don't want to be here any more than you want me here. But I thought we should talk. Again."

"I told you the last time—" Queen says.

"Always the class act, Jimmy," Murdoch says, his voice weary.

Queen ignores Murdoch and scribbles his signature on the various things Mike hands him. It's quite the collection: the toy Nightmobile, action figures, trading cards, postcards, even a (very) mini-Nightplex. Queen uses a silver sharpie, thus ensuring permanence on everything signed. When finished, Queen studies his face in the mirror. Mike stuffs the memorabilia into his backpack, then turns toward Murdoch.

"I'd love to get your signature as well, Mr. Murdoch," he says.

"It would be my pleasure," Murdoch says, shifting the cane from one hand to the other. He picks up the mini-Nightplex. "This brings back memories."

Mike's voice is high-pitched and nervous. "I didn't know you ever saw this stuff."

Murdoch is amused. When he's calm, his voice takes on a lilting, Pepperidge Farm quality. "I consulted on all the designs for the show. The set, the toys, the actual Nightmobile out there. With the toys, I helped them figure out where the secret compartments go and such." He flicks a switch on the Nightplex and a door slides back, revealing a tiny staircase.

Mike hunches over the toy. "The secret entrance to the Nightplex." He whistles. "Cool."

Mike has probably played with that toy a hundred times, so I'm pretty certain the "Cool" is evoked by the sight of Hal Murdoch playing with it. Queen looks over his shoulder.

"I'd rather you not have my signature and Murdoch's on the same items," he says.

Murdoch points the cane at Queen. "I'll sign what I want for who I want. You don't have any say in *that*."

Queen scoops up his own toy Nightmobile on the makeup table. He scribbles his signature on it and shoves it away. "Here you go, kid. The signature of an actual star. If you leave Murdoch's name off it, you can have it. I'll even personalize the signature if you can guarantee that."

The toy Nightmobile sits on the end of the makeup table. Murdoch and Queen glare at each other. Mike bounces on the balls of his feet, caught between the two of them. I contemplate running for the hills, leaving this whole sorry scene behind me. Before the scene can get sorrier, Lars glides into the room, clasping his hands in front of him.

"It's all taken care of, Mr. Queen," Lars says, "The bottled water is on the way and your room at the Kiefer is secured."

Murdoch's face is red. "Still a demanding ass, eh, Jimmy?" he says, short of breath.

"Don't call me *Jimmy*," Queen says, clenching his fists.

"Whatever you say, Jimbo," Murdoch says, a mischievous smile playing on his face.

Queen runs his hand over a small leather case on the table. "I don't have time for this. I've got to get ready for the show." He points toward the door. "I want all of you out. Now."

I'm happy to comply. Mike does some last-minute genuflecting as he scurries away. Murdoch turns to follow us. Lars assures Queen the bottled water is just a minute away. Queen tucks the leather case under his arm and looks at Lars like he's never heard of bottled water. Lars shuts the door behind us.

"He's a difficult man to please," Lars says, "But having him here is completely worth it."

"I used to think that, too," Murdoch says, "You'll learn."

With that, Murdoch disappears into the darkness of the backstage area. Lars follows him. Mike and I go back to the convention. We're quiet until we're past Chuck and back on the convention floor. If I thought Mike would be disillusioned by his meeting with James Queen, I'm sadly mistaken.

"That was incredible," Mike says, "James Queen and Hal Murdoch in the same room. I can die now."

"If you'd spent another minute there, you might have," I say.

Mike, though, is in the seventhest of heavens. He bounces around, moving past the back-issue tables. For my part, I wonder how I get myself into these situations. Stuck in a large room that smells increasingly of sweat and spandex (and those are just the people who've bathed). I admit, though, I'm a hypocrite. I'm not only into stuff like Batman and Star Trek and Star Wars and Game of Thrones and such, I make a living writing about that stuff. I don't have a geek high horse to get on. But I refuse to leave the house dressed like Batman unless St. Paul is, in fact, threatened by The Joker (or I'm with a chick who's really into Batman).

While Mike searches for more funny books, something catches my eye. I'm not sure I'm seeing it correctly at first. This is one of those moments when life hands you a juxtaposition. You see someone in a setting you'd never imagine them to be in. But I'm right on this one. My pulse quickens. I tap Mike on the shoulder.

"Is that Casey Mara?" I ask.

"Who?" Then it hits him. He follows my look. "Casey Mara from college?"

"I think that's her working the coffee stand."

The stand in question is sponsored by Jitters Coffee, a small chain in the Twin Cities area. I recognize the name, even though I rarely patronize the place. That has less to do with the quality of Jitters' coffee and more to do with having a kickass coffee shop right in my neighborhood (Glacier's, up on Cathedral Hill).

"That's her, alright," Mike says, "She still looks great."

"No doubt. I should go over and say hi."

"Definitely," Mike says, "Give her a brief visit."

I shoot him a look. His shit-eating grin is firmly in place. It's an old joke and I don't feel like getting into it right now. Mike looks in the backpack then he starts digging through it frantically, muttering "Shit, shit, shit." He's thrashing around, heedless of others, threating to make a scene. I grab his arm.

"What the hell's going on?" I ask.

"I forgot the toy Nightmobile," he says, looking like he's about to cry, "The one James Queen signed. I must have left it in his dressing room. I was in such a rush to get out." He slaps a fist against his Cro-Magnon forehead. "I don't fucking believe it. Once in a lifetime chance to get it signed by James Queen and I fucking lose it."

I don't know if I'm ever going to have kids. There are no prospects that direction and I can't say I'm champing at the bit. But dealing with Mike has prepared me for the misbehavior and tantrums I might face in a parental situation.

"Relax, alright?" I say, "We'll just go back to Queen's dressing room and get it. And hey, you'll get a chance to drool over him again."

Mike ignores the sarcasm (for the first and possibly only time in his life) and leads us back through the Sea of Geeks to the opening in the curtain. However, once we get there, the path is again blocked by Lars's friend and co-promoter, Chuck.

"Authorized personnel only," he says.

Chuck is an imposing guy, in his own weird way. He's a little shorter than us and a tad dumpy. His blonde bowl cut is brushed to one side, revealing a scar over one eyebrow. There's always a look in his fierce dark eyes that, along with the permanent scowl on his face, gives you the impression he's thinking of ways to dispose of your corpse. That said, there are two times when you don't want to mess with Mike: when he's been drinking whiskey and when he's determined to get a valuable collectible back.

"We *are* authorized," Mike says, getting up into what passes for Chuck's grill, "We were just back there. We met James Queen. I forgot something and I just need to get it."

"No can do," Chuck says, looking past Mike, speaking in a voice that sounds like a meat grinder, "There's an issue with Mr. Queen. Lars is taking care of it. They can't be disturbed."

Mike's voice rises, slightly. "Look, James Queen signed some stuff for me. I forgot one of the things. It's valuable. I just need two minutes."

"Authorized personnel only," Chuck says.

Mike squares his shoulders. Carnage and brutality (or a reasonable facsimile) are about to go down. I put a hand on Mike's shoulder and pull him aside.

"We can get back there after the show," I say.

Mike vigorously shakes his head. "Forget it. If I don't get that toy Nightmobile back, some asshole will have it up on eBay inside an hour."

"How do you plan to get back there?" I ask, with a due sense of trepidation.

He runs a hand through his hair. "You create a distraction. Get Chuck out of the way and I'll get through."

I nearly swallow my gum (and I'm not chewing any). "What am I supposed to do? Hit him with a folding chair?"

"I like it, but you don't have to go that far. We just do the old pick-and-roll. Remember?"

Sadly, I do. It might be more accurately described as the old *look away-and-slink*. We did it all the time in college. Though in that case, it usually involved Mike sneaking a girl out of a party while I distracted her friend and/or roommate and/or boyfriend. But we've never tried it with a borderline psychopath like Chuck.

"Why don't *you* keep him talking and *I'll* sneak back there?" I say.

"Can't take the chance," Mike says, "I don't want anybody getting their hands on that stuff but me. You're going to have to do the talking."

I could, of course, tell Mike I am a human being with free will and don't *have* to do anything. But that would be like explaining physics to a chimpanzee. Best to just fling the poo and get it over with.

"Hey Chuck," I say. He doesn't respond. Three seconds in and I'm already getting flop sweats. "I had a, a thing I wanted to talk to you about." Still nothing. "It's a…business thing."

That gets a reaction from him. His beady eyes narrow to where they practically disappear. From brief experience, I know this is a sign he's thinking. (And, from brief experience, I've never decided if this is a good thing or a bad thing.)

"Business, huh?" he says, his voice in the usual monotone, "What kind of business?"

I don't have a fucking clue. If I were Mike, of course, I would have already considered and thrown away about fifteen ideas. But I'm a writer. Give me a little space to think, some room for trial and error, and I'll be fine. Improv is not my specialty.

"It's just an idea," I say, "Something I was thinking about. You know. How you think."

"Uh-huh," Chuck says, probably assuming I've been hitting the hooch (if only), "What were you thinking about?"

I say the first thing that pops into my head. "You know the vendors at ballparks? *Cold beer here.* That kind of thing? I was thinking we could have them at movie theaters."

Even *I* think that's the stupidest goddamn idea I've ever heard. Chuck, however, gets this faraway look, as if he's trying to picture the whole thing. Mike slips past him, heading backstage. Chuck doesn't notice a thing.

"I can see it," Chuck says, "But how are they going to call out what they're selling? It'll interrupt the movie."

Well, I've gotten this far by ignoring common sense. "They'll wear wireless headphones. No talking necessary."

"How will they take orders? How will they know what people want?"

"There's an app for that."

"There is?" Chuck asks.

"There will be when you create one."

Son of a bitch. After years of mocking the nitwit ideas Chuck and Lars come up with, I'm feeding them one. I hope Mike's toy Nightmobile is worth the pain and suffering I'm causing the general public. Chuck holds up a finger, stopping my internal celebration/horror.

"One other problem with the vendors," he says, "They'll be wandering around. That'll get in the way of people seeing the movies."

"Are you kidding me?" I say, wishing I were kidding, "The way movie theaters are constructed now? The stadium seating and the giant screens? There could be a riot going on and no one would notice."

Chuck bobs his head. "I like it. I like it a lot. I'll talk to Lars." He gives me the fisheye. "What's your cut of this?"

"It would be enough to know I've contributed."

"You're not going to come back later and want a piece of this?"

I offer my hand. "I can fucking guarantee it."

His grip is disconcertingly strong. He goes back to his impression of a lion statue at the library. I keep an eye out for Mike. He returns a minute later, blowing by Chuck like nothing happened. Chuck, maybe lost in the new idea, maybe slipping into spontaneous catatonia, doesn't register his presence. Mike bounds up to me, beaming like a schoolboy just let out of detention. (A sensation Mike is probably familiar with.) He pats the backpack holding the memorabilia.

"Got it," he says, "No fuss, no muss. Which is more than you can say for Lars. James Queen was giving him what-for. I hope he's going to do the show."

"As long as the check clears, I'm sure he'll be good."

Mike gives me the stinkeye. He might be blind to the fact James Queen is a contemptible ass, but I'm not. The crowd is buzzing, ready for the show to start. We find a spot not far from the stage. We can see a small opening in the curtain for the Nightmobile, the *real* Nightmobile, to get on to the stage. Assuming, of course, that Wing Red doesn't drive the damn thing right *through* the curtain and into a crowd of unsuspecting dorks.

"This is gonna be cool," Mike says, his geek mojo in full force, "The Nightmobile in action. Didn't you dream about that when you were a kid?"

I did. I was never what you'd call a car guy, but the Nightmobile was something special. Who wouldn't dream of racing through the streets, cape flying in the breeze, knowing evil doers are shaking in their boots? I guess anyone who was dating girls wouldn't have dreamt of such a thing, but the rest of us had room to indulge. Speaking of girls…

"We've got a minute," I say, "I'm going to go say hi to Casey."

"Good idea," Mike says, his grin spreading, "Just make it a quick visit."

I stop for a moment. I'm tempted to turn back and say something, but there's no sense in opening old wounds. Besides, he'd just give me more grief.

I double-time it through the crowd. The general flow of traffic is *toward* the stage rather than away from it, so I find plenty of space. I button up my jean jacket, covering the Flash t-shirt. The crowd at the Jitters stand is thinning out. I run a hand lightly over my chin, wishing I had shaved.

As the name would imply, Casey is Irish, but she looks more Scandinavian. Blonde hair, big blue eyes, Romanesque nose. She's waif-like, with long arms and legs, yet she's pleasantly rounded in all the right places. Her smile is bright. She wears a black polo shirt and black slacks. A nametag rests over her left breast. Watching her work the counter, I'm taken back to those thrilling days of yesteryear when we'd hang out with our idiot friends at the various watering holes around Adams College. It's enough to make me forget our one regrettable moment. Hopefully, she's forgotten it as well.

Casey catches eyes with me as I approach and her face lights up. She stops wiping down the espresso machine and meets me at a corner of the booth.

"Joe Davis!" she says, taking my hands, "Oh my God, what are you doing here?"

"Suffering for my art," I tell her. I fill her in on my reasons for attending the convention.

"I should have known," she says, "I've read your column. I absolutely love it."

I give her my well-practiced shy smile; my standard reaction to praise or recognition regarding my weenie bit of celebrity. *Enjoy your success*, my parents would tell me, *but don't get the big head*. I don't know that I practice that, but I fake it very well.

"I didn't realize you were in the Cities," I say, "I thought you had moved to Seattle."

"I did," Casey says, "Got tired of the rain. Got homesick. I thought the Twin Cities would be more fun. I've been here about a month." Casey's voice is lilting, but with that old edge for banter. Just like I remember. "I'm glad to see you," she says, "I was thinking of looking you up."

That's good news. "Which Jitters do you work at?"

"The one on Grand Avenue. Over by St. Thomas."

Ah-ha. I live no more than two miles away from there. That presents some possibilities. "I'm on Summit and Dale," I say, "Over by the Cathedral."

"You should stop in some time," Casey says, running a thumb over the back of my hand, "I work evenings and weekends."

"I will stop in."

She looks at her co-workers. "I've got to get back. But it was good seeing you. Stop in when you get a chance."

Casey slides back down the counter. She gives me a mischievous look. I make my way back to Mike, feeling pretty good about the conversation. An exchange of pleasantries. Evidence that the past has been forgiven, if not forgotten. Now, if Mike could just keep his trap shut…

When I catch up with him, Mike's trap, and the rest of his person, is preoccupied by The Night Hawk's pending appearance. Judging by the buzz rippling through the crowd of superhero wannabes, he's not alone.

"I can't wait to see him get flown in," he says, "You remember on the show? When the Night Hawk would come crashing in on the bad guys?"

"I do remember," I say, "I thought Gemini City had an abnormal number of skylights."

Mike misses my sarcasm, though I doubt he was even listening. I turn off the snark and let him have his good time. It's the same thing I do when my nephew, Ty, freaks out about trains. It's easy to make fun, but hard to find something in my own life that brings me as much joy. Best to give the floor to the true believers.

Finally, the lights drop. A roar goes up from the crowd. Search lights play around the convention floor, as if looking for an escaped prisoner. A projection of the Gemini City skyline, seen countless times over the closing credits, bursts on to the curtain. The familiar voice of the show's narrator booms over the PA system.

"On a quiet night in Gemini City," the voice is deep and melodramatic, "the citizens little realize the danger that lurks in the shadows. But their sleep is peaceful. Because a beacon of justice shines in the darkness." A guitar line rattles like a machine gun, accompanied by horns and a cheesy organ. The crowd roars, recognizing the theme from *The Night Hawk*. "Two heroes, man and boy, protect the honest citizens of Gemini City. Together, they strike terror into the dark heart of the underworld."

The curtains part. Rolling drums from the theme song provide the perfect entrance for the Nightmobile. The engine roars as the car comes through the curtains and eases to a halt on the stage. Give Tim Hefflin credit, he's managed to execute the simplest of maneuvers. The crowd absolutely eats it up. The gullwing doors open and Wing Red, in all his paunchy glory, stumbles out. He weaves around to the front. The crowd greets him with a huge cheer.

The voice drones on. "With their rolling fortress, the Nightmobile, and the help of a dedicated police force, they fight crime in all forms. They are the Teen Sensation, Wing Red, and his mentor, the dreaded…Night Hawk!"

The music explodes with a catchy, throbbing guitar rift and full orchestral accompaniment (probably courtesy of a synthesizer). The spotlights come together on the ceiling. After a moment, The Night Hawk himself drops into view.

Lit up just so, the costume looks fierce and imposing. The Night Hawk stands aloof, just like on the show. His descent is just fast enough to give the impression he's dropping in on some bad guy's lair. It's enough to make me forgive James Queen his earlier truculence and get caught up in the general hysteria.

"This is it," Mike says, bouncing on his toes, "I finally know why I'm alive. I needed to see this."

The Night Hawk reaches the stage. Wing Red lurches to centerstage. For a moment, they're side-by-side again. The Terrifying Twosome. The cheering hits a crescendo, then quiets in anticipation of what The Night Hawk will say. Everyone holds their breath.

And nothing happens.

The Night Hawk's not moving. His head is hanging. Wing Red puts a hand on Night Hawk's shoulder and gives him a shake. Then he jumps back, his hand over his mouth.

"Holy shit!" Wing Red says, in a voice audible in Guam, "He's fucking dead!"

James Queen can rest easy. He's certainly the center of attention now.

CHAPTER TWO

A side effect of growing up and growing older is the increasing realization that people are just no damn good. It's even worse when we realize our heroes are no exception.

As far as I can tell, only two celebrities in history have been completely worthy of our love and admiration: Mr. Rogers and Betty White. Everyone else is open to charges ranging from Impoliteness to High Douchebaggery. It's only a matter of time before their found guilty.

The tough part is figuring out what we're supposed to do with the parts of disgraced celebrities that we admire. Do you pretend you never found Bill Cosby or Louis CK funny? Do you mentally erase Kevin Spacey from every movie he's ever done? Do you scrutinize the Naked Gun *movies and wonder what it was about O.J. Simpson you were missing? It's a slippery slope.*

Made more slippery when a celebrity has the nerve to drop dead in the middle of a show.

We're in an abandoned whipped cream factory on the wrong side of town. A young woman in a tight black and gold outfit, her hands bound, hangs from a chain that (we assume) stretches to the ceiling. The domino mask can't cover the strain on her face as she struggles against her bonds. Below her is a giant vat of white stuff marked *Whipped Cream*. Nearby, a fat man in a white suit struts across a platform, unwrapping a piece of candy.

"Struggle all you want, Night Girl," the fat man says in a bleating voice, "You can't avoid your fate. But don't worry. I hear drowning in whipped cream is a real…treat."

Night Girl (in reality, the mayor's niece, Diana Rushman) turns the struggle up to eleven. "You're not going to get away with this, Candy Man! Even if you get me, The Night Hawk and Wing Red will stop you!"

Candy Man and his henchmen (dressed in black suits and ties) break into belly laughs. Candy Man's jowls flap as he shakes with mirth.

"The so-called Terrifying Twosome have no idea where we are," Candy Man says, "My hideout is impenetrable. They'll never find you in time."

Candy Man signals the henchmen. One of them throws a switch on a garish machine. Night Girl is lowered toward the vat of whipped cream. She struggles to get free.

Sitting next to me on the futon, my friend Carol power-rolls her eyes. "Whipped cream and low-grade bondage," she says, "I'm guessing a guy wrote this?"

"Keep it down," Mike says, "Don't ruin it."

Carol holds up her hands in mock surrender. We watch my TV. Night Girl continues to struggle. The whipped cream gets closer and closer. Dramatic music builds, creating a sense of doom. We wait for the end. But we know it's not going to end badly.

Sure enough, just when all appears to be lost, the roar of a car fills the air. Candy Man and his henchman stop laughing. One of the walls explodes. Glass and plaster fly in all directions. The Nightmobile, in all its sleek and powerful glory, barrels through and screeches to a halt. The gullwing doors open and Night Hawk (secretly high school teacher, Tony Rogers) leaps from the bucket seat, his cape flowing about him. Wing Red (actually Tony Rogers's nephew, Roy Parker) follows, smacking fist into palm. Night Hawk turns to his partner.

"What do you think, pal?" Night Hawk asks, "A little of the old bang-pow?"

Wing Red raises his fists. "A *lot* of the old bang-pow, I think."

Night Hawk and Wing Red leap into action. Candy Man lingers nearby, cheering his men on. Night Hawk sends one henchman flying with a stiff uppercut. Wing Red knocks another senseless with a round kick. Night Hawk grabs another by the tie and whips him into a karate chop from Wing Red. Within seconds, the henchmen are wiped out.

From her corner of the futon, Carol giggles, her dark hair falling across her face. "Oh my God, you can *see* these are stuntmen! The Wing Red guy has a receding hairline."

Mike shushes her, frantically. "Would you be quiet? Don't ruin this!"

Carol's still shaking with silent laughter. Onscreen, Night Hawk and Wing Red stalk toward Candy Man. The fat man unwraps another piece of candy.

"Fine work, Terrifying Twosome," he says, popping the candy into his mouth, "but I'm afraid it's not going to be enough. You see, I talked with our mutual friend, Psycho Billy. He was willing to loan me some of his friends, the Murder Clowns!"

Four garishly dressed clowns fly into view, as if sprung from giant springs. They land in a circle around Night Hawk and Wing Red. The Terrifying Twosome stands back-to-back. The Murder Clowns draw a variety of weapons: swords, tasers, nunchucks, baseball bats. They flourish them while Night Hawk and Wing Red stand their ground.

"Looks like the circus has come to town," Wing Red says, clenching his fists.

"Indeed, pal," Night Hawk says, his eyes steely, "Time to fold the big tent."

The battle begins. At first, all four Murder Clowns are repulsed through a combination of karate sweeps and parries and good old-fashioned bare-knuckle brawling. But the clown with the baseball bat recovers and lays it across Wing Red's back. When his partner crumbles, Night Hawk spins toward him, leaving him open to a sting from the clown with the taser. Night Hawk crumples to the floor, struggling to keep his equilibrium. The Murder Clowns start laying waste to the Terrifying Twosome. From his perch, Candy Man's bulbous body shakes with laughter.

However, he's taken his eyes off Night Girl. She kicks her legs, causing the chain to sway back and forth. She looks not unlike a trapeze artist going to work. The path takes her closer and closer to an oblivious Candy Man. Suddenly, Night Girl wraps her legs around Candy Man's neck. She tightens her legs, choking the fat man, who spits out his candy.

"Give me the keys, Candy Man," she says, "or it's the end for you."

Candy Man pulls at Night Girl's legs but realizes it's hopeless. His face turns red and his eyes bulge. He gets the keys from his coat and hastily tosses them to Night Girl, who catches them in her teeth. While still holding Candy Man in her grip, Night Girl uses the keys to free herself. Her hands loose, she lets Candy Man go and drops to the platform. It takes only two spectacular kicks to dispose of the fat man. Night Girl laughs in triumph, then turns toward the ailing Night Hawk and Wing Red.

"Okay, that's pretty cool," Carol says.

Mike pats his lap. "See? What did I tell you?"

Night Girl leaps off the platform and tackles one of the Murder Clowns. She relieves him of his sword and uses the hilt to jab him in the stomach and then in the face. She ducks a swing from the clown with the nunchucks, causing him to hit one of the other clowns. But the clown with the baseball bat strikes again. He catches Night Girl in the stomach. She hits the floor, holding her midsection. The Murder Clowns gather around, ready to finish her off. The clown with the baseball bat raises it high overhead, a maniacal look on his already maniacal face.

And he gets clobbered with a right cross coming from out of the frame.

The baseball bat clown hits the deck, losing the bat in the process. The other Murder Clowns back off. Night Hawk and Wing Red stand guard over Night Girl while she gets her senses back. Wing Red helps her to her feet. The three of them are poised for a fight.

"Thanks for the assist," Night Girl says.

Night Hawk turns toward the Clowns. "We could say the same to you." He raises his dukes. "What do you say, gang? Should we finish this thing?"

Night Girl strikes a judo pose. "I'd say the odds are a little more even."

Wing Red smacks his fist into his palm. "No. I'd say they're in our favor."

The Murder Clowns charge. Night Hawk uses a right hook to take down the clown with the taser. Wing Red ducks a blow from the nunchucks and uses a pair of karate chops to take out another clown. Night Girl dances away from the sword. Night Hawk and Wing Red hoist her up, allowing her to take out the clown with a kick. The clown with the baseball bat takes a futile swing, brings the bat over his head and dives at The Night Hawk. Night Hawk deftly avoids him and finishes the clown with a left cross. Night Girl laughs, the Murder Clowns at her feet. The Candy Man groans. Night Hawk and Wing Red stand over him.

"Feeling a little sleepy, Candy Man?" Night Hawk asks, "Must be a sugar crash."

Wing Red clenches his fists. "He's just lucky it's not *me* taking out his teeth."

Night Hawk lays a hand on his partner's shoulder. "Agreed, Wing Red."

"Hey!" Wing Red says, looking around, "Where's Night Girl? She disappeared!"

"Just like always," Night Hawk muses.

"Where do you think she goes?" Wing Red asks.

Night Hawk muses. "Perhaps she has some secret lair, like ours. Speaking of which, I think we can leave this for the police."

"Into the Nightmobile?" Wing Red asks.

"And home," Night Hawk says.

With that, the Terrifying Twosome race to the Nightmobile. The music swells. The scene fades to black. Roll credits.

Mike hits *Stop* on the remote control and gets up to retrieve the DVD. It's the day after James Queen's untimely demise and we're all gathered in my apartment. It's a simple one-bedroom affair, located on the third floor of a converted rowhouse. There's a nice little living room with three arch windows overlooking Summit Avenue, a breakfast bar separating the living from the thin kitchen and a hallway leading to the deck out back. Somewhere around here my cats, Lenny and Squiggy, keep the place safe for democracy. Everything your bachelor of simple means would need.

I go into the kitchen for a refill of my coffee. Carol follows, holding her own coffee cup. I bring the pot over to the breakfast bar and pour us both a cup. Mike joins us. Carol turns to him.

"So, that's your childhood highlight?" she asks.

"Hey, I just like the show, okay?" Mike says, "You gotta spoil everything for me?"

We're strolling into minefield territory here. Mike and Carol dated for about a year, once upon a time. It wasn't hard to see Mike's attraction to Carol: laser blue eyes, long dark hair, perfect cheekbones and the like. And she's smart and funny. (Too smart, really, to date Mike. That's something I've never gotten to the bottom of.) Their breakup came as a real shock. To Mike. While he and Carol have maintained enough of a truce that we can all be friends, the old tension bubbles up from time to time. This conversation could dovetail into Mike listing *other* things Carol has ruined for him. I move to forestall an argument.

"Hey, it's like pro wrestling," I tell him, "If you love it, no explanation is needed. If you don't, no explanation will ever do."

Mike accepts that. I fish a can of grape soda out of the fridge and set it in front of him. If it's not a peace offering, it's at least a placating one. It takes some of the air out of Carol. She sips her coffee.

"Sounds like it was a pretty crazy scene," she says, "After James Queen died."

It was all of that. Tim Hefflin's pronouncement of Queen's death touched off a giant panic. People moved in all directions but weren't sure which was the right one. Given that everyone was dressed as a costumed character, it bore a strange resemblance to a climactic scene in a Marvel Universe movie. Ella Jones, still wearing her street clothes, hit the stage and ran up to Queen. Hefflin wandered over to the Nightmobile, as if he were going to drive it back to his hotel. Hal Murdoch stood in the wings, looking helpless. Lars (yes, *Lars* of all people) came to the rescue, hitting the stage with a collection of volunteers to form a human screen and preserve some of James Queen's dignity.

"That's not how I want to go," Mike says, sipping his soda, "Having a heart attack while dressed in a superhero costume you wore thirty years ago? Forget it. Overdosing in a hotel room while a hooker steals my wallet. That's how I want to go."

Carol pats Mike's hand. "I'm sure you'll get there." She sips her coffee. "Are they certain it was a heart attack?"

"That seems to be the working theory," I say, setting my *Writers Do It Between The Covers* mug on the breakfast bar.

Carol checks her reflection in the hall mirror and straightens the necklace inside her wine-colored blouse. "I feel bad for Lars. He and Chuck put a lot of work into that comic book convention. They actually pulled it off. Then something like this happens."

She's got a point. All of Lars's and Chuck's endeavors come to naught. But usually due to piss poor planning. This is the first time I recall plain old-fashioned bad luck rearing its ugly head. Or heading its ugly rear.

As if on cue, the front door opens and Lars pops into the room. His stride is more purposeful than his usual sashay. He produces a wad of bills from the pocket of his slacks and sets them on the breakfast bar.

"Here you go," he says.

"What is this?" I ask. I'm afraid to even touch the money. Knowing Lars, there's a distinct possibility I'd be trafficking in stolen money.

"It's the hundred dollars I owe you," Lars says, "Remember? You loaned it to me so I could buy the sound system for the haunted brothel tour Chuck and I put together. I'm paying you back."

"Lars, that was like three years ago," I say.

"I need to pay my debts. Hope this makes us square."

There's little chance of that. If I added up all the booze Lars has mooched from me over time, he'd still owe me enough money to mortgage a house. But I'll take what I can get. Mike studies the cash, probably wondering how much Lars owes *him*.

"Where did you get it?" Mike asks.

"Profits off the comic book convention," Lars says, sounding matter of fact, "The final accounting has yet to be done, but it should prove to be very lucrative."

Carol's neatly trimmed eyebrows go up. "Even with James Queen dying?"

"I don't want to be mercenary about it," Lars says, "but Mr. Queen had the good taste to pass away *after* the customers had paid their admission fees."

"A pro to the end," I say.

"Say what you will," Mike muses, "death makes a hell of a floor show."

Carol turns to me. "That would make a good book title."

"I can't see it," I say, turning to Lars. "I appreciate you paying me back. Even if it was kind of unnecessary."

"I need to pay my debts," Lars says, "My mentor assures me this is the right way to do these things."

I pocket the cash. "Ah, yes, the famous mentor. Who is this guy?"

He flinches, as if I've blasphemed. "This *guy*, as you so casually put it," Lars says, "is Mr. Bobby Vitality. A wise and learned man."

At the mention of the mentor's name, all of us—Lars, excepted, of course—struggle not to laugh. Lars remains the picture of dignity and grace (a real testament to Mr. Vitality's work). I chew the inside of my cheek.

"Bobby Vitality," I say, "Guessing that's not his given name."

"Probably not," Lars says, "But that's of little concern. Bobby Vitality recreated himself from whatever he was before. Just as he's teaching me to do now."

I, personally, would have chosen a different name than Bobby Vitality (Maximum Funk springs to mind) but the idea of recreating yourself isn't bad. It's certainly having a good effect on Lars. Best to just let him go at his own pace.

"It looks like it's working out so far," I say.

"It is," Lars says, his eyes lighting up, "You should meet him. It would be good for you."

I'm not certain how to respond. I don't want to offend Lars, but I've never felt like I'm drifting through life, purposeless. I have my column, my weenie bit of celebrity, my cats…um, my fantasy football league. A rich, full life.

"I'll think about it," I say, using the same vague line my mother would use when she didn't want to tell me *no* and hoped I would eventually forget what I was asking for.

Usually, Lars would accompany such a thing with a smack of his hands, maybe a little war whoop, and assurances I would not regret the thing I will almost certainly regret. This time, though, he just slips his hands into his pockets.

"I certainly hope you'll consider it," he says, simply, "Mr. Vitality has been a great help to me. He's even consulting me on the memorial for James Queen."

Mike turns toward Lars. "A memorial? When?"

"Or more to the point," I say, "why?"

"*When* is yet to be determined," Lars says, briskly, "I'm looking into available venues. *Why* is because James Queen has no family to speak of and he should be honored. On a personal note, my last interaction with Mr. Queen was not, um, cordial. It would be setting things right, spiritually, if I did this for him. Serve him in death in a way that I was never able to adequately serve him in life."

"Mike said he was reading you the riot act backstage," I say, "Just before the, uh, incident."

Lars shakes his head, mournfully. "He wanted to make sure everyone stayed out of his dressing room. I assured him I would take care of everything, but I don't think he believed me. I think he had lost faith in me. It's a regret."

I'm tempted to comfort Lars by telling him there was very little he could have done to placate a demanding ass like James Queen. But he wouldn't believe me, and Mike would get his undies in a twist at the blasphemy. Lars turns on his heel and glides toward the door.

"If you'll excuse me," he says, "I have to attend to the stopped drain in Mrs. Conner's apartment."

I nearly fall off my stool. "You're doing superintendent work?"

Lars looks confused that I'm asking. "It's my job, isn't it? You all have a good day."

Yep. I'm perplexed. Not concerned, mind you, just perplexed. Lars is the building's superintendent, but he works about as often as George R.R. Martin puts out a book. This must be the influence of the advisor. Strange. Lars's life has been built on a solid foundation of listening to nobody but Chuck and the voices in his head. Now he's not only listening to someone else, he's even acting on it. It's disquieting. Carol checks her phone and takes a hasty sip of her coffee.

"I need to get going," she says, "I'm meeting some people."

"I was wondering why you were dressed up on a Saturday."

Truth be told, Carol is dressed up all the time, at least by the low standards of our group. The occasional black t-shirt with jeans is as dressed down as she gets. Carol rests her arms on the breakfast bar.

"I'm going to a bachelorette party," she says, "For an old boyfriend."

I open my mouth to reply, then catch what Carol said. "Bachelorette…you mean for your old boyfriend's fiancé?"

"No," she says, looking exceedingly pleased, "I mean for the boyfriend himself."

"Bachelorette for the…" Then it hits me. "Oh…so he…"

"Was Christopher when we dated," Carol says, "And now her name is Christine."

Mike throws a look at Carol. "How long did you guys date?"

Carol flits a hand. "Just a couple of months and it was years ago. We've been friends since then. She's a great person. She just needed to…figure out a few things."

Don't we all? I sip my covfefe. "Where's the party going to be?"

"A bunch of places," Carol says, grabbing her purse off the futon, "We're all going barhopping in downtown Minneapolis."

I put on my best Ward Cleaver voice. "Now, you be careful when you're down there, young lady. I've heard about how these bachelorette parties can be. Have a sober ride, don't talk to strange men, practice safe sex, each your vegetables and all the rest of that shit."

Carol gives me a mock salute. "What about you?" she asks, "What have you got going?"

"Nothing much," I say, staring at my coffee cup, "Just thought I'd go to Jitters."

Carol's face scrunches up. "What about Glacier's? You two having a fight?"

"No," I say, "Just figured I'd check out a different place, that's all."

I'm not doing a good job of concealing my motives. It's hard enough to lie to Carol, given the sodium pentothal qualities of her eyes. It's worse when Mike is more than willing to rat me out.

"There's someone he wants to see," Mike says, turning to me, "You're going to see Casey, right?"

Carol returns to the breakfast bar. "Who's Casey?"

I set the coffee aside. "Don't ask." Then I turn to Mike. "Don't tell."

Mike speaks out of the corner of his mouth, "It's that timely humor of his. That's why he makes the big bucks."

"*Not*," Carol says.

The two of them giggle like Wayne and Garth. All we need are some guys in flannel shirts and Bill Clinton and the whole Nineties party will be complete. I use my coffee cup to point to the front door.

"Weren't you two going someplace" I say.

"I was," Carol says.

"I wasn't," Mike says.

I again gesture toward the door. "Feel free to go anyway."

Carol grabs her coat and moves to the front door. Mike pushes his grape soda aside and joins her. She lowers her voice.

"You'll tell me all about it?" she asks.

"Oh yeah," he says.

I put my coffee cup down on the breakfast bar with enough authority to get their attention. Mike catches eyes with me. It only takes the look to tell him he's going to keep quiet. See, this is the thing with Mike: I have more blackmail info on him than he could ever have on me. Mike grew up a military brat; the scion of two over-protective parents. Once he got to college and was no longer under their eternal gaze, he not only embraced his freedom, he locked it in the basement and told it things like, "It puts the lotion in the basket." I witnessed all of it. And remember all of it. Mike's shoulders sag.

"Forget it," he tells Carol, "I have to respect Joe's privacy."

"You have to?"

"I *have* to," Mike says, glaring at me.

Carol puts her hands up, dismissing the whole thing. She flips open the front door. "Fine, keep it to yourselves. But you know I'll find out, sooner or later."

That's what frightens me.

***

It's a beautiful night to visit Jitters, one of those ridiculously pleasant fall evenings, warm and clear. It's what they call Indian Summer. (At least, they used to. I should check into whether that's still the accepted nomenclature.) It's a nice drive down Summit Avenue. St. Thomas University, in all its sandstone brick and old money glory, appears on my right. I turn my Saturn Ion toward Grand Avenue, just a block away, and glide into the parking lot for Jitters.

As I head inside, I check my look in the window next to the door. My hair is tousled just so; neither messy nor overly coiffed. My black t-shirt is wrinkle-free, and the jean jacket is just worn enough. Check, one-two. Ready to go.

Jitters is a nice little place. Clean faux-marble floor. Dark wood tables and straight back chairs. Atmospheric lighting. A long bar next to the cash register. A coffee grinder bearing a strange resemblance to an old locomotive dominates one wall. (My nephew, Ty, would love this.) It gives the place a little character. It could use it. Everything's fine, just a little…antiseptic. Like *cozy* as defined by a think tank. It's nothing as genuine as Glacier's, my neighborhood coffee shop. Then again, I'm not here for the coffee or the atmosphere.

Casey is behind the bar, looking at her phone, when I walk in. She's wearing a red polka dot summer dress dropped over a white long-sleeved tee. The shorter hair takes some getting used to, but it's rapidly growing on me. The place is sleepy, so I certainly won't hold the phone gazing against her. If there weren't five colleges in the vicinity, the place probably wouldn't be open this late on a Saturday. But there are a few tables of college kids, engaged in some sort of deep conversation. (Beer bong construction, if their college experience is anything like mine was.) Casey looks up from the phone. She breaks into a bright smile.

"Hey you," she says, coming down to my side of the bar, "Come here. Let me give you a proper hug."

"Works for me," I say.

We exchange the best embrace we can considering the metal barrier between us. Casey waves a hand toward an empty stool. She wipes down the bar, more as a show of working than anything.

"What brings you by?" she asks.

"Thought I'd grab some coffee. Say hi."

"Glad you did. Hang on just a second."

Casey slides over to the three large metal coffee pots and pours a dark roast into a large mug. She sets it in front of me and slides the sugar shaker my direction. I can't help smiling.

"You remembered," I say.

She squares me with a coy look, just like the old days. "We had coffee often enough at school. And lunch. You still got a thing for chimichangas?"

"Lost my taste for them, I'm afraid."

"Probably for the best."

That leads us into the obligatory chat about the old days. I update her on most of the guys I used to hang around with. She does the same with her part of the crew. She briefly mentions her time in Seattle, and I talk about moving to the Twin Cities and getting settled. We feel our way into the conversation, which happens when you haven't seen someone in more than ten years. And when you're dancing around some past unpleasantness.

I sip my dark roast (which is fine, but not nearly as rich as the stuff at Glacier's). "I was surprised to see you yesterday."

Casey tucks a hand below her chin and lowers her voice, as if making a confession. "It wasn't exactly my kind of crowd." Then her eyes get wide, the same kind of emotional turn-on-a-dime she'd do back in the day. "Wasn't that nuts? What happened to that Night Hawk guy?"

"It was all of that."

"Do they know what caused it?" Casey asks.

"I'm hearing a heart attack. No one knows for sure, though."

"At least you get a story out of it."

"I suppose. Not generally the kind of story I prefer, though."

She gives me a knowing look. "You were there to make fun of them, right?"

"Not *The Night Hawk* cast. Just the convention folks."

"And they gave you a *ton* of material to work with?"

"It was the gift that kept on giving."

We're both laughing. Then we realize it's not polite to laugh about a man's death and we stop at the same time. Then start again when we realize we've had the same thought. Yep. The same conversational *simpatico* we had in the old days. Casey tries to assume a serious look.

"It's too bad, though," she says, "It would have made a great column. Like the one you did on your friend from high school. Steve Nylund?"

"You read my column?"

"Absolutely," Casey says. Then she looks down, embarrassed. "I looked you up a few years ago. Just wanted to see what you were up to. I found your column. I've read all of them."

I'm flattered. Before I comment, though, one of the college kids approaches the counter, looking for a refill. Casey excuses herself. Her walk has a bit of sashay in it, just like the old days. This is nice. Casey and I were always great pals and I enjoyed chatting with her. She makes her way back. I toy with my coffee mug.

"How's it feel to be back in the Cities?" I ask.

"I'm still getting used to it." She gives me a warm look. "It's nice to see a friendly face."

"That's what it's here for." I'm aware of how close we are. "What time do you get out of here?"

"Ten. A little after. It takes me about fifteen minutes to clean and lock up."

"You want to grab a drink? There's a great little hangout in my neighborhood."

"I'd like that." She taps my coffee mug. "You want me to top that off?"

"Sounds good."

She takes my mug back over to the coffee machine. The evening is going exactly how I hoped. My phone buzzes in my pocket. I take it out, annoyed, wondering which soulless bastard would call me at a time like this. It's Mike. (Well, ask a silly question…) I debate answering. I do it; to tell him off if nothing else. The second he hears my voice, though, Mike starts babbling. When I get what he's saying, I abandon any thought of telling him off. I ring off just as Casey returns with my coffee.

"I hate to do this," I say, getting up, "But can I get a raincheck on the drink?"

She looks confused. "Sure. Is something…?"

"Going on? Definitely. Mike just got attacked."

CHAPTER THREE

My mom once said the secret to a good relationship is to be best friends with your significant other. Looking at my choice of best friends, I get a clue as to why my romantic relationships have turned out the way they have.

Friends can get in the way of a decent relationship and vice-versa. Many of my girlfriends have developed mysterious illnesses to avoid hanging out with my friends, particularly Mike. (One girl claimed to have diarrhea just to steer clear of Mike. Sort of took the sting out of the relationship.) But one must tread carefully. When the relationship is over, the friends will still be there. To constantly remind you what a shrew the girlfriend was and to ask what you ever saw in her.

In a perfect world, of course, I would have that drink with Casey. But when your best friend calls you up in a blind panic because he's been attacked, that is the time for all good men to come to the aid of the party. So, off I go. It takes ten minutes to get to Mike's apartment building. Thankfully, he's still among the living.

"'Bout damn time," he says, answering his buzzer. Still living and friendly as ever.

Mike's building is among the converted factories that make up Lowertown. It's not a bad neighborhood, what with the beautiful Union Depot station and the St. Paul Saints home field nearby. It's just a little…industrial for my taste. I prefer a real neighborhood. The building itself has a certain charm, with its exposed brickwork and thick support beams. Given Mike's uncertain employment status these days, I wonder how much longer he can afford living here. I make my way up to his fourth-floor apartment

Mike whips open the door as soon as I knock. "This is fucked up," he says. He stops and looks at me. "You get dressed up for Casey?"

"How can you tell?"

"Sure, because I just met you last week."

I follow Mike into the apartment. It's a one-bedroom-plus place. (The "plus" is a raised area near the front door that could be used as a study. If Mike didn't use it to store comic books.) Its got your basic furniture and gets cleaned every change of season. Mike, never the calmest soul, paces the carpeted floor (or at least the parts that don't require him to step over anything too large). He drinks deeply from a bottle of Grand Brewing Oktoberfest. I consider sitting down but can't find a surface that wouldn't require extensive excavation. I stand on the edge of the living room and try not to imagine the garbage creature from *Star Wars* slithering about.

"What the hell happened?" I ask.

Mike places the beer bottle against the top of his head. "Okay, after I left your place, I went to The Tav. Hooked up with Robbie and Stoner. Watched the Gopher game." Just hanging out with Robbie and Stoner might have resulted in an attack. They're college buddies of ours. Decent guys, if you lower your standards for decency. "After we were done, I came home," Mike continues, "Second I walk in the door, I know something's up. All the lights are off."

Something that comes from knowing someone sixteen years is knowledge of their quirks. Among many of Mike's other quirks, he's afraid of the dark. Mind you, it's not an across-the-board fear. He doesn't sleep with a nightlight. He's broken into any number of places under the cover of darkness. (More on that later.) But he hates opening the door to his place and walking into a darkened room. It's why we've never had a surprise party for him. The sheer carnage and brutality that would ensue could keep us tied up in litigation for years.

"What did you do?" I ask.

"I stood there. I might have said, 'What the fuck?' I'm not sure. I went to get the light switch, and someone clonked me on the fucking head."

I gesture for him to move the beer bottle, so I can get a look at his cranium. I feel around (an activity Mike is less-than-thrilled with) and find a small knot on top of his head. He winces the second my fingers brush it. I apologize and let him go to back to his beer bottle therapy.

"What happened then?" I ask.

"First, I fell down," he says, "That's what you do when someone hits you on the fucking head. I landed on my vacuum cleaner."

"Why was your vacuum cleaner out?"

"I took it out a few months ago. I was looking for some old porn in the closet. I keep meaning to put it back."

"The porn or…?"

"The vacuum cleaner."

It was a fair question. "So, you fell down…"

"And whoever the hell it was stood over me, going, 'What do you know?'"

"What the hell do you know?"

"Nothing! That's what I tried telling this guy," Mike says, "Or girl. Whoever it was."

"It might not have been a guy?"

Mike runs the beer bottle over his face. "Whoever it was sounded weird. All raspy and guttural."

"Like Christian Bale in *The Dark Knight*?"

"More like Christian Bale in *The Dark Knight* if he had a sore throat and his underwear was a little tight."

"They were covering their voice."

"That's what it sounded like."

I shove some clothes off a chair and sit (hoping like hell the chair holds me up). "Did you get a look at the guy?"

"No. It was dark, and he was behind me. I was afraid if I moved, he'd hit me again. Then he said, 'Just tell me what you know.' I told him again that I don't know anything. Then he said…" Mike squints, trying to remember the exact words. "'Queen is dead. He had it coming. Unless you want to get killed, you'll talk to me.'"

"Shit," I say.

"I damn near did. I told him I didn't know what he was talking about. Then he slapped me on the back of the head, real hard. I realized I wasn't going to talk my way out of this. This fucking guy was going to kill me. I had to do something."

"What did you do?"

"I whipped creamed his ass."

There's nothing one can say except, "Excuse me?"

Mike reaches down to the floor and comes up with a can of Reddi-wip. "This was lying next to me. I grabbed it, rolled over and shot it into the guy's eyes. Direct hit. The guy started screeching, kind of high-pitched, and stumbled toward the door. Right before he left, he said, 'I will be back, and I will fucking kill you.'"

"Did you go after him?" I ask.

"And let him fucking kill me? No. I locked the door and called you."

Holy shit. I never thought this rat trap of an apartment would save Mike from an attacker. It's frightening to think a less slovenly man would be dead now.

I look around for a clue. "Did he take anything?"

"No," Mike says, "I went over the whole place while I was waiting for you and I didn't find anything missing."

Here's a weird thing I've discovered about messy people. You'd think someone who lives in a place that looks like a trailer park had an up-close-and-personal with an F-5 couldn't keep track of anything. And yet, move one piece of their decrepitude and it's as if their whole slobby ecosystem has collapsed. I, on the other hand, keep my apartment as clean as an operating room and am frequently unable to find a pen or my car keys. So, I'll take Mike's word on this.

"Did you call the cops?" I ask.

"No fucking way. I don't want the cops around here."

I can't blame Mike for his reluctance. Just a year ago, he was jailed on suspicion of killing his neighbor. Falsely accused, as it were. The sort of thing that undermines one's faith in our institutions. Still, there's common sense to be considered.

"You need to call the police," I say, "Report this."

"What are the cops going to do? Look around, take my story and say, 'We'll get in touch with you if we find anything.' And you know they won't find anything. No, fuck that."

Mike goes into the kitchen and comes back with two beers. He hands one to me and sits in the beanbag chair. I sip my beer and tuck the bottle under my chin.

"You realize what this attack means?" I say.

"Security in my building is for shit?" Mike says.

"No. Well, yes, but that's not where I was going with that." I lean forward. "James Queen was murdered."

It takes a few seconds for that to register with Mike. "I hadn't even thought about that. I was so preoccupied with the guy attacking me, I didn't think about what he said."

"*Queen got himself killed.* That's what the guy said?"

"I'm positive."

"That doesn't sound like a heart attack," I say, "That sounds like James Queen was murdered."

I have to say it again, just solidify the enormity of what we're talking about. James Queen might have been a has-been, the punchline to jokes told behind his back, but he was still a celebrity. To have him die in our fair city was bad enough. To have him murdered…

Mike rolls out of the beanbag. "Why did the guy come here? What was he looking for?"

"Couldn't tell you." I ponder it. "But the guy obviously thinks you know something. Maybe something that tells us who killed James Queen."

"What could I possibly know?" Mike says, his agitation turned up to eleven, "The one thing everyone knows about me is I'm a goddamned moron!"

I hold my hands out. "The guy didn't break in here to get your collection of Green Arrow back issues."

"I met James Queen, he autographed my stuff and that was that."

We're quiet while we sip our beers. The guy who attacked Mike thinks he saw something. Mike insists he didn't see anything. Of course, right now he's probably too freaked out to recall much of anything. He'll probably calm down after a few beers, but that's not exactly going to help his memory.

I set my beer down. "You *sure* you don't want me to call the cops?"

"Last time the cops were here," he says, wagging a finger at me, "*I* got hauled off to jail. No. Nothing doing."

I don't know what it's like to get locked up for murder, although I got awfully close last spring. I only avoided it because the guy who locked Mike up chose not to do the same to me. Come to think of it, that might be the ticket out of this.

"I'll talk to Sergeant Pike," I say, "See what he says."

Mike looks like I just proposed urinating on the floor. "Oh good. Deputy Fife will be looking out for me."

Sergeant Frank Pike of the St. Paul Police Department's Homicide Division. He was the lead investigator in the murder of Mike's neighbor across the hall. While Mike was ultimately proven innocent (and Pike saved my life in the bargain), Mike hasn't forgiven the good sergeant.

"It'll be fine," I say, "Maybe Pike can get something going. Maybe he already has."

"Excuse me if I don't hold my breath," Mike says.

We finish our beers. I set my bottle on the kitchen counter (where it will likely remain at least through the holidays) and go to the door. Mike follows. I get the sinking feeling he's not just walking me to the door.

"Are you going somewhere?" I ask, my hand on the doorknob.

"I can't stay here," Mike says, "This guy tried to kill me. What if he comes back?"

Shit. He's right. Maybe the guy will be scared off for an evening, but there's nothing preventing him from making a return visit. But that's not what's bothering me.

"Where are you going to stay?" I ask.

Mike looks hurt that I even asked. "I thought I could crash at your place."

Oy vey. In sixteen years of close friendship, the one thing Mike and I have never been—save for crashing in the odd hotel room on a road trip—is roommates. We may be best friends, but when it comes to household management, we are direct opposites. I look around his place and get nightmare images of him doing the same thing to mine.

"You don't want to stay at my place," I say, "Remember what happened with my cousin Micky last summer? I'll keep telling you to use a coaster, keep your feet off the coffee table, put your empty bottles in the recycling bin. I mean, we get on each other's nerves when you *visit*. You really think we can live together?"

Mike ask, in a small voice, "Where else can I go?"

Ah fuck. Whether by design or simple good fortune, Mike's gotten to me. I can't stand to see a dumb animal suffer. I sag against the door.

"All right, you can crash on the couch tonight," I say, "But that's all I can promise. Tomorrow, we'll figure something out."

"I appreciate it," Mike says.

We stand there for an awkward moment. Mike shows no inclination to move. "Aren't you going to pack some stuff?" I ask, "Toothpaste, change of clothes, pajamas?"

"Nah, I don't need that stuff."

"Not even the pajamas?"

"I'll just sleep in my underwear."

Great. Tomorrow, I'm going to have to throw the couch out. And move.

CHAPTER FOUR

The basic problem with roommates, of course, is that people were not meant to live together.

Now, I know you'll think this the position of some twisted introvert (and it is) but I believe this applies to human beings of all stripes. It's not as if two extroverts won't argue over stuff like, "Who used my parmesan cheese? Dammit, I had it marked." It doesn't matter if you're male or female, gay or straight, Caucasian or African American, a Vikings' fan or a Packers' fan, we are all united by our mutual ability to bug the shit out of each other.

On top of that, there's just that unending feeling of someone being there. If they're not at work or on a date or visiting family or something, you're stuck with them. No separate corners to retreat to.

BTW, these are also the reasons I'm probably not married. Don't tell my mom.

Mike is up and on his way to his temp job early. He grabs some toast and coffee before he leaves. In the process, he leaves the bag for the bread open and doesn't throw away the used basket in the Keurig. On the bright side, he left his clothes scattered all over hell. (*Hell* will be an apt description of my apartment if it contains Mike for any length of time.) I spent a good chunk of my morning cleaning and disinfecting.

I trade a few text messages with Casey, apologizing again for ditching her last night. She's perfectly understanding and perfectly willing to meet me for a drink at The Tav at the earliest convenience.

Having settled crises both foreign and domestic, I work on a column on relationships and redemption. My typical workday starts shortly after I wake up and ends, depending on the kind of roll I find myself on or the number of distractions I'm subject to, a few hours later. It's not exactly slave labor. It affords me a wee bit of celebrity and a constant creative outlet. And it keeps me (barely) above the poverty line.

My desk is tucked into a corner of the room, next to the arch windows at the front. I enjoy a large mug of pumpkin spice coffee and throw the view of the fall colors on Summit. The morning is crisp, frosting the window slightly. The cats snuggle together on the shelf over the radiator. Things are going swimmingly, which is the international signal that I'll be interrupted sooner or later. Sure enough, I'm three-quarters of the way through the column when the front door buzzer sounds. I consider ignoring it, as I frequently do, but decide to answer. I look forward to giving the heartless bastard a piece of my mind.

"Yeah?" I say, in my least friendly tone of voice.

"Please tell me you have coffee on," is the reply.

Whoever is at the door is doing a wonderful impression of Carol after she's emerged from a coma. This is an intruder trying to get into the building. I decide to live dangerously and buzz in this "Carol." Truthfully, I'm certain it's her, but just to be on the safe side, I grab an old tennis racket, the only weapon I keep in the house.

Nearly a minute later, there's a weak knock on the door. I find the artist formerly known as Carol on the landing, gently waving in the breeze. Her hair hangs down over her bloodshot eyes and she's got a hand against the doorjamb, as if it's the only thing holding her up. Her face is blotchy and her eyes glossy. It's in sharp contrast to the usual professional appearance (dark blue blouse, suit coat, black slacks, black trench coat). She looks like a goth chick who's really sold out.

"I'll get you that coffee," I say, "Try not to expire before I bring it to you."

"I'll be fine," she says, weaving toward the futon, her movements brought to you by the law firm of Languid and Tentative, "I just need to get to the couch. You can bury me there."

I decide against telling her Mike slept there last night, wearing nothing but his boxer briefs. (Then again, Carol slept with Mike for a year. It probably won't dissuade her as much as it will bring back bad memories.) I slip into the kitchen and pour the requested java. When I get back to the living room, Carol is stretched out on the futon, having not bothered to remove her trench coat. Her forearm lays across her eyes. Lenny and Squiggy take up their positions. Squiggy settles in the crook of Carol's arm. Lenny stands guard on the back of the futon. They love Carol above all my other friends, but they seem uncertain she'll survive this experience. I set the mug down on the coffee table near her and grab a seat in the comfy chair.

"I guess the bachelorette party was a to-do?" I say.

"It was to-done all right," she says, "I don't want to talk about it."

"Oh, come on. You can't show up at my place, looking you'd have to work your way up to Death Warmed Over and not give me any details."

Carol moves her arm slightly. "Joe, when I'm ready to discuss it—assuming I'm ever ready to discuss it—that's when we'll discuss it. And not a minute sooner. I'd appreciate it if you just let me decompose in peace."

On the bright side, Carol and I are perfectly comfortable sitting around, not saying anything. I sip my coffee and mentally write the rest of my column. The cats stand guard over Carol.

Lenny and Squiggy are littermates and they run my household (since they spend slightly more time here than I do). Lenny is a handsome butterscotch tabby whose methods of demanding attention would never fly if the #metoo movement extended to the feline set. Squiggy has more decorum. With his black-and-white coloring and obsequious manner, I often picture him as my butler, ready to lend aid and comfort. It certainly seems Carol is in that boat.

I set my own mug on the coffee table. "At least you had a better night than Mike."

Carol barely moves. "What happened?"

I fill her in on the break-in at Mike's place and the subsequent attack. She doesn't register any kind of reaction. When I'm finished, she says, "You're going to talk to Pike?"

"He's meeting me at Glacier's later," I say.

Carol still looks fuzzy. "You're going to tell him about the thing with Mike?"

"No, I figured we'd come back here. Do each other's hair and nails. Get all girly."

She closes her eyes. "Tell me how it goes."

I tap the coffee table. "What the hell happened to you last night?"

"I'm not saying." Carol opens her eyes. "What about you? Did you go see this Casey person?"

"I did."

"And what's the story with her? Why don't you want Mike to talk about her?"

I sit back in my chair. "I don't believe I'm legally obligated to answer that. It will remain redacted from the files and hidden from the general public."

Carol rolls on her side and tries to level an intimidating stare at me. The best she can do, though, is resemble a divorce attorney with an astigmatism.

"Joe, why are we doing this?" she asks, "You know exactly what will happen. I'll stay on you and you'll tell me everything that happened. Why don't you just save us both the effort and tell me what happened with this Casey?"

She's got a point. When it comes to getting information, Carol is like a badger. She'll sink her cute little claws in, and you will have no hope of escape until the information is released. Since I can't avoid the inevitable, I'm forced to negotiate.

"Okay, I'll tell you," I say, "but we're going to need some quid pro quo, mofo. Before I tell you the story, I need the skinny on what happened to you last night."

Carol debates this, then sits up. The effort appears to cost her, either in terms of a headache or a sloshing stomach.

Whichever it is, she quickly recovers, even if she doesn't quite hold her head up.

"There's not a lot to tell," she says, "Because I don't remember a lot of it."

"What *do* you remember?" I ask.

Carol brushes the hair out of her eyes. "I remember we started at Big Ben's Distillery. Karen, the maid of honor, bought the first couple rounds. We were doing Kool-Aid shooters. You ever had those? They're tasty."

That's my problem with a lot of mixed drinks. The tastiness. I've learned, after several vodka lemonade incidents, that hiding hard liquor in an innocuous fruity beverage is a recipe for disaster. If I'm going to drink vodka, I'll drink it over ice or in martini form. I need my liquor to taste like liquor. That way I at least have an idea what I'm getting myself into. Mixed drinks, tough, lull you into a false sense of security. They taste like Kool Aid or lemonade or fruit juice. It's only when you're yakking your guts out the next morning that you realize you've fallen for an alcoholic Trojan Horse.

"I'm guessing things devolved after the Kool-Aid shooters?" I ask.

"That would be a word for it. We moved on to a couple other clubs and we kept up with the shots. After that, things get hazy. I remember taking selfies with the other bridesmaids. I remember having a long talk with Chris in the bathroom."

"About what?"

"I have no earthly idea," Carol says, rubbing the bags under her eyes, "We could have been plotting world domination. We could have been talking about the best way to get stains out of carpeting. I *do* remember the word *Panda* was involved. And it was intense."

"Panda? How the hell do you have an intense conversation involving the word *panda*? It can't be done. Even if you hear on the news, 'The mother panda smothered her cub,' you think, 'Aw, that must have been adorable.'"

"Are you finished?"

"I am."

Carol twists her mouth to one side as she thinks. "I remember walking along First Avenue, shouting at a passing car—I have no idea what I said or why I said it—and I remember dancing at a club. At least, I think it was a club. It might have been a grocery store." She brushes some hair from her forehead. "Then I woke up at home. No idea how I got there or who got me there."

"That's a little scary," I say.

"No doubt. I didn't see any evidence that I threw up. Oh, and I was naked. Judging by the way my clothes were in a pile, I think being naked was my idea. I probably got my clothes off but didn't have enough steam left to put on my pajamas."

I sit back in the comfy chair. "And that's *all* you remember?"

Carol hangs her head. "Uh…yeah."

"You don't sound sure."

"I'm not. It's weird. It's like…you ever woke up with the feeling something bad went down? You can't remember what it was, but you're sure it wasn't good?"

"Couple of times."

"I've got that," Carol says, "But I cannot, for the life of me, tell you what it was. Maybe it'll come to me later."

"You could ask someone in the wedding party."

Carol waves that off. "No, I don't want to admit how plastered I was."

"You sure they haven't cottoned to that already?"

"I don't think so. I'm pretty good at holding my liquor."

Or so Carol likes to think. She's usually okay for a few drinks. But after that, she gets chatty and wild-eyed and advocates the kind of civil disobedience a sober Carol would never speak of. The only more obvious drunk is my younger brother, Owen, who I can tell is shit-faced when he cracks an actual smile.

I sip my coffee. "Good luck piecing things together."

Carol pets Squiggy, who's taken up residence on her lap. "Okay, your turn. Tell me about this Casey person."

Oh boy. I had vowed never to tell this tale. All my college friends know it, but they don't speak of it (at least not to my face). I've compromised it for a collection of unreliable, drunken memories from Carol. Talk about selling the cow for magic beans...

"All right," I say, running a hand through my hair, "But this goes no further."

"That's the agreement."

I hide behind my coffee mug. "Okay, Casey and I knew each other in college. We had a Shakespeare class and were in a play together. We were part of the same social circle. Hanging out at Boomtown on Friday nights. Having coffee and lunch together. That sort of thing. Casey and I always had a flirty relationship. We'd banter. She gave good banter."

"Banter is important," Carol says

"Indeed. But despite all the flirting, we'd never act on it. When I first met her, she was dating somebody. By the time she broke up with that guy, I was dating somebody. It went back and forth like that. The timing was always off." I set my mug on the table. "So, one day, Casey and I are at lunch, chatting about our dating lives. And it dawns on us that we're both single. For the first time since we've known each other. Plus, it's spring and in spring, a young person's mind turns to sap. I remember she was wearing this sexy little sundress." My mind is threatening to drift off to old sexual fantasies. "Somewhere in this conversation, we decide it's high time we consummate this little flirtation of ours."

"Like you do."

"Like you do. Since I didn't have afternoon classes that day—and I would have skipped the damn things if I had—we decide to go back to my place. As soon as we get through the door, Casey's all over me."

Carol winces. "Should I be listening to this?"

"I'm not bragging. I'm setting something up." I return to that thrilling day of yesteryear. "All right, the sundress disappears and Casey's pulling off my clothes, dragging me toward the bed. It was like my life did a movie edit. We walk in the door. We're naked in bed. And Casey's crawling on top of me. No foreplay, no time for me to get set up, no time to think about baseball. Nothing. Boom! We're doing it. Quick as that. And then it was over. Also…quickly."

Carol bites her lip, suppressing a laugh. "How quickly?"

"Oh…on days when I feel like flattering myself, I like to think I lasted thirty seconds."

"Ouch."

"Ouch, indeed. When Casey realized I had finished, she said, 'Is that it?' I didn't know what to say. Nothing like that had ever happened to me before."

Carol arches an eyebrow. "Never?"

"Okay, the first couple times with my high school girlfriend didn't set any records for stamina. But I was new to the game. This thing with Casey? That caught me totally off-guard."

"Understood."

I squirm in my seat. "So, I'm sitting there, tongue-tied. Casey just goes, 'All right.' Then she put on her clothes and left. Didn't give me a second chance. Worse, she went around telling everyone I was lousy in the sack."

Carol cringes. "That had to put a crimp in your dating life."

"A little. Fortunately, there were other young ladies who could offer a dissenting opinion. Create some reasonable doubt. The worst part is it got back to my idiot friends."

Carol's met these guys. She knows why that was the worst part. "Got rough, did it?"

I sit back in the chair. "Robbie started calling me *Quickdraw*. Mike came up with *Hair Trigger*. T.J. started calling me *Sixty Minute Man* with full irony. I mean, when fucking T.J. is scoring off you…" I shake my head. "Stoner said my

Native American name was *Can't Satisfy Woman*. I thought that one was kind of funny."

"Did you ever live it down?"

"I did. About a month later, T.J. was running for home in a softball game and he shit his pants. Gave everybody—including me—a new target. Took the heat off."

"I'm guessing you never settled things with Casey?" Carol asks.

"Nope. That was the end of lunches and coffee and hanging out at Boomtown. We lost track of each other. A mutual friend mentioned she moved to Seattle after graduation. The other day was the first time I saw her in about ten years."

I go to the kitchen for more coffee. I'd offer Carol a warmup, but I don't think she's taken a sip of the coffee I first poured her.

"What's your plan with this Casey?" Carol finally gets a trace of a smile. "Are you going to try and have sex with her to prove that you're good in the sack?" When she gets no response from me, the smile disappears. "Oh my God, *that's* your plan?"

"Look, I'm not saying I'm Warren fucking Beatty—"

"Jesus, you *do* need to update your references."

"But that thing with Casey was a stain on an otherwise spotless reputation. I need to correct that."

"Why?" Carol asks, "So you can go back and brag to your idiot friends?"

"No. They're going to be idiots no matter who I have sex with. I want to do this for me. And Casey, of course."

"Of course. Good luck with that."

Carol finally takes a sip of her coffee. She looks a bit more like herself. She gets up from the futon, displacing Squiggy. She pats him on the back by way of apology.

"I have to get back to work," she says, "I've got a meeting."

Carol's an ad writer, one of the better ones you'll find. While we're both loosely in the same line of work, Carol will tell you hers is the real job. She grabs her purse and struggles to her feet. That done, she sways toward the front door.

"Keep me updated on the thing with Mike," she says, "and the thing with Casey."

"Will do. It's all I've got going on."

Carol makes her exit. I pick up her coffee cup and put it in the sink. A few hours to go before meeting with Sergeant Pike. Maybe this will all be for nothing. Maybe the whole thing is just what it seems: a heart attack suffered by an aging actor performing a stunt he should have reconsidered.

Why am I having a hard time believing it will be that easy?

***

Sergeant Pike was not thrilled to hear from me. He probably regrets giving me his card. Truth be told, I could live without his constant snark and disapproval. But the guy saved my life once. And he also didn't put me in jail when it would have (at least temporarily) served his best interests. Ergo, he's a standup guy. Just one I don't always want to be in the same room with.

He's agreed to meet me at Glacier's coffee shop. This place is much more my speed. Glacier's is a converted café with checkerboard tile floors, straight-back chairs, brass rails and picture windows. Glacier's draws the young and artistic denizens from the upscale side of my neighborhood, meaning there's a lot of self-involvement and very little conversation. It's great when I want to write. Maybe not so much when I want to have a conversation with a cop. But this is the only place Pike was willing to meet, so here I am. I've got a table next to the picture window and a pumpkin latte in front of me. How bad can things be?

Pike arrives, ignoring the bell over the door. He isn't intimidating on the surface. He's short and balding. His wire rim glasses rest low on his nose, exposing a pair of sad eyes. His cheap suit appears to be permanently rumpled and his tie is even more askew than usual. He looks permanently tired and stressed. But all it takes is a slight narrowing of the eyes and a certain cold tone in his voice to know you're dealing with someone formidable. He approaches the counter and orders a plain coffee to go. A minute later, he joins me at the table, ignoring the view out the window.

"Counselor," he says, a smirk on his face, "Good to see you."

The *Counselor* nickname dates back to the first time I met Pike, about a year ago. Mike, nervous under questioning about the death of his neighbor, introduced me as his lawyer. While Pike was wrong about Mike being guilty, he's never let the nickname go. I ignore it, as usual.

"Thanks for meeting me," I say, "Glad to see you haven't been killed in the line of duty. If *glad* is the word I'm looking for."

He gives that a *You got me* bow. "Why am I here?"

"Do you know who's working on the James Queen case?"

"Intimately. It's me. But I wouldn't really call it a case. The guy died of a heart attack."

I should have known. If there's one problem with Sergeant Pike—I mean, if I could isolate it to just one—it's that he's stubborn. And dismissive. And unimaginative. (Okay, I can't really isolate it to just one.) I gently move the pumpkin latte aside.

"The coroner said this?" I ask.

"Haven't gotten the report back. But that's what everything indicates."

"Then why are you assigned to it?"

"There's just a few things we need to check out."

"Such as?"

His eyes narrow. "You hunting around for a story?"

"Not exactly. I mean, I'm probably going to write about him. Pop culture icon drops dead and I'm there to witness it? I can't let that pass without comment." I lower my voice. "I've got another reason for asking, though. You remember my friend Mike?"

"Sadly, I do."

"Someone broke into his apartment and attacked him last night. They said he knew something. But he has no idea what that something is. They also said, 'Queen got himself killed. He got what he had coming.'"

Pike pushes up his glasses and pinches the bridge of his nose. Frequently, when I'm dealing with Lars, I get a headache that starts in my sinuses and spiderwebs out. I get the sinking feeling Pike experiences the same headache when dealing with me.

"Tell me what happened," Pike says, his glasses sliding back into place.

I go through what I know: our visit with James Queen, his untimely demise and the break-in at Mike's place.

Pike peers over the top of his wire frames; the look that always makes me feel like an idiot. I rush to the finish. Pike pushes his glasses further up his nose.

"You didn't call the police?" Pike says.

"I wanted to. But Mike has a little trouble trusting you guys."

"The feeling's mutual. As I recall, your friend *does* have trouble telling the truth."

I can't help getting annoyed with Pike. I also can't help agreeing with him. Mike told Pike about four lies in their first five minutes of acquaintance. Hard to come back from a thing like that.

"Mike only lies to get himself out of trouble or to get something he wants," I say, "Neither of those apply here."

Pike checks his watch (yes, he still wears a watch). "Let's back up. If I take your friend at face value—and I'm really reaching here—you're telling me James Queen was murdered. And this person who came after your friend thinks he knows something incriminating?"

"That's how I read it. I don't know what Mike could know. He only met James Queen briefly. Mike asked Queen to autograph some stuff and then Queen threw us out."

"No sign of violence to the body," Pike says, "I can tell you that. If it was murder, how was it done?"

That's the question I've been contemplating. There's only one answer to it. It would be easier to provide if Pike weren't looking at me like he wanted to challenge me to a fistfight. I take a casual sip of my latte, trying to calm myself.

"It had to be poison," I say, "I'm not sure *how* Queen could have been poisoned. But that's the only answer I've come up with."

"Toxicology will tell us that." Pike says. He doesn't seem willing to go along with what I'm telling him. (Not a new sensation, believe me.) "You say your friend got hit on the head?" he asks.

"I felt the lump myself."

"Did he admit to being dazed or disoriented during this attack?"

My heart sinks. I know exactly how this conversation will play out. "I don't think Mike was dreaming the whole thing."

"But you don't *know* that," Pike says, "because you didn't call the police. The same police who would have told your friend to go to the hospital and get his injuries checked. Then we might have an idea how bad his bell was rung and if we can believe what he tells us."

I slide the pumpkin latte aside, lest I throw it at him. "So, you're just going to ignore this whole thing?"

Pike raises a hand. "I'll wait for the coroner's report."

"Meantime, my friend gets to live in fear of his life because you think the Phantom of Lowertown clonked him on the head."

"He's welcomed to file a police report," Pike says, "Unless he decides to do that, there's nothing we can do."

"You're kidding me. Look at what the guy said about Queen—"

"Everything I've seen tells me this was a heart attack or a stroke. I'm not changing that based on the word of a guy whose specialty is lying."

Mike's inability to tell the truth to any authority figure strikes again. Besides, even if I could talk Mike into filing a police report, the cops would only confirm his worst fears: *we'll look into it and are you sure you didn't dream this up after getting hit on the head?*

"The other people from *The Night Hawk*," I say, "are they still in town?"

"They agreed to hang around until we get the coroner's report back."

"Oh?" I say, "You're not *entirely* convinced it's a heart attack or a stroke?"

"It's a precaution," Pike says, "I would suggest not bothering them."

I hold up my hands in mock surrender. I've gone as far as I can consulting Pike. "Thanks for your time," I say, cradling my latte, "Always a pleasure. We should go chase broads some time."

Pike gets to his feet with the kind of alacrity one normally associates with a kid leaving his desk on the last day of school. He only gets a few feet before stopping and looking at me.

"You're not going to blunder into this, are you?" Pike asks.

I hold my hands out; Mr. Innocent. "Why would I do that?"

"To find a murder that just isn't there. Believe me, all you're going to do is piss people off. For once in your life, take my word and let this thing go. Do you understand?"

"I understand every word you're saying."

Pike scrutinizes me, then exits. I let Pike put some distance between us, then I pick up my cell phone and dial Lars's number. He can put me in touch with the cast of *The Night Hawk*.

Hey, I told Pike I understood what he was saying. I didn't say I'd go along with it.

CHAPTER FIVE

When I was a kid, attending fourth grade at Cobb-Cook Elementary School in Porter's Bay, they tried to drum a Don't Do Drugs *message into our heads. The guy in charge of the program was Mr. Kearney, the school's football coach. All the guys liked Mr. Kearney, despite our growing suspicion he was a crappy coach (our school's flag football team being Exhibit A). For him and nobody else (certainly not our parents) we would avoid the evils of drugs. For Mr. Kearney, we'd stay on the straight and narrow.*

Thus, you can imagine my shock when I was walking into the Memorial Arena for a hockey game and saw Mr. Kearney out front, having a smoke. It was all I could do not to stop and gape at the scene. (The four-below temperatures may have helped me on my way.) When we got inside, my father wondered what was going on. I told him about my teacher having a smoke.

"John Kearney?" Dad said, "He's one of your teachers? The guy who was thrown out of Nick's Corner Bar for dirty dancing with some woman on a tabletop?"

All I could get out was: "Huh?"

Dad realized he had gone too far in his explanation but wasn't sure how to walk it back. "It was okay. He was drunk as a skunk."

That wasn't exactly the way to do it. I don't remember the rest of that night or large swaths of the fourth grade. My disillusionment was such, I blocked Mr. Kearney out of my memory. But I vowed I would never have anything to do with drugs or alcohol.

If only I hadn't gone to college.

In the current division of labor, Mike is handling the disillusionment while I'm contemplating drugs and alcohol.

"This woman introduced me to puberty," Mike says, checking his reflection from the passenger window, "She was the first one I ever looked at and thought, 'Nice gazongas.'"

I grip the wheel and talk myself out of driving into oncoming traffic. "She was hot. No doubt about it. Still is."

Mike tugs at the collar of his gray sweater. "You have any idea the number of my masturbation fantasies that woman starred in?"

"Can we keep it a mystery?"

I'm not sure he's prepared for this meeting. I *know* I'm not. We're driving down to the Ambassador Suites, a luxury hotel on the east end of downtown St. Paul. According to Lars, it's where the cast and crew of *The Night Hawk* are sequestered until they get the all-clear to leave town. He even called Ella Jones and set up the meeting.

Mike drums his fingers on the dash (even though I've told him that irritates the hell out of me). "You sure this is a good idea? The woman lost her ex-husband. You think we should go barging in there, asking a lot of personal questions?"

"We've got to start someplace," I say, "Whoever is after you thinks you know something." I pull up to a stoplight and turn to Mike. "If you saw something, it had to be when you went back to get the backpack. What do you remember?"

"I just wanted to get the bag back and get the hell out of there," he says, "I went in the dressing room, grabbed my bag, grabbed the toy Nightmobile off the table, and got the hell out. All I saw the whole time was James Queen bitching out Lars."

That's what I was afraid of. We've got no physical evidence. Nothing that Mike saw that we can go on. But if someone killed James Queen, it had to be someone from *The Night Hawk*. No one else would have reason or access to James Queen. So, we'll start with them.

A few minutes later, we pull into the parking lot of the Ambassador Suites. It's a luxury hotel on the east edge of downtown St. Paul. We've had a few adventures here, most recently involving my ex-girlfriend, Norah. For all the hotel's pretentions to Old World glory, it doesn't have much of a parking lot. It's paved near the hotel entrance and has dirt on the far side. I find a spot in the dirt portion.

Mike fusses with the cuffs on his leather jacket. "Why start with Ella Jones?"

"Like you said, she's Queen's ex-wife. We saw her leaving his dressing room, upset about something. It seems like she's the best person to start with."

We go through the revolving doors at the front and through the spacious lobby. The hotel's twelve floors are grouped in a square around a sunken area in the middle. Said sunken area houses a café, largely screened off by potted plants and other foliage. Mike spots the nearest reflective surface and checks his look for the three-hundredth time

"I hope she doesn't mind," he says.

"We'll tell her I'm doing an article on James Queen. I need some information on him. And I certainly can't write the article without talking about his death."

"Best cover story possible," Mike says, "More or less the truth."

More or less the truth. The story of my life.

The hotel bar is to the left, off the lobby. It's a dark wood and brass rail affair; a manufactured mix of pub and lounge. About half the tables are occupied. Ella Jones's table is situated behind a decorative trellis. It allows a bit of privacy. There's a glass of red wine in front of her.

You'd be hard-pressed to tell Ella Jones is in her fifties. Her dark hair is a little longer than the bob she wore on the show. The red sweater and black slacks show off a figure more shapely than her petite frame might otherwise indicate. Her face is open, but there's a hint of mischief in her green eyes. *Pixie-ish* was always the word that came to mind back in the day. She might have a few more lines on her face, but she's as attractive as she was on the show. She gets up from the table as we approach.

"You must be Joe Davis," she says, offering a slim hand to Mike.

He coughs, embarrassed. "Actually, my friend here is Joe Davis. My name's Mike Griffin. But I'm a big fan."

Ella takes the mistake in stride. "Glad to know you, Mike."

We shake hands and Ella gestures toward adjoining chairs. Her movements are fluid and her hands strike semi-balletic poses when not in motion. Most of the light comes from the votive candle on the table. It shows off Ella Jones's striking face to best effect. Mike tries not to stare (and fails). Ella speaks to me but keeps her gaze on Mike.

"What is it you wanted to talk about?" she asks.

"I think my friend Lars mentioned I have a column for *The Daily Bugle*," I say, "I'm doing an article on James Queen. I wanted to talk to his castmates."

Ella gives us a coy look. "And ex-wives?"

Well, that elephant is working the room. Ella Jones and James Queen started dating during the final season of *The Night Hawk* and were married shortly after the show ended. They were divorced several years later. There were no salacious details or undue publicity. About as amicable as the divorce of two Hollywood has-beens could be.

"It seems like you'd know James Queen best," I say.

Ella thinks about that as she sips her wine. "I'm not sure how well anyone knew James. He kept people at arm's length. Or really, he was too self-involved to share himself with others. I suppose I was closer to him than anybody else. I'm not sure that counts for anything."

Mike fumbles with a napkin. "Was he like that on the show?"

"More or less," Ella says, looking into her wine glass, "I didn't notice at first. I was new. He was a celebrity. I was star-struck. You forgive a lot in those cases. I forgave for a long time. Until I finally saw him for who he was."

"Did he change after the show went off the air?" I ask.

"Yes and no," Ella says, "He was still self-centered. But something did change. People stopped caring."

"And he didn't handle it well?" I say.

"No, he didn't," Ella says, "It was one thing when he was a big star. People genuflected and did what he wanted. And he abused that privilege. He had no time for his co-stars, let alone the people on the crew."

Mike props an elbow on the table. "Sounds like the stuff Tim Hefflin wrote in his book."

A sad look crosses Ella's face. "Some of it was like that. Tim distorted a lot of things. James was dismissive of people, but he wasn't a raving lunatic. And he had…a wandering eye."

"Was it worse than Tim Hefflin?" Mike asks, "In the book, it sounds like Tim was pretty…active."

Ella chuckles. "I don't think that's exactly accurate. Tim wasn't a monk by any means. But he wasn't as *active* as he makes himself out to be in the book."

I signal the bar, hoping for some service. "How did James feel about the book?"

"He wasn't happy," Ella says, "He mentioned it on the phone with me. What an ungrateful son of a bitch Tim was. On the bright side, Tim didn't sell a lot of books."

The bartender comes over and takes our order. Mike and I each get a beer. Ella asks for a refill on her wine. She keeps her eyes on Mike while the bartender is here. A slight smile crosses her face. Mike catches it and looks down. Son of a bitch, he's blushing. I feel like a third wheel.

"I didn't realize you were in touch with James," I say.

"Here and there," Ella says, "We'd talk on the phone. He spoke to my class once."

"You teach a class?" I ask.

Ella folds her hands on the table. "I teach acting. I have a class that meets once a week. Kids looking to become working actors. I know that's supposed to sound sad. *Those who can, do; those who can't, teach.* But I really love it."

She takes out her phone, swipes through a few things, then she hands it to Mike. I look over his shoulder. It's a picture of Ella surrounded by a bunch of bright-eyed twentysomethings.

"Nice grouping," I say.

"That's my class," Ella says, "Talented kids. Some of them have real potential."

Mike points to a particularly attractive blonde next to Ella in the picture. "Who's that?"

"That's Alison. She's my star pupil. She's already had a few small roles in movies and on TV. She's going to make it big. Trust me."

Mike hands the phone back. "She's a hottie."

Ella's mouth tightens as she puts the phone away. "I'm trying to mentor her. Help her to be…careful."

She doesn't expand on that and I don't ask her to. I assume she's talking about the various predators that stalk

Hollywood. I don't have firsthand knowledge of these people, but one only needs to look at Harvey Weinstein and imagine it's not an isolated incident. Probably good to have someone looking out for you.

"What was that like?" Mike asks, "Having James Queen talk to your class?"

"It was fine," Ella says, with no trace of enthusiasm, "The students were polite. I don't know if they were all that interested. James was interested in them, though."

"How so?" I ask.

"Just what they were doing," Ella says, "That sort of thing."

She follows that up with a hasty sip of wine. She doesn't seem anxious to talk about Queen's appearance or Queen himself. Can't say I blame her. I don't wax eloquent about any of my exes. And I've never married any of them.

"Was it weird seeing James at the convention?" I say.

"It's never exactly a good time," Ella says, looking into her wine glass.

"How did he get along with the others?" I ask, "Tim mHefflin and Hal Murdoch?"

"He didn't," Ella says, "He and Tim had a few unfriendly words. And he had a big argument with Hal."

Mike beats me to it. "About what?"

"I'm not sure. Neither of them would talk about it."

We're quiet while the drinks arrive. I drain more of my glass of beer than I intended. Mike, normally a guzzler himself, takes only a small sip, perhaps aware that Ella is watching him. I swirl the beer in my glass.

"We saw you coming out of James Queen's dressing room," I say, "It looked like you were crying. I don't know if you remember us being there…"

"I'm sorry, I don't."

"Did something happen with you two?"

Ella's face is a mask. Not anger, not even disapproval. Just a face that gives away nothing. She considers her answer.

"I thought…maybe this was an opportunity to settle a few things," she says, "Make peace. But he wasn't in the mood." Ella runs a finger around the rim of her wine glass. "He said horrible things. And now, that's the last image I have of him."

Ella drops her hand to the table beside her wine glass. Mike makes a half-move, as if he's going take her hand. He stops himself. He's imperceptibly slid his chair closer to hers. I try to not feel like a complete heel, having intruded on someone's…well, I guess *mourning* is the word for it. And I've done it under slightly false pretenses. But I'm in this far…

"You were backstage when James was…um, found?" I ask.

"I was next to Hal Murdoch," Ella says, "I went backstage after the argument with James. Hal came over to talk to me, just before the show started. He's a good man."

"Did he come over right after you left James's dressing room?" I ask.

"No, not right away," she says, "I was alone for a while. Probably for the best."

Mike again starts to reach for Ella's hand. This time, she meets him halfway, laying her hand over his. Mike chuckles (almost a giggle) and looks down. Cripe. It's like I'm back at the lunch table in junior high.

"What did you and Mr. Murdoch talk about?" I ask.

"Just what an ass James is," Ella says, "The usual stuff, I'm afraid."

I toy with my beer glass. "And you're okay with the heart attack theory?"

Ella looks startled. "Of course. Why wouldn't I be?"

Why not, indeed? Here's the tricky part: I'd like to dig deeper, but I can't do that without looking suspicious. *You didn't see anyone slip James Queen a poisonous mickey, did you? Come to that, what do you know about poisons? You ever had to cover up a murder? How good are you at picking locks? Executing sneak attacks? Disguising your voice? You ever thought about being evil? I mean, really evil.*

"It's just surprising," I say, trying to sound casual, "I only met him briefly, but James seemed to be in good shape."

"He was," Ella says, "as far as I knew. He was obsessed with his health. But you know what they say about heart disease. The silent killer."

"So I've heard," I say.

The heart disease theory is hard to crack without an autopsy to discredit it. Since there's no point of attack here, I let the conversation drift back into casual areas, mainly talking about St. Paul and if there's anything to do here. (There isn't.) Ella focuses on Mike, which is something of a relief to me. I'm not a fan of small talk. I finish my beer and stand up.

"Thank you so much for your time, Ms. Jones," I say.

"Please call me Ella," she says, still looking at Mike.

"Ella," I say, "Thanks again. I've got to get going."

"You're welcome to stay."

She might be talking to both of us, but she's only looking at Mike. His face turns a deeper shade of red. I'm worried he's going to start hyperventilating. I can't help feeling like a third wheel.

"I appreciate that," I say, "but I need to get going."

Ella withdraws her hand from Mike's. "I suppose the two of you rode together."

"We did," I say, "but Mike doesn't have to come with me."

Mike's building is only a handful of blocks away from The Ambassador. On a night as nice as this, it's walking distance. Of course, he's not going to go back there, for fear of his life. He's going to come back to my place. Unless he has a better offer. Mike breaks into a sweat and pops to his feet.

"Sorry," Mike says, "I need to get going, too. Stuff to do. Work and…stuff."

Ella offers an understanding nod. "Have a good night. I hope to see you again." She's looking at Mike and Mike alone.

We say our goodbyes and head for the door. Mike stumbles over a chair. Once we're clear of the bar, he runs a hand through his hair and tries to control his breathing. I'm not sure if he's relieved or thinking about going back.

"I might be mistaken," I say, "but I think you had an opportunity back there."

"You're not mistaken," Mike says, "I did."

"And you're not into it?"

"No, I'm totally into it."

I stop. "You want to go back?"

"Not at all."

"So, you're into it, but you don't—"

"Exactly," Mike says, "Let's get the hell out of here."

Yep, that clears that right fucking up.

***

"The key is realizing vision is not enough," Lars says, leading me down a hallway, "That's where I was going wrong before. I was so consumed by my vision—well, mine and Chuck's—that I thought the vision was the be all and end all. It's not. You need discipline. Rigor. That way, you relax and own the vision instead of *it* owning *you*. There's serenity in knowing you're doing everything you can to live your best life. You understand?"

I'll be honest: I wasn't really following that. I caught all the words, but the train of thought lost me. It sounds like someone playing Mad-Libs with the Self-Help section at the bookstore. But it means something to Lars, so I pretend to be into this shit.

"Fascinating," I say. Hey, if you're going to express interest without any real emotion behind it, who better to emulate than Mr. Spock?

We're in a small office building just off University Avenue in St. Paul. The neighborhood used to be more glamorous and, between the light rail line and the new soccer stadium, is in line for some serious gentrification. For now, it's still largely rundown and shady. The building housing *Vitalicity* is nice enough, what with the brickwork and the marble floors. It's not the kind of place I'd normally venture, unless I had a dentist's appointment or had to see Lars. Frankly, I would have preferred the dental appointment.

"I'm very happy for you," I tell him, "but I just want to know if you set up the meeting with Hal Murdoch."

I've had trouble tracking down Lars today. The greeting on his voicemail said he would be at the offices of Vitalicity Inc. all day. So, here I am. For better or worse. Worse, really.

We go into the main office. It's filled with various staffers, all with business casual clothes and drab hairstyles. There are a series of desks and cubicles. The walls are festooned with posters bearing motivational messages. (*If You Can Dream It, You Can Do It; Don't Limit Your Challenges, Challenge Your Limits; The Key to Success is to Focus on the Goals, Not the Obstacles.*) Everyone is scurrying about, frantically working at…something.

Lars fits in with the other staffers (which might be the only time I've ever used *Lars* and *fits in* within the same sentence). He wears a new (off the rack) suitcoat over a white dress shirt, thin tie and dark slacks. His quasi-pompadour has again been squashed down and slicked back. His dress shoes squeak against the floor. He reminds me of Christian Bale in *American Psycho*.

"What exactly do you guys do here?" I ask, dodging the staffers.

"A variety of things," Lars says, gesturing around the room, his movements fluid, "Charity events, motivational seminars, self-realization workshops, things such as that. We have a belief that fulfilled people are happy people. And happy people contribute to society."

"Must be why we have all those pot smokers in leadership positions," I say.

Lars tucks his hands behind his back. "You're sure you don't want Mr. Vitality's advice? It's invaluable, I find."

"I appreciate that," I say, "But I don't really need his advice."

"Or so you think," Lars says, "But I'm not going to pressure you. True change must come from within. I ask you to stay open to everything. Allow yourself new experiences."

"Sure, what the hell?"

We move through the office, stopping at an undecorated cubicle. Lars glides into a little desk chair.

"My home away from home," he says, "I get my best thinking done here."

How far he's come. He used to do his best thinking on the shitter, generally while smoking a joint. Instead, I prop an arm on the entrance to the cubicle.

"I'm happy for you," I say, "How's the memorial for James Queen coming along?"

Lars digs through some paperwork. "We're looking at next Friday. It's a little ways out, but it's the best we could do. It's probably going to be at the History Center. I'm going to stop in and check it out when I get a chance. Make sure it's appropriate."

I'm sure it will be. The Minnesota History Center functions not only as a museum, but a pretty damn good events center. I'm not surprised they'd be willing to hold a memorial for James Queen. I'm more surprised they'd be willing to meet with Lars. Then again, everything is topsy-turvy these days.

"Sounds like a plan," I say.

"I have Mr. Vitality to thank," Lars says, "You sure you don't want to meet him? I think it would be a real treat."

Ugh. How do I get myself out of this? I absolutely *do not* want to meet Bobby Vitality. But I don't want to hurt Lars's feelings. The dude has been doing me favors. I can't just spit in his face, can I? (Seriously, I can't, right? Damn it.)

"I suppose it wouldn't hurt," I say.

Lars leaps out of the chair, as if spring-loaded. He regains control of his dignity and says, "Follow me."

We stroll over Mr. Vitality's office. The door is partially closed, but the gold plate reading *Bobby Vitality* is visible at a hundred yards. Lars speaks to me in hushed tones.

"All I ask is that you treat Mr. Vitality with respect," he says, "He doesn't reach out to many people."

"I'll act like I'm honored by it," I say, fighting off some queasiness.

Lars approaches the door of the office like it's the Most Holy Place in the center of the Temple. He knocks, tentatively. A voice comes from the inside.

"Yes?"

"It's me, Mr. Vitality," he says, his voice squeaking, "Lars. I'm here with my friend."

Bobby Vitality emerges from the office. I'm not sure what I was expecting. Probably a cross between the Maharashi Yogi and Bob Ross. Instead, I get a guy with slicked back black hair, graying at the temples, and a mouth full of white teeth. He's burly, a bit like Dean Martin if he had been a linebacker (and God help Jerry Lewis if that had been the case). His gait is casual and unhurried. The tan slacks, white dress shirt and gold necklace accent the whole image. His intense blue eyes look into mine and he extends a hand.

"Joe Davis," he says, his voice moderate and calm, "it's a pleasure to meet you."

I take his hand. "Lars has told you about me."

"He mentioned he had a friend who was a writer and a bit of a celebrity," Mr. Vitality says, "And I recognize you from the picture on your column."

Ah, the joys of weenie celebrity. You never know where and when you're going to be recognized. I put on my best faux humility. "I didn't know you read my column."

"I don't," Mr. Vitality says, never losing the million-dollar smile, "I saw your picture on the website while I was looking at other things."

I drop his hand. If Mr. Vitality notices anything in my attitude, he doesn't say. Lars remains awed by his mentor. Again, I wonder what kind of influence this guy has over Lars. And if it's a good thing or a bad thing.

"Lars was telling me about the memorial he's planning," I say.

Mr. Vitality fingers the gold necklace. "He's made arrangements with Mr. Queen's co-workers to speak at his obsequies."

"Seems appropriate," I say.

"Come to think of it," Mr. Vitality says, bringing his index finger to his chin, "local celebrities would add some color. You would be a great choice to speak at the service."

True, I don't want to go along with anything Mr. Vitality thinks up; certainly not one that involves public speaking. But I'm so impressed he used the word *obsequies* in a sentence, that I have to consider it.

"I was going to write an article on Queen anyway," I say, "Kind of a retrospective. I can make the two of them work together."

"Excellent," Mr. Vitality says, as if he expected that answer all along.

"Glad I could help."

Mr. Vitality turns to go back to his office. Then he stops and turns to me. He comes close, invading my space.

"You seem like a very unhappy fellow," he says.

"On the contrary, I'm very happy," I say, "I've got good friends, a job I enjoy, an apartment I like and two cats to keep me company. Everything a man could want."

"Except fulfillment," Mr. Vitality says, nodding to back up his opinion.

"Fulfillment is in the eye of the beholder," I say, trying not to whither under his look, "There isn't anything missing from my life."

He wags a finger, as if he's hit on the solution. "It's relationships, right? You haven't found that certain someone and it's starting to bother you."

"Sorry, no," I say, trying not to be smug about it, "I had a breakup a few months ago that was rough. At the time. I'm over it now. I just broke it off with another girl, but we weren't all that serious. It was just sex."

Son of a…why the hell did I tell him that last part? I mean, it's true. Annika and I were only in it for the physical stuff and when it ran its course, we parted as friends (or at least people who weren't going to key each other's cars). None of that, though, is information I need to share with Mr. Vitality. So, why did I do it? He doesn't seem thrown by my confession.

"I know what it is," he says, "You *did* find that certain someone, once, and you don't think you'll ever find anyone like her again."

Holy shit, this guy is good. No wonder Lars is taking advice from him. And why *I* have no desire to take advice from him. (I'm not thrilled when my close friends seem to know me well, let alone this yahoo.)

"I've got to get going," I say, stumbling toward the exit, "It was nice talking to you."

I slip toward the door, anxious for freedom. Lars follows. Mr. Vitality watches me, smiling slightly. My tension unwinds once Lars and I get to the hallway. Lars beams.

"You must be glad you met Mr. Vitality," Lars says.

"I'm bursting at the seams," I say, "Hard to sit still."

Usually, my sarcasm passes right by Lars, as his brain tends to run several seconds ahead of humor. This time, though, he fixes me with a look that's half-disappointment, half-reprimand.

"I had hoped you'd keep an open mind," Lars says, "Your cynicism runs awfully deep."

"Okay, enough with the *Let's analyze Joe* shit," I say, "When can I meet Hal Murdoch?"

"Four o'clock, sharp, at his suite at the hotel."

I'm embarrassed. Here I am, getting snippy with Lars and he's helping me out. I can hear my mother's voice. *You should be more grateful with people, Joe.* I shuffle my feet.

"Uh, thank you for that," I tell him, "I appreciate it. You've been a…big help."

"I'm glad to do it," Lars says, "You've helped me a number of times. It's only right that I pay it back. And eventually pay it forward." I turn to go, but Lars's voice stops me. "One more thing," he says, "Please don't encourage Chuck with any wild schemes. We both know the movie theater vendor app is a terrible idea. I don't know your reasons for suggesting it—frankly, I don't want to know— but please don't feed him any more ideas. Thank you."

With that, he goes back into the office. What the hell is going on? *Lars* is reprimanding *me* for some ridiculous scheme? I've got to get out of here. There's a cocoon of creepiness enveloping this building. I need to make my escape.

Of course, with my luck, I'll probably find Bizarro waiting for me in the parking lot.

CHAPTER SIX

When we take a trip of any kind—vacation, business trip, flight from the DEA, what have you—we discover just how much we can live without the so-called essentials in life. When you get right down to it, most of the things in our lives are inessential. A trip just underscores this.

Once we return, we must face how well we did without all that crap. "Gee," we should be thinking, "I was on the road for a week, managed to feed and bathe myself, and lose money at the blackjack table and never once needed my collection of scented candles or my antique Happy Days *lamp. I wonder if I could actually…downsize?"*

We won't do that, of course. We're loyal to our shit and our shit alone. Now, if you'll excuse me, I'm going to pour coffee into my It's The Great Pumpkin, Charlie Brown *mug and listen to my Herb Alpert CDs.*

Hal Murdoch, it seems, takes stuff with him when he travels.

His suite is on the eighth floor of the Ambassador, along with the other people from *The Night Hawk*. Clearly, he's being treated with a certain amount of deference. A sort of visiting royalty. And, in our little world, he's exactly that. As soon as Mike and I step off the elevator and walk to Murdoch's room, we're nervous and fidgety, hoping to make a good impression on the great man.

Hal Murdoch started as a staff writer on several TV shows, then got his break with *The Night Hawk*. When the show was finished, he either wasn't offered any other work or wasn't interested. Maybe *The Night Hawk* was his life's work. He's a widower with no children. From what I gather (largely via Wikipedia), he's been content to live off the residuals from the show.

The woman who answers the door is about our age. She's short and her dark hair is pulled back into a bun. She wears black-rimmed-glasses and her long black shirt hangs down over a pair of black tights. But for the severity in her manner, she'd be attractive. She leads us into the room.

"My name is Billie," she says, her voice surprisingly high-pitched, "I'm Mr. Murdoch's assistant."

She marches into the room. There's a hint of muscularity in the legs and I can't help wondering if it extends to the rest of her. There's a bit of curviness when she looks back and I see her chest in profile. Mike, though, concentrates on Hal Murdoch. Murdoch is in a comfortable chair in the corner, his legs stretched out in front of him. He wears a gray patterned dressing gown over a dress shirt, a tie, and gray slacks. Brown slippers adorn the feet. The late afternoon sun shines in from the deck and shrouds Murdoch's face in shadow. He puffs serenely on a cigar. (The Ambassador is a nonsmoking hotel, but Murdoch doesn't seem to mind.) Even though it's his second time meeting Murdoch, Mike's still in a fawning mood. He bows slightly as he approaches Murdoch.

"Thanks for meeting us," Mike says, "It's great to see you. Again."

Murdoch removes the cigar from his mouth. "A pleasure. Have a seat. Billie, would you mind getting us some coffee?"

Billie goes to the kitchenette and pours three cups of coffee from an ornate silver pot. Mike and I wedge ourselves into chairs facing Murdoch. Billie brings us the coffee, then fades into the background.

"I don't remember seeing Billie at the convention," I say.

"She was outside in case I needed anything," Murdoch says, "A bit of vanity, I'm afraid. I don't like to be attended to when I'm in public. Makes me look like a doddering old man."

I can understand. If I reach that age and can afford a personal assistant…ah, who am I kidding? I probably won't do either of those. I sip my coffee. I'm pleasantly surprised it's not the brown grit one generally finds in a hotel.

"This is really good," I say, holding up the cup.

Murdoch grins. "It's a Guatemalan blend I bring from home. I can't drink what most hotels pass off as coffee. One of those comforts of home, I guess."

He seems to have brought a few other comforts of home. Photos of him with various celebrities are spread across the credenza. Mike, never much of a decorator or a coffee snob, couldn't care less.

"It's a real honor, sir," Mike says.

"Relax, son," Murdoch says, "I'm just a writer. A *former* writer, really."

The modesty doesn't allay Mike's enthusiasm. "I'm a huge fan."

"You said the same thing about Jimmy. And you met him. Sorry you had to see that." Murdoch slowly spreads his hands. "What can I do for you fellows?"

I launch into my cover story about writing an article on James Queen and what happened at the convention. Murdoch listens patiently, bringing his fingers together in a steeple. I feel scrutinized. That always brings out the flop sweats in me. I rush to the finish.

"I'm hoping we can talk about your history with Mr. Queen," I say, my mouth dry.

"If that's your job, go ahead," Murdoch says.

I take out my phone and bring up the recorder app. "Is this okay?"

"You're going to make a phone call?" Murdoch asks.

"Uh, no," I say, "I have a recorder app. I'd like to record the conversation." I swallow, hoping to get some saliva back. "If that's okay."

"Perfectly."

I relax, ever-so-slightly, and put the phone on the table between us. "If I could get a few words about Mr. Queen…"

Murdoch sniffs. "What? More words?" He crosses his legs. "James Queen was absolutely the best choice for The Night Hawk. First time I saw his screen test, I knew that. He hadn't done much. Some theatre, a couple commercials, guest spots on shows, walk on parts in movies. But he had that look, that presence. And he understood comedy. How to play drama right to the hilt but still make it funny. He knew where that fine line was. If the network was going to insist we make a comedy, James Queen was the perfect Night Hawk."

"That's right," I say, "You didn't want to do a comedy originally."

Murdoch frowns, deepening the lines in his face. "No, I didn't. I wanted to do a show that resembled *The Night Hawk* comics I read when I was a boy. They had the edginess of real life, but with all the action and derring-do. It was a great adventure, not a laughingstock. But the networks didn't trust 'serious' superhero stories then. The only way to get the show on the air was to make it…" He searches for the word.

"Campy?" I say.

Murdoch gives me a sour look. "I guess that's the word for it. James could have pulled it off if we had played the show straight. But he was also just subtle enough to play the comedy. He was a hell of an actor. Too bad he wasn't as good a person."

Mike's face falls. He doesn't like getting the dirt on his favorite childhood show. I can sympathize. I never got over finding out the whole cast of *Saved by The Bell* was fucking. (Although, I should have suspected it.)

"James Queen changed once the show became successful?" I ask.

"He did," Murdoch says, "Success went to his head. I don't know. Maybe he was always like that and I didn't realize it. Whatever it was, he was a raging asshole. To his castmates, to the crew. To me."

Mike interjects. "How so?"

"He'd demand changes to the script," Murdoch says, "make sure he was featured in every shot, demand that other cast members' lines were cut so he'd get more. He was hell on wheels. And that was before we had to negotiate money."

I shoot him a quizzical look. "Negotiate? Didn't he have a contract?"

Murdoch sighs, ruefully. "There are contracts and there are contracts. Jim Queen became a huge star overnight. Bigger than the show. And he knew it. He could demand what he wanted and there was nothing we could to about it. After the first season, he wanted to completely redo his deal. The network wanted to fire him. But I knew that would ruin the show. To the public, Jim Queen was The Night Hawk. The only way I could save the show was to re-sign him. And give him what he wanted."

"And what was that?" I ask.

"A piece of the show," Murdoch says, "Part ownership in my production company and my rights to The Night Hawk. Smartest move he could have made. I gave in. Dumbest move I could have made."

Mike looks afraid to ask. "He got worse?"

Murdoch nods. "And there was nothing I could do about it. I tied myself to him. Forever. It ruined my chance to make things right!"

The last part comes out a little louder. Murdoch puts a hand to his chest. His body curls around it. Billie appears as if out of thin air. Murdoch waves her away. She fades into a corner, looking uneasy. Mike's eyes get wide.

"You're talking about *Night Hawk: The Movie*, right?" Mike asks.

Everyone in the room recoils, like a sewer pipe broke open. Bringing up *Night Hawk: The Movie* to Hal Murdoch is like inviting Jeff Bridges to a career retrospective and spending the whole time asking about *Heaven's Gate*. The movie came out about ten years after the cancellation of the TV series. The show's popularity in syndication sparked interest in a movie. A number of A-list stars were rumored to be attached. Instead, the cast of the original series were reunited. The result was a ninety-minute version of the show that amped up all the campiness and shitty comedy and lost nearly all the derring-do and subtle characterization. It was cinematic root canal. The critics roasted it. Box office returns were roughly equivalent to the income of the guy on the exit ramp holding the *Will Work for Food* sign. A bomb of epic proportions. Career mass suicide for everyone involved. Hal Murdoch included.

Murdoch rests his head against the steeple of his fingers. "That was supposed to be my redemption." He catches himself. "*The Night Hawk*'s redemption. We were going to have The Night Hawk from the comic books. Dark, dangerous, edgy. The original script was terrific. Me and this kid, Christopher Schmidt, worked on it. He was going to direct it as well. We had some big names interested. I was over the moon about it. But there was a problem."

"James Queen," I say.

Murdoch clenches a fist. "I couldn't get the film made unless I got that son of a bitch out of the way. I offered him a cameo. Maybe a supporting part. No dice. He wanted to be The Night Hawk again. He wanted a comeback. The only way I could get the movie made was to make him The Night Hawk." Murdoch glances languidly toward the window. "It was a damn shame. James could have played it straight if he had wanted. But he didn't trust himself. Didn't think the public would accept him. He made us rewrite everything. Drove that Schmidt kid right off the picture. Right out of the business. Queen brought in his own director, some geek who did comedies. And that was that." He throws his hands out, simulating something going up in smoke. "Poof. The critics couldn't get the knives out fast enough. Then the public followed."

Mike tugs at his hands. "It was…uh…"

"You don't have to be nice, son," Murdoch says, "I know a stink burger when I see one. I walked out of that premiere knowing it was over, knowing no one would ever give me money to make another film. And all for one mistake. For giving in to that son of a bitch!"

Again, Murdoch raises his voice. It's guttural and harsh. His fist swishes the air. He starts to get out of the chair. Before he can get there, he puts a hand to his chest and falls back into the chair. His face is red. Sweat beads pop out on his forehead. He gasps for air. Billie materializes next to Murdoch. She produces a tiny pill from a small box and slips it directly into Murdoch's mouth. After a few moments, Murdoch breathes easier. Billie hovers until Murdoch pats her on the arm.

"Sorry," he tells us, in a raspy voice.

Billie almost screens Murdoch from us. "I think Mr. Murdoch needs some rest."

Murdoch, though, places a hand on Billie's hip and gently moves her aside. "It's all right," he says, "I'll be fine." Billie hesitates, then fades into the background once more. Murdoch gives us a flip of his hand. "You have to forgive Billie. She was a bodyguard before she became my assistant. The old instincts still kick in from time to time."

"It's okay," Mike says.

This is an awkward moment. There is more I want to ask Murdoch, but it feels like badgering a guy in ICU. Billie gives me a forbidding look. If I had to guess, she'd love to grab my phone and chuck it off the deck. I look away from her and decide to keep going.

"I want to ask about the day James Queen died," I say, "You talked with him in his dressing room. And then you came back later. What were you two talking about?"

"Just trying to make friendly conversation," Murdoch says, "With James, that wasn't easy. I tried to be polite. Then he made nasty remarks about the other people in the cast. I got disgusted and I told him off. We argued and I thought it was best to leave. I stewed about it and then I decided to return. I don't know what I was looking for. Maybe some conciliatory words. Maybe another chance to tell him what a son of a bitch he is. In any event, you two were already there. Then he got nasty again. After that, there was no chance to talk to him."

"Then you just went backstage?" I ask.

"I was alone for a bit," Murdoch says, "Trying to calm down."

"And you didn't see James Queen again?" I ask, "Until, uh, the incident?"

"That's correct." Then he catches himself. "No, I stand corrected. I saw him chewing out your friend. I assume it was about the bottled water. I didn't want to get involved. I'd had enough of James."

"That's when you ran into Ella Jones?" I say, "She said the two of you were backstage when Mr. Queen died."

"Yes, we were," Murdoch says, "She seemed upset."

"She had been in Queen's dressing room," I say, "Do you know what they were talking about?"

"Not word for word. I think Ella was asking for Queen's help with something."

That's interesting. "With what?" I ask.

"I don't know," Murdoch says, "She only said she asked for James's help and he was horrible."

Ella didn't mention anything about asking for James Queen's help. Why the omission? Or is Murdoch not remembering things correctly? Mentally, though, he's pretty sharp. Before I contemplate it much, Billie ushers us away.

"I think Mr. Murdoch should rest," she says.

This time, Murdoch doesn't object. Billie isn't tall, but her stare is penetrating and her presence formidable. I scoop my phone off the table.

"Thanks for your time," I say.

"It's been my pleasure," Murdoch says.

Mike leaps over to Murdoch and shakes his hand once more. Murdoch gives Mike an indulgent smile even as Mike threatens to pump the man's arm right off his body. Billie puts a hand on Mike's back and gently, but firmly moves him to the door. I open the door and start to lead the way out. Murdoch's voice calls after me.

"Send me a copy of the article," he says.

"Absolutely," I say, "I'll send you the link."

Murdoch's face falls. "Link?" Then he mutters, "Goddamn internet."

Some days, I feel the same way.

***

"The problem with Brad," Casey says, a glass of beer just below her lips, "was that he would do anything for me."

"Sounds like a good problem to have," I say, toying with my pint of Grand Brewing Oktoberfest.

"Well, it was, and it wasn't. It could get…" She searches for the right word, "complicated."

I prop my chin in my hand. "How so?"

Casey gives me a shy look, as if totally unaware I would ask the question she's invited. It's fun. I haven't had a teasing conversation in a while. And Casey was always great at it. It's nice to have her here on my home turf.

The Tav is walking distance from my place—even in the winter—and is my favorite watering hole. It's a combination sports bar/pub. The atmosphere is cozy, the staff knows me and there's a collection of quality craft beers. The thin lighting illuminates Casey's bright eyes. If the coy looks and playful tone in Casey's voice mean anything (and I certainly hope they do), I am on my game.

Casey thinks about good old Brad and his complicated willingness to do anything. "Okay, for example," she says, "did you know Brad could do a really good Scottish accent?"

I was not. I vaguely remember Brad. He was in our Brit Lit class, junior year. A nice enough guy, in a bland sort of way. He and Casey dated for about six months and I never quite knew what she saw in him. He wore wire-rim glasses and button-up shirts and looked like the kind of guy who steps out of the shower to pee. To hear he would do something as daring as a Scottish accent is downright shocking.

"I did not know that," I say, "Our Brad had hidden talents."

"He could do it pretty well. And I'll admit…it was kind of a turn on."

All right, *now* I can see what Casey saw in Brad. "You learn something new every day."

"But like I said, it could be trouble." She leans close, as if she's going to share a state secret. "There was this one time. We were in his dorm room, in bed together. And, just to kind of kickstart things…I asked him to do the accent."

"Why, Miss Kinky Boots."

Casey looks down, faux-embarrassed. "But there was a problem. See, Brad couldn't really whisper and do the accent. He could only do it at the top of his lungs. Which is fine if you're in a car or going for a walk by the river, but not so much in a dorm room in the middle of the night."

"Thus, you weren't the only one getting turned on."

"Exactly. The whole floor must have thought we were doing a porn version of *Braveheart*."

"Which, viewed from a certain angle…"

Casey crumples a napkin and throws it at me. It bounces off my face and lands next to my beer. We're laughing, just like we're back on the Adams College campus, sharing our various misadventures. But it feels like there's something more here. We're both trying to cultivate a sense this tete-a-tete is important, but not *too* important. (Studied casualness, you see.) I'm wearing a maroon dress shirt with my jeans. Casey has just a hint of makeup. We're giving each other the same faux-casual vibe. The laughing subsides and we can clink glasses in a toast.

"You're writing an article on James Queen," she says.

"I am. His life and untimely death."

Casey props her chin in her hand. "Is there anything about James Queen's death that the general public doesn't know?"

"A few things," I say, "I'm not sure if I should go into details…"

"And why not?" Casey asks, picking up on my teasing tone.

"At the end of the day, I'm still a journalist. I can't give away scoops to just anybody."

"Who am I going to tell?" she says, teasing, "I only run into the geeks at Jitters and—okay, they'd be interested. But I promise I won't say anything."

I make a show of thinking about it. Casey strikes a pose, like a puppy begging for food. I can't help but laugh. I set my beer aside and tell her the story: Mike being attacked, the potential suspects and what I've found so far. Casey gradually forgets about her drink.

"You think James Queen was killed?" she asks.

"It's a possibility," I say, "Why would someone come after Mike for something he's supposed to know? And James Queen was mentioned specifically. Something's up."

"You've got a point," Casey says, "How's Mike handling it?"

"He's freaking out. As expected. I'm keeping an eye on him, though."

"How so?"

"He's living with me."

Casey covers her mouth, trying—and spectacularly failing—to cover her laugh. She hung out with Mike enough to know what he's like. And to know that whatever strange brew that creates my friendship with Mike will curdle when we're forced to live together.

"How is that going so far?" she asks

"If the murderer doesn't get him, I just might."

We laugh, despite Mike's misery. (Cut us some slack. It doesn't take much to make Mike miserable.) We enjoy the moment. Our faces are close, and it feels uncomfortable.

"I've missed this," Casey says.

"Me too."

"We always had such a great time together."

I grimace slightly. "Maybe not always."

And there it is, folks. Come one, come all and see the eight-hundred-pound gorilla in the room. To her credit, Casey doesn't play dumb and ask what I'm talking about. She looks down, a little embarrassed.

"I'm sorry about that," she says.

"You're apologizing to *me*?" I say.

"It was really mean of me. Going around…saying what I said. I guess I was just embarrassed. Maybe a little…"

"Disappointed?"

Casey keeps her eyes on the table. "I think I built things up in my mind. We had such a great chemistry and I thought it meant we…" She swirls her beer. "It doesn't matter. The point is, I shouldn't have gone around saying what I said." She sneaks a look at me. "Can you forgive me?"

I dismiss it with a light laugh. "Of course. I wouldn't be sitting here if I couldn't."

Casey lets out a breath, relieved. "I'm glad to hear that. This is what we always did best, anyway."

Obviously, I can't let it go at that. (I wouldn't be sitting here if I could.) "I don't think we really gave that other thing a chance."

"Really?" Casey says, "I hate to break this to you, but when people talk about going 'all the way', they're talking about what we did."

"I get that," I say, "but I think we could have done better. *I* could have done better."

Casey studies me over her beer. "What are you saying?"

"It's just that…I didn't really have any complaints before. And none since. With you and me, I get the feeling it was…just one of those things."

There's a long silence. Casey gets that Cheshire Cat grin. The light from the candle on the table flickers against her soft face. "Just one of those things?"

"A freak occurrence," I say, "One I've regretted ever since."

We gaze at each other. There's a fluttering in my stomach. Casey pushes aside her beer and folds her arms on the table.

"I'll be honest," she says, "I've always wondered what might have happened if we had given it another shot. It feels like there's…"

"Unfinished business?"

"Exactly. I was so glad to bump into you at the convention. And to see you walk into Jitters."

My face feels warm. "That's nice to know." I take her hands. "What should we do?"

"Not sure," Casey says, "Seems like we should do something, though."

My eyes cut toward the door. "You want to get out of here?"

"Absolutely."

I run to the bar and throw some money at Nick, the bartender. He squints at me beneath his shaggy eyebrows. Then he gets a look at Casey and all becomes clear. He scoops the money off the bar and gives me a wink. Casey and I hurry out into the night.

It's chilly, but not uncomfortable. Casey walks ahead of me. We only get as far as her Toyota Corolla before she grabs me and kisses me. We wind up in an embrace against the driver's door. It's as intense as the old days (well, old *day*). Casey slides her hands over my ass. I kiss her neck as she lets out little gasps.

"I just want you to know," Casey says, "that I think we should take this slow."

"Slow, yes, completely."

"We can go back to your place…and play…but maybe it should stop there. For now."

"For now. Of course." I'd agree to join the Taliban at this point. Anything to get Casey back to my place. Everything is going exactly as I had hoped.

So, naturally, my cell phone rings and fucks everything up.

I should ignore it, of course. But the phone shatters the mood. I have nothing to lose in answering it. I offer my apologies to Casey and take the phone out of my pocket (a more delicate operation than it would have been a few minutes ago). Mike is on the other end. I should have known. He better have a damn good reason for calling.

"What is it?" I ask, trying—and failing—not to sound out of breath.

"I need your help," he says, sounding equally out of breath (though I'm hoping for an entirely different reason), "Someone's following me."

I'll hand it to him. It's an entirely different reason.

CHAPTER SEVEN

I know people are fond of saying things like, "I would do anything for my friends." And they're completely sincere about that. Until someone calls their bluff.

I don't know if it's my cynicism or my hatred of blanket statements, but, come on, anything for your friends? First off, "friends" is a broad category. I don't have a ton of friends, but even within that small group, I've developed a hierarchy. Mike, Carol and Lars can expect me to go further in assisting them than, say, Sully who chats me up while we're on the exercise bikes at the health club. If you're honest, you've developed a hierarchy, too. If your bosom companion of many years calls you up and tells you they're stranded on the roadside on a winter night and they need you to come get them, you'll quickly struggle into your coat and boots and grab your car keys. (While secretly bitching about it the whole time.) On the other hand, if Phil from Accounting gives you that same call, you're likely to go, "Sorry, Phil, I've had a few beers——" (Slugs first beer, hastily cracks a second.) "You, uh, you sure you don't have AAA or something?" It's just reality. Don't shoot me. I'm only the messenger.

While Mike is on top of the hierarchy, where does that hierarchy stand as compared to nookie or the warm-up-to-nookie? The few seconds break from Casey has allowed the blood flow to divert back to my brain. I'm able to think critically (if not happily).

"Being followed?" I ask, "What do you mean 'being followed?'"

"As in someone is following me, you gibbering moron!" All right, it was a stupid question, I'll give him that. "I walked up to the convenience store to get a few things," he says, "and I noticed someone following me on the way back. I tried to run back to my building, but he cut me off. I don't know where to go. I need help."

I rest my knuckles against my head. I need to help Mike. I'm struggling with the want-to. However, the mood here is shattered. Casey tilts her head to one side, wondering what the hell is going on. I return the phone to my ear.

"Where are you now?" I ask.

"I'm walking around Mears Park," he says, "As long as there are people here, I'm safe. I don't know how long that's going to last. How soon can you get down here?"

That's a bit of a sticky wicket (and other Britishisms I really ought to drop from my vocabulary). I didn't drive to The Tav, since the place is in walking distance. Time is of the essence. I turn to Casey.

"Can you give me a ride downtown?" I ask.

"Sure," Casey says, "Is everything okay?"

"I don't know. It's a thing with Mike. I'll tell you on the way." I speak into the phone again. "I'll be there in less than ten minutes. I'm getting a ride from Casey."

I can tell Mike is smirking, even over the phone. "Good. Then I know you'll be quick."

Yep. Our Mike. Really knows how to ask a favor, he does.

****

On the bright side, I don't have to explain the urgency of the situation to Casey. She tears out of The Tav parking lot and down Cathedral Hill as if she has no fear of the police. I fill her in on the call from Mike. Casey's jaw drops, slightly.

"Who is the guy following him?" she asks.

"No idea. If I had to guess, the same person who attacked Mike in his apartment. And, possibly, the same person who killed James Queen."

"We're trying to get Mike away from a murderer?"

Casey doesn't seem disturbed by that conclusion. Her eyes flash with excitement. At least I won't have to apologize for this little misadventure.

If Mears Park conjures up images of a sprawling park in the center of the city (like a low-rent Central Park), allow me to correct your misconception. Mears Park is, in fact, a "park" in name only. It's a square the size of a city block, hemmed in by apartment buildings and retail. The "park" is more concrete than grass. While it hosts a kickass jazz festival for one weekend in the summer, it mainly houses the local homeless population and staffs the occasional mugging.

Casey turns on Fifth Street and follows it across downtown. We pass a sad little skyscraper called Cray Plaza and the park opens before it. I scan the park for Mike. He's powerwalking down the sidewalk closest to Sixth Street, on the north end of the park. Casey sees him and takes a left on Sibley, heedless of the traffic. (It's downtown St. Paul after five. There's never traffic here.) I look for Mike's pursuer. There's no shortage of shady-looking personae around the park. It makes an incriminating sort hard to distinguish. I lower the window, preparing to call to Mike.

Just as he gets jumped.

It happens too fast to immediately process. There's a flash of something, then Mike goes down on all fours. He's stunned. I hop out of Casey's car, not waiting for her to stop. She's going slow enough that I'm able to stay on my feet. No TV-cop-roll-on-the-pavement required. I slip between two parked cars and run for Mike.

"Hey!" I shout. Because one really shouldn't show up unannounced in these situations.

The guy standing over Mike looks like something out of a Terry Gilliam movie. He's fat, with a black trench coat covering much of the bulk. He wears a black felt hat that obscures the part of his face not obscured by a ski mask. He brandishes a nightstick. For a moment, the guy doesn't move. I'm not sure if it's surprise or indecision. Then he turns and runs.

I kneel next to Mike. "You okay?"

He looks up, glassy-eyed. "Oh hello, Joe. What are you doing at the prom?"

The guy is getting away. Casey stops at the curb and hops out. I pop to my feet and shout to her.

"Make sure Mike's okay. I'll be right back."

I'm wildly optimistic about the *Be right back* thing, of course. Casey shouts something to me as I take off. I don't catch all of it, but it sounds like concern that I'm taking on a fool's errand. Like I don't know that. But I've come this far…

The guy hustles down the sidewalk, jumps between two parked cars and cuts a diagonal path across Sixth. I follow his route. He's fast for someone his size. I'm a decent runner, but I'm not gaining on him. Once across Sixth, he swings around a building and runs up Wacouta toward Seventh Street.

Seventh Street is a higher-traffic zone. It leads to Highway 94 one direction and bends through downtown the other. There's a chance we might get someone's attention. (Again, downtown St. Paul after dark? No guarantees.) The guy cuts around a building, disappearing from my sight, and runs down Seventh Street.

Or so I think.

The second I round the building, something hits me in the stomach. It's been a while since I've had all the wind knocked out of me. I haven't missed it. My knees buckle and my stomach seizes up. It's like a giant invisible hand is squeezing the life out of me.

A muffled voice comes from above. "Did your friend tell you?"

I struggle to form words. "Tell me what?"

There's silence, then: "Stay out of this. Your friend is a fucking dead man."

Some air starts to return, flooding me with relief. Footsteps fade into the distance. When my vision clears, there's no sign of the guy. No witnesses. Downtown St. Paul. Where you have the freedom to commit felonious assault in anonymity.

I slowly get to my feet and feel around my ribcage. Nothing broken (although I have no idea what broken ribs feel like). I spit into my hand. No blood in the saliva. No internal bleeding. So, I've got that going for me, which is nice.

I walk back to Mears Park, moving more gingerly than when I left. Mike and Casey are at the corner of Sixth and Sibley. Casey, seeing me holding my stomach, runs up to me, a concerned look on her face. I hold up a hand, silently assuring her I'm all right. I look to Mike.

"Are you okay?" I ask.

"Jiffy swell," Mike says, stretching his back, "Just knocked the wind out of me a little. How about you?"

"Knocked the wind out of me a lot," I say.

I relay the story to Mike and Casey. Mike's face gets tense. Casey's mouth drops open. One of them is more used to this kind of thing. Casey puts a hand on my stomach.

"You sure you're all right?" she asks.

Given the charge I get from her touch, I'm tempted to play up the injury. Unfortunately, Mike is here. If I play injured hero, Mike will greet it with a series of eyerolls. I give Casey's arm a squeeze.

"I'm fine," I say, "Just pissed I didn't catch the guy."

Mike looks toward Seventh. "He moves fast for a fat ass."

"He does," I say, "Was that the guy who attacked you in your apartment?"

"I didn't get a good look at him," Mike says.

Swell. Two attacks, no identification. Yes, we could go to the police and report this. But Mike won't agree to it.

And I would feel like an idiot telling a skeptical cop we were assaulted by a fat guy wearing a fedora and a ski mask. The cop would smell the beer on my breath and probably give me a "Move along, rummy." (Assuming, of course, the cop was from the 1940s.) I put a hand on Mike's shoulder.

"You sure you're okay?" I ask.

"I'm fine," Mike says, "Let's just get back to your place."

Casey and I exchange a look. I had planned on having company at my place, but needless to say, it was *not* going to be Mike. However, the dude was just attacked. I can't abandon him to his fate just because I've got a decent shot at some nookie. (To be clear, I *can't* do that, right? Dammit.)

"Casey, would you, uh, would you mind giving us a ride back to my place?" I say.

She doesn't hesitate. "Of course not. You didn't even have to ask."

Mike's body sags with relief. "Thank you."

We walk back to Casey's car. Mike hops into the backseat. Casey and I linger on the sidewalk. I put my hands in my coat pockets.

"Thanks for helping out," I say.

"Quite an adventure," Casey says.

"I guess Mike being at my place kills our…earlier plans."

"I guess it does."

I clear my throat. "I hope you're not…uh…"

A corner of Casey's mouth curls up. "I'll take a raincheck."

The relief drives me to give her a quick kiss. It could easily turn into a longer kiss, but Mike starts rapping on the window. Casey gives me an embarrassed grin before walking around to the driver's side. I slide over to the passenger door, trying not to think about the night I'm missing out on.

I hope Mike is worth all this. Although I'm almost certain he isn't.

***

While I like to believe we're moving toward a more enlightened era, one in which people are not strictly defined by gender roles, and we're all seen as equal and worthy, I'll admit it's quite an uphill battle. Yes, guys are generally unwilling to give up certain cliched roles they've assumed over the centuries. But women have to be aware of their own stereotyping. As evidence, I present any girl I've dated who assumed I knew *a lot* more about auto mechanics than I do. And, of course, there's my good friend Carol.

"This guy kicked *both* your asses?" she asks, staring over her coffee cup at Mike and me.

Mike and I look at each other. This wasn't quite the happy hour we were expecting. Apparently, a sympathetic ear

145

while relating our adventures from the night before was a bit too much to ask.

"It was a sneak attack," I say, "Both times.

Mike slaps the bar. "Damn skippy."

"Uh-huh," Carol says, "Keep telling yourselves that."

I grab another Grand Brewing Oktoberfest out of the fridge. Lenny is underfoot, letting me know it's time for dinner. Squiggy stands nearby, allowing Lenny to do the dirty work. I toss some dry food into their dish, sidestep the ensuing stampede and return to the breakfast bar.

"You sure you don't want something stronger?" I ask.

"No, thanks," Carol says, quickly, "I don't…really have the taste for it. Right now."

Mike shoots her a look. "Why not?"

"I just don't," she says.

Carol glares at me, letting me know I am not to share the bachelorette party story with Mike. I give her a small tilt of the head, assuring her everything will remain on the downlow.

"I've been thinking about the whole thing," I say, "Now that I've had a minute. There was some weird stuff going on."

"Weird stuff?" Carol says, "It just sounded like your typical masked guy in a fedora stalking and attacking two people in downtown St. Paul. Nothing to see there."

I ignore Carol and slide on to one of the stools. "Mike said it last night. The attacker moved pretty fast for a fat guy."

"But that's not a deal-breaker," Mike says, "You remember J.J. Joyce? From the touch football tournament? He moves pretty fast for a big fat ass."

"He did until you broke his leg," I say.

"I was going for the ball," Mike says.

"The ball that was on the other side of the field?" I ask.

Mike sips his beer. "Whoops."

Carol, as she's wont to do, steps into the middle of our vaudeville routine. "All right, the guy moved fast for someone who's overweight. What does that mean?"

"That maybe he isn't fat," I say, "Maybe the trench coat was a disguise. You stuff it with a few layers of clothes or something and there you are. Makes a thin person hard to identify."

Carol twists her mouth to one side as she considers this. "It would certainly fit with the rest of the outfit."

"And there was something about the guy's voice," I say, "It was gravelly and raspy. It didn't sound…natural."

Mike perks up. "Like when I got attacked. He was disguising his voice."

Carol holds up a finger. "Or *her* voice."

Mike gets a pained look, not liking the implication. Whether it's the idea Ella Jones might be the attacker or that we got our asses kicked by a girl is less clear. He gets up from the breakfast bar and strolls into the living room (without putting his beer bottle in the recycling).

"That doesn't mean it's Ella Jones," he says, reading the room, "A guy could disguise his voice, too. Or maybe it *is* a fast fat guy. What about Tim Hefflin? I don't want to think it's him. But if it *had* to be one of the people on *The Night Hawk*…" Mike trails off.

"Have you talked to Tim Hefflin yet?" Carol asks.

"Next on the agenda," I say, "I'm just not sure how to do it. Lars is busy planning the memorial for Queen and working for his…mentor. I know Hefflin's staying at the Ambassador Suites, but that's about it. I don't know how to get ahold of him."

"Or if he'd even talk to us if we *did* get ahold of him," Mike says.

"You could always spy on him and follow him," Carol says, "If he's the guy who's stalking you, turnabout would be fair play."

Mike and I look at each other. Yes, the sarcasm in Carol's voice was unmistakable, but that doesn't mean she's wrong. If we can't figure out how to get ahold of Tim

Hefflin, we have to manufacture a way. Mike seems to be on my wavelength.

"You may have something there," he says.

Carol's head swivels between the two of us. "I don't have anything. It was a joke."

I wag a finger at her. "But the best humor has a ring of truth in it. We need to talk to Hefflin. This might be the only way we can do it."

"What's the plan then?" Carol asks, "You loiter around the lobby of the Ambassador Suites and hope that Tim Hefflin walks thr…that's exactly what you're going to do, isn't it?"

"It is," I say.

Mike fetches his jacket from the coat tree (where I put it after he'd thrown it over the back of the futon). "We can finish happy hour down there."

I grab my jean jacket and look to Carol, now stranded at the breakfast bar. "You want to come along? It was your idea."

"What am I supposed to do?" Carol says, "Babysit you two? Keep an eye on you so you don't get into any…that's exactly what I'm going to need to do, isn't it?"

"It is," I say.

She drains the rest of her drink and grabs her coat. Carol is probably wishing she kept her mouth shut.

That's the story of *Carol's* life.

***

While it wasn't as spectacular as some rock stars you've heard about, Tim Hefflin did have an Icarus-like flight through the entertainment industry. At twenty-five, the star (or at least, lead supporting character) of a popular TV series, bundles of money, appearances on the covers of magazines (back when those were a thing), women throwing themselves at him (at least, that's how he chooses to remember it), invitations to all the big parties and meetings with all the high-powered people. The world at his feet.

And then…

At twenty-eight, an out-of-work actor typecast by the role that made him famous. He realized he wasn't going to get any serious roles and after a while, realized he wasn't going to get *any* roles. Not even thirty and his dreams had come and gone. Fortunately, there was drinking. Hefflin got really good at that.

It's a talent that still serves him well.

Since we're not guests at The Ambassador Suites and respectable hotels don't generally take loiterers, Carol, Mike and I find a table in the hotel bar. The general public is allowed to congregate there. The place is a bit crowded, but not so much so that you have to wait forever for a drink. A Nancy Sinatra tune plays on the stereo system. A pretty okay time if we weren't on low-grade stakeout. We keep an eye on the lobby. If Hefflin comes through, we'll know it.

"You going to use the cover story about writing an article," Mike says, swirling the Oktoberfest in his glass.

"It's worked so far," I say, sipping my own beer.

Mike greets this by getting up and going to the bathroom. (I'll try not to take that as a lack of faith in me.) Carol and I are left alone. She looks at her Coke and frowns. I think she no longer enjoys the ride on the wagon.

"You found out anything more about the bachelorette party?" I ask.

"No. The mystery is still there. And getting deeper."

I prop my chin in one hand. "Do tell."

Carol sneaks a look in the direction of the restrooms. No sign of Mike. "I got a text message from Shannon. She's in the wedding party. It said *Way to go.*"

"Way to go? Way to go what?"

"I have no earthly idea. And I wasn't sure how to ask Shannon. I just texted back *Thanks.* That was that."

"Have you talked to Chris, the bride? Or anyone else in the wedding party?"

"No. There's a rehearsal in a few days, at the History Center. That's where the wedding's going to be. Maybe I'll find out something. Maybe I don't want to, though."

I toy with my beer glass. "You realize nothing might have happened? It's just a feeling you've got. I've gotten strange feelings after a bender. Most of the time, they don't amount to anything."

"Most of the time?"

"There was the incident on Front Street. But my lack of memory probably helped with the police questioning."

Mike comes back to the table and Carol clams up. She finishes her soda and shoves the empty glass aside. After few minutes, our waiting pays off. The elevator doors open, and Tim Hefflin emerges. He wears a pair of shades, lest anyone recognize him. (Probably not much of a worry.) A black sweater is draped halfway over his gut, looking not unlike a muumuu. His black hair is already a bit mussed and his face is blotchy as ever. He orders a whiskey at the bar, then makes his way to a corner table behind the trellis (very near the one Ella used). He slumps over the drink, his only friend. We follow his movements.

"Are you going to go talk to him?" Carol asks.

I drain the rest of my Oktoberfest. "Let's do it."

Mike and I stop at the bar for refills, then head for Hefflin's table. He doesn't notice us until we're right up on him. He doesn't greet us. Since it's my cover story, I get to do the honors.

"Hi," I say, trying to sound confident, "You're Tim Hefflin, right?"

Hefflin takes off the shades. "Who are you?"

"My name's Joe Davis. I work for *The Daily Bugle.* Have you heard of it?"

"No."

Kind of reach. Yes, *The Bugle* is on the worldwide web, but our following is mainly in the Twin Cities. Still, Hefflin's manner isn't putting me at ease. Strange that I'd be intimidated by a guy who hasn't been famous in more than thirty years.

"We met you backstage at the convention," I say.

"I don't remember that," Hefflin says.

No surprise there. "It was, uh, it was right before..." I look for the right words.

"Jim Queen dropped dead?"

That'll cover it. "That's right. At any rate, I'm doing an article on James Queen and I was hoping—"

Hefflin slips the shades on. "Look, no offense, but I just want to sit here and enjoy my drink. I don't want to be bothered by some fucking fanboy with a WordPress page and a hard-on for old memories."

I mutter. "Why would I be offended by that?"

Mike elbows me in the gut. He backs away from the table, pulling me in his wake. "Sorry to bother you," he says, "Maybe some other time."

Hefflin flicks his hand, like he's getting rid of a gnat. We make the walk of shame back to our table.

"That was a mistake," Mike says, "We shouldn't have bothered him."

I'm not sure whether to be irritated or exasperated. Probably a combination of both. (What would that be? Irrasperated? Exitated? I'll work on it.) Mike has been ready to go down among the spittoons with people who have done or said far less. And yet, he's willing to give Tim Hefflin—a guy with only a slightly better claim to fame than either of us—a free pass for being an asshole.

Carol looks up as we take our seats. "That was fast."

"Tim Hefflin wasn't in the mood to talk," I say.

Mike and I sip our drinks. Carol chews the ice in her glass. We keep an eye on Hefflin's table. I follow the occasional movements of his head. It's *what* gets his attention that I find interesting.

I tap Mike on the arm. "You notice what Hefflin is looking at?"

"No," Mike says, "I was busy looking at the blonde with the bazongas."

Carol drops her head into one hand, but I plow forth. "You weren't the only one," I say, "Hefflin was looking at the same thing. In fact, he's looked at just about every woman who's walked past his table."

Mike smiles. "You're thinking…"

"We sent the wrong people for the job? Yep."

We both turn to Carol. She picks up on our vibe and gets a stricken look. She lays her hands on the table.

"You've got to be kidding me," she says.

"Suit up, Carol," I say, "You're in this half."

She wags her finger at me. "No way. The last time you said that, it was a complete clusterfuck."

She's got a point. When we last pressed Carol into this kind of service, she wound up in the ladies' room fending off a lawyer covered in fake cocaine. (Like you do.) So, I get where the hesitation is coming from, I really do. But we don't have time to rehash old disasters.

"It won't be like that," I say.

Carol levels a look at me. "How do you know?"

I struggle to come up with a reason. "Because I have faith in you."

Mike nods in agreement. Carol groans. "Let me guess this straight," she says, "you two idiots get yourself into this situation and I have to bail you out?"

"Part of our charm," I say. Carol looks ready to come over the table and strangle me. I back off. "Just ask him a few questions. Get some information."

It's a big favor, granted. A challenge, one might say. And like proud, borderline arrogant people everywhere, Carol can't back down from a challenge. She stands and straightens her skirt.

"This better be worth it," she says.

Carol stalks toward the bar and orders a drink. While she waits, she takes her hair down and fluffs it out, checking her look in the mirror behind the bar. Hefflin perks up, looking her direction. The bartender puts a Cosmo in front of Carol. Down with the wagon, up with liquid courage. Carol subtly undoes a few buttons on her blouse, then flicks the neckline open.

I lean toward Mike. "I'm not sure Carol can get away with the *Here's a view of Cleveland* thing."

"Actually, Carol's got a pretty decent rack."

"Really?"

"You wouldn't think to look at her. I don't know if it's the way she dresses or the way she carries herself. But the shirt and bra come off and you're like, 'Whoa!'"

We each bring up the mental image. In my case, it's based on imagination and in Mike's, it's based on fact. I throw a look at Mike.

"Should we be thinking about this?" I ask.

"Can't see where it's going to do us any good."

We go back to our surveillance work. Carol slowly turns and props her elbows on the bar. She's got Tim Hefflin's undivided attention. Mike taps me on the arm.

"There's a table on the other side of the trellis," Mike says, "We can probably hear and see everything."

We grab our beers and take a circuitous route to the table. Hefflin doesn't see us arrive. Then again, we could be toting a nuclear bomb and Hefflin wouldn't notice. His attention is strictly on Carol. She slinks toward Hefflin's table. Mike and I slide into our seats just as Carol reaches Hefflin. He removes his shades. Carol brushes the table with her fingertips.

"Hi," she says, "Anyone sitting here?"

"Um, you," Hefflin says, his mouth slack, "If you want."

"I want."

Carol glides into the chair opposite Hefflin. He fumbles with his drink, visibly sweating.

"I'm, uh…" he says.

"You're Tim Hefflin," Carol says, her voice smoother than the whiskey Hefflin's drinking, "I know exactly who you are. I'm a huge fan of *The Night Hawk*."

"Oh, you're too young to remember that show."

"I am," Carol says. Then she catches herself. "But that's what Netflix is for, right?"

Hefflin chuckles, nervously. He downs his drink and signals for another. "I'm glad you like the show."

"I did. I loved…" Carol's eyes widen. She's drawn a blank on Hefflin's role in the show. "Your character."

"Wing Red."

Carol props her chin on her hand, her stride restored. "I loved seeing you in action. You were amazing."

Another drink arrives. Hefflin grabs it and gulps it. He spills some on the table but doesn't seem to care.

"You liked me on the show, huh?" he says, "Most people talk about how great James Queen was."

"No," Carol says, a finger stroking her jaw, "There is only one reason I watch that show."

Hefflin's laugh is a little high-pitched. He slugs the rest of his drink and nearly drops the glass on the table. Carol rests a hand on his forearm.

"You didn't get along with James Queen?" she asks.

Hefflin signals for another drink. His voice is thick. "He was an ass. I suppose he was okay at first. But then he started treating me and the rest of the cast like peons."

There's a bit of sympathy in Carol's eyes. "It must have been rough."

"It got worse after the show," Hefflin says, "Queen went after me."

"How did he go after you?" Carol asks.

"He kept me from getting work." He sways a bit. "See, I'd get sent out on auditions, but I wouldn't get anything. Every time I thought something was going to develop, it got shut down. Took a lot of years, but I found out why it was happening. Who was responsible."

"James Queen," Carol says.

"Exactly," Hefflin says, lurching forward, "He practically fucking admitted it. The old cast, we did some damn commercial. Spaying and neutering your pets. Anyway, Queen asked if I was able to find any work. I told him I wasn't. He said he knew all about it. Then he walked away. When I asked my agent, she said word had gotten around that I was hard to work with. Unreliable. I didn't have to think too hard about who was saying that. I wanted to kill the motherfucker. But I wasn't sure I'd make it in jail."

Hefflin's new drink arrives. Carol looks away and spots us through the trellis. Mike gives her a thumbs up. She ignores him.

"Is that why you wrote your book?" Carol asks.

"Oh, that," Hefflin says, "The stuff in the book might not have been completely…factual." He lowers his voice. Mike and I lean closer to the trellis. "My agent told me the book would sell better with more…salacious details. She didn't care if the stuff actually happened. I just wrote whatever came into my head. And then I started to enjoy it. It was like a whole alternate history. I started to live in it. I didn't even think about people reading it and believing it was the truth. I was having fun."

"And Queen was upset?" Carol asks.

Hefflin laughs, practically spitting. "You might say that. Prick talked to me backstage, right before he died. Said he hired a lawyer and he was going to sue me. You believe that? Fucker could never take a joke."

This is a new wrinkle. No one mentioned that Queen was going to sue Hefflin. Maybe they didn't know. Carol looks concerned.

"You think he was serious?" she asks.

Hefflin takes a big swig. "Queen was always serious. Especially about himself. He wouldn't just threaten to sue me. He'd sue me." He runs a hand over his face. "Queen could afford a good lawyer. I couldn't. He was going to take everything from me. Didn't matter that I don't have anything to give."

Hefflin downs the rest of his drink and signals for another. He's listing to port. Carol pushes her Cosmo away.

"Could anyone have helped you?" she asks.

"Hal Murdoch, maybe," Hefflin says, slurring, "Hal always treated me well. I talked to him the day Queen was killed. Asked him what I should do about the lawsuit. He was willing to help. We didn't get into specifics. But I had hopes."

Okay, what the fuck? We had a conversation with Hal Murdoch, and he didn't say anything about the lawsuit. Then again, I didn't ask, and it isn't the sort of thing Murdoch would volunteer for an article about James Queen's career. That "doing an article" cover story only gets me so far.

"Could anyone else have helped?" Carol asks, "Ella Jones, maybe?"

Hefflin rests his chin in his hand. "Maybe. It's the kind of thing Ella would do. She's a sweetheart."

Another drink arrives. Hefflin grabs it greedily and takes a healthy sip. Carol speaks gently.

"You really like her," she says.

"I love her," Hefflin says, more high-pitched, like the old days. He looks quickly at Carol, as if he's given something away. Then he shrugs. "I always have. From the first time I met her. She's beautiful. A beautiful person."

"Did you ever tell her that?"

Hefflin sits back and bangs his head on the back of the booth. "No, she wouldn't want to hear that from me. She loves…someone who didn't deserve her. End of story."

"I thought Ella and James Queen were divorced," Carol says.

"They are. But it wasn't her idea. Queen cheated on her. With everyone and everything. More or less forced her hand. But she still doted on him. Still at his beck and fucking call." He swigs his drink. "Just the way Queen liked it."

Carol glances toward me and Mike. We're glued to the conversation, almost forgetting we're looking for incriminating evidence. She returns to Hefflin, now listing to starboard.

"Were you and Ella close?" I ask, "When you were filming the show, I mean?"

Hefflin drains most of his drink. "I guess. We talked a lot. She said once I was the only person she really *could* talk to. Including James."

"Did Queen know you loved Ella?" Carol asks.

"He did," Hefflin says, "And he loved rubbing my face in it. I bet it's why he talked shit about me. Ruined my career. He knew I'd do anything to protect Ella. Especially from guys like him."

"Anything?"

"Abso-fucking-lutely anything."

Carol looks to us, needing direction. I jerk a thumb toward Mike and mouth, "Ask about him." Carol turns back to Hefflin, who hasn't moved. (Given the amount Hefflin's had to drink, we have to consider the possibility he's dead.)

"You had an argument with James Queen the day he died," she says, "Did you see anything else?"

"Not really," Hefflin says, "I was busy puking."

"Puking?"

"I wasn't feeling well," Hefflin says, looking away, "I was talking with Mr. Murdoch and then I…had to step away. I had a lot of…cold medicine. You know? A fuckload of cold medicine." He clears his throat. "I got the, uh, vomiting over with and then I went over to the Nightmobile. Hung out there until I had to go on stage."

Not much to add. Carol sneaks a look to me and Mike. We give her the wrap up signal, letting her off the hook. She then realizes the difficulty: how to extract herself from this situation without looking suspicious. For his part, Hefflin isn't moving. Carol touches the table in front of him.

"Are you all right?" she asks.

Hefflin snaps a look at her, nearly falling over. "I'm fine. Fine. You're fine. Everybody's fine."

"Fine," Carol says.

There are a few seconds of silence. Hefflin struggles to keep his head up. "I've got to tell you," he says, slurring, "You're a very attractive woman."

"Thank you," Carol says, her face frozen.

"I've got a bottle of vodka up in my room. I can make you something. I'd love to."

He reaches for Carol's hand. She strategically picks up her Cosmo and finishes it in one swallow.

"Look, you're really sweet, but…"

Carol tries to think of something to go with that but is at a loss. Can't say I blame her. There's no shortage of reasons to avoid going upstairs with Tim Hefflin, but all of them, while true, are still insulting. Hefflin, though, will not be deterred.

"It'll be great," he says, "Just you and me and a few drinks. Sky's the limit. The idiot who put this convention together is still covering the hotel bill."

Carol struggles not to take off at a dead run. "That's nice, but—"

"Think about it," Hefflin says, "Just the two of us and…"

Sadly, we'll never find out what would have followed *and*. Because the next thing Tim Hefflin does is vomit. On Carol.

Yep, going to play hell getting her to do anything like this again.

CHAPTER EIGHT

A thing I didn't like about my teen years, but came to appreciate later, was how my parents prepared me for adulthood. (Not that I'll ever tell them that, mind you.)

All the time we were teenagers, my brothers and I were drilled in certain domestic skills. My parents were determined their boys were not going out into the big, bad world without a degree of self-sufficiency. Mom and Dad divided the teaching according to their specialties. Mom taught us how to cook, do dishes, make our beds, clean and straighten, and sew a button. Dad handled yardwork, simple repairs, balancing a checkbook and basic auto maintenance.

The division of labor created a division of success. Kevin and Owen took to my dad's teaching, handling their own repairs and car maintenance. I can cook and clean house. The division hasn't hurt us. I don't mind calling building maintenance for repairs or bringing my car into the shop for an oil change. My brothers leave domestic chores to others: Owen to his wife Mary and Kevin to his cleaning service and the local Chinese takeout. I only wish my brothers would stop making cracks about how I'll make someone a good little wife one day.

There are, of course, benefits to cooking that have nothing to do with sustaining life. (Don't get me wrong, sustaining life is a big one.) It comes in handy the morning after a first sleepover date. ("Hmm, he didn't totally embarrass himself as a lover *and* he can cook? This merits further exploration.") It also relaxes me and helps me think. This morning, for example, a simple omelet is in order.

It's bright and warm outside. The cats lounge in a sunny spot on the hardwood floor. The aroma of pumpkin spice coffee wafts through the air. The apartment is in decent shape, since I was able to clean up once Mike left for work. I slide an apron on over my red Adams College sweatshirt and get the ingredients out of the fridge.

I think about the chat with Hefflin as I sauté the onions and peppers. Three potential suspects, all of whom had unfriendly conversations with James Queen before his untimely demise. All of whom claim to have just gone about their business before said demise. Of the three, Hefflin's claim is the least reliable, given his level of, uh, cold medication.

I take the little frying pan with the onions and peppers off the burner and replace it with a larger frying pan. A healthy pat of butter is tossed into the larger pan. While that takes a few seconds to melt, I crack three eggs and drop the yolks into a silver mixing bowl, along with a splash of water and a dash of salt and pepper. I whisk and think.

Poison is the only way Queen could have died. Okay, so if Queen was poisoned, what kind of poison and who administered it? And when? What did Mike see that he shouldn't have seen? Should I be thinking about poison when I'm preparing a meal?

I spin back to the frying pan and slide the melting pat of butter around the pan. I pour the egg mixture into the frying pan and stand guard with my trusty spatula. The eggs set along the edges. I use the spatula to pull the eggs from the sides then drop in the sautéed onions and peppers. I toss some shredded cheddar over the top then use the spatula to carefully fold the omelet over and slide it on to a nearby plate. Voila! See, Mom? All those cooking lessons didn't go to waste. (Not that she will ever hear me say that.)

I set my omelet on the breakfast bar and pour a fresh cup of coffee. I think about what to do next. There were a few intriguing things to come out of chatting with the cast of *The Night Hawk*. Ella Jones asked for Queen's help. With what? She didn't bring it up. A second chat with her is in order. James Queen was going to bring a lawsuit against Tim Hefflin. No one mentioned that. Seems like I should have another chat with everyone from *The Night Hawk*. I'm just not sure how far I can get without telling them the real reason I'm asking these questions.

Then again, maybe I can approach this from another angle. I could bother Pike about the toxicology results. See what that turns up. Maybe I should have some breakfast and figure it out from there.

I'm at the breakfast bar when there's a knock at the door. I set my coffee down. I'm missing the Lars who would burst into my apartment unannounced. I didn't realize how much work it saved me. I answer the door. Sure enough, Lars is on the landing, dressed in his work suit.

"Good to see you, brother," he says, "Okay if I come in?"

"Lars, can we just have an understanding that you are allowed to come into my apartment unannounced any time between the hours of ten a.m. and ten p.m.?"

"Not sure I'm comfortable with that," he says, "You should always respect a person's privacy. When someone's at home, they are in the cocoon of—"

"Shut the fuck up and get in here."

Lars passes me, drops his hands into his pants pockets and looks around. He spots the omelet and coffee sitting on the breakfast bar.

"Breakfast, huh?" he says, "Looks good."

"You want some?"

"Oh no," he says, "Absolutely not. That's not why I came up here."

"It's no problem."

"Can't do it. I wouldn't want you thinking of me as a moocher."

Up to a few weeks ago, that's *exactly* how I thought of Lars. Even now, full in the knowledge of his changing ways, I fight the instinct to believe he came up here to score a free breakfast. Regardless, I have no intention of eating the damn thing in front of him.

"Lars, it's a three-egg omelet," I say, "That's way more breakfast than I normally eat. My eyes were bigger than my stomach. You'd be doing *me* a favor."

"I don't know…"

"I'm getting a plate for you. Sit down and help me eat this damn thing before it gets cold. That's an order!"

Lars sits at the breakfast bar while I fetch a plate and silverware. I plunk the plate down in front of him, use a butter knife to cut the omelet in two and slide his half on to his plate. Lars grabs a napkin from the dispenser on the breakfast bar and drops it in his lap. I slide a cup of coffee in front for him. We settle down for breakfast.

Quite the happy couple, we are.

Lars eats more slowly than usual. He taps his plate with his fork. "Good work here, my friend. Thank you."

"Glad I could help," I say, "What brings you by?"

"Just wanted to update you on the memorial," he says, "It's definitely going to be at the History Center. I'm going there in a few days to finalize the details. And, of course, Mr. Vitality and myself would still like you to speak."

Something about "History Center" gets my Spidey-Sense tingling, but I'm not sure why. "Is there anything you would like me to say?" I ask.

"I don't want to dictate," he says, "but I think you can stick to the facts of James Queen's career. Throw in a witty anecdote or two. Think you can handle it?"

"The wit? I can probably handle it." It's what I get paid for, after all.

Lars goes back to his breakfast. We make small talk until we're finished. Not a bad start to the day. I offer to put Lars's plate in the sink, but he insists on doing it himself. He even uses the dish scrubber to clean the dish. When he's done, I have a fresh cup of coffee waiting for him. He holds it up in a toast as he takes his seat.

"Mr. Vitality is interested in you," Lars says.

My own coffee cup stops shy of my lips. "Let him know I'm flattered, but unavailable."

"Not interested like that," he says, "Although you have a rather oppressive view of things. He's interested in helping your career."

"I seem to be doing fine," I say.

"But you could be doing more. Writing books. Plays. Maybe even a movie or a TV series. God knows you've got the time on your hands."

Speaking of hands, I offer Lars the back of mine. "I'm fine writing dick jokes three times a week."

Lars opens his mouth as if to argue, then he holds up his hands. "Just think about it. That's all I ask. You might not be living up to your potential."

"I think I am."

Which is a depressing thought, in a way. But not as depressing as becoming the kind of automaton Lars is evolving into. But I'm not going to argue with Lars. Not on a full stomach.

"It would be a good time for you to help Mr. Vitality," he says, "The organization is working on a big project."

"Oh? And what's that?"

Lars tugs at his tie. "It's, uh, on the QT. Only those closest to Mr. Vitality know. Can't let just anyone in on the big plan."

"You're not in on it, are you?"

"Not as such. No."

I should have figured. Mentor or no, you can't let Lars get too close to an important project. Perhaps out of embarrassment, Lars changes the subject.

"How are things going with Mike?" he asks, "Anything new on that front?"

I share with him the thoughts I've been having and update him on the conversation with Hefflin. I have to mention the vomiting. Lars winces.

"How's Carol?" he asks.

"Hard to tell. She's not speaking to me or Mike."

He doesn't seem concerned. "She'll get over it. A little vomit should never ruin a friendship."

I wonder if that's an affirmation from Mr. Vitality or if Lars came up with that on his own. I'm not sure I want to know. I pour another cup of coffee and try not to think of vomiting. Upsets the digestion, you understand.

Lars finishes his coffee and carries the cup to the sink. "I haven't heard an update about your friend Casey."

"Not a lot to tell," I say, "She helped me and Mike the other night. We've exchanged a couple of texts since then. We're trying to find a time to get together. Mike being here gets in the way. Until it's safe, he's not going back to his place. And Casey's got a roommate. Kind of puts a damper on things."

Lars folds his arms. "What are your intentions toward this young lady?"

Once upon a time—and I mean, like, a month ago—this might have been a sarcastic question. An opening to banter, at the very least. But Lars is serious. It's like I'm meeting a prospective father-in-law (one I don't really *want* to be my father-in-law).

"We're just…looking to have a good time," I say.

"A good time, huh?" Lars says, "Do you love this woman?"

"I love…*parts* of her."

Lars's head drops. (Hey, no fair. That's *my* gesture toward *him*!) "You're looking on this as another shallow sexual relationship?"

"If I play my cards right."

"Joe, I'm going to tell you something," he says, "You deserve to be happy. Do you think another in a series of brief sexual relationships is going to bring you that happiness?"

"If it happens, I'll let my ear-to-ear grin do the talking for me."

Lars reaches for me like he's going to grab my shoulders. Then he stops and pulls his hands back. "I'll leave it up to you," he says, "Just ask yourself—really ask yourself—what will make you happy."

At the moment, it would be Lars leaving my apartment without further lecturing me. (He's awfully pissy for a guy who just scored a free breakfast.) I tell him I'll think about it. (I won't, of course.) Lars strides to the front door. He opens it and pauses.

"If you want to meet with Ella Jones," he says, "You might want to talk to Mike."

"Mike? Why Mike?"

"He's gotten together with her a few times. Just talking on the phone, having coffee. That's your 'in' with her, brother."

I'm flummoxed. It's like finding out your dad is actually an international superspy. But this is less cool. "I didn't know that," I say.

Lars shrugs. "He has a life outside of you, Joe."

With that, he leaves, his Disapproval Quota apparently fulfilled. I grab my cell phone off the desk and punch in Mike's number. He's got some 'splaining to do.

And, after that, so does Ella Jones.

***

"It's not like we're carrying on a torrid affair," Mike says, tucking his hands into the pockets of his leather jacket, "We've just been talking."

"Oh, I see," I say, hitting the button for the *Walk* signal, "Your life is being threatened. You're holed up at my

174

place because somebody killed James Queen and is going to kill you next. And you're hanging out with one of the suspects. Why would you want to mention *that*?"

Mike keeps his distance. His face drops into a mask I've seen before. It's one part placid, one part disappointed. It's the look he adopts when being chewed out by authority figures (teachers, bosses, Carol). I never thought he'd use it on me. But I'm not feeling too terribly bad about that.

It's a chilly night on Grand Avenue. A cold wind blows. Not as bad as it will be in a few months, but chilly, nonetheless. Dead leaves drift across the street. I huddle into my pea coat (cold enough for the winter coat, not cold enough for a scarf) and avoid looking at Mike. Our destination is The Riverland, a little coffee/wine bar on Grand. Walking distance from my place. For me, anyway. Mike is huffing and grumbling.

"It's not like we've been talking about James Queen," Mike says, running a hand over his freshly shaven face (a rarity in itself), "We're just talking. About life and stuff. She's holed up in that hotel, bored out of her mind. She just needs some company."

"Is that why you suggested we meet at the Riverland?" I ask.

"Yep. Getting her out of the hotel will do her a world of good. And maybe she'll be more willing to talk."

I'll concede that one to Mike. If it leads to Ella Jones being more open, I'm all for it. I'm still annoyed to find out things about Mike from other people. Particularly when he's living under my roof (a situation that is a whole different annoyance).

"Seriously, though," I say, as the *Walk* signal pops on, "Why didn't you tell me you were talking to Ella Jones?"

"You didn't ask."

"Mike!"

"Because it's weird, all right!" He runs a hand through his hair. "I should be thrilled because it's Ella Fucking Jones. The woman I've fantasized about since I was a kid. But…I don't know. What's that saying about how you should never meet your heroes?"

"You should never meet your heroes?" I say.

"Oh, it's that exactly? Whatever. It's true. Ella's really nice and everything. And I'm flattered she wants to talk to me. But it's just…I don't know. Sad?"

"Sad how?"

"It's not what I expected. All the time I spent imagining what Ella Jones was like, what her life must be like. I didn't picture her being sad." He runs a hand through his hair. "She had about a minute-and-a-half's worth of success and that's all she's ever known for. She has no husband, no kids, no family. She's got her students. And she loves them.

She's gotten really close with that one student. Ashley. But they aren't here and she's trying to deal with her ex-husband's death. She just needs someone to talk to. I'm fine listening."

"And you haven't talked about James Queen at all?" I ask, "Or Tim Hefflin or Hal Murdoch?"

"Nope. She'll mention them in passing. *That was when James and I were still married,* or *Tim used to say something like that.* But nothing about Queen dying or me being stalked."

Swell. Not only is Mike hanging out behind enemy lines, he's missing a golden opportunity to get information. Then again, maybe this could work to Mike's advantage. If Ella killed James Queen and is trying to get information out of Mike, she'll soon realize he doesn't know anything. Then again, they haven't talked about James Queen's murder. Maybe I have to take their get-togethers at face value. As we cross the street, Mike speaks without looking at me.

"You heard anything from Carol?" he asks.

"Not yet," I say, "You?"

"Nope," Mike says, "I think we're getting the full-blown silent treatment."

"So it would seem. Think she'll come around?"

"Vomit's a tough thing to get over," Mike says.

"And get out."

"And get out."

We come up on the entrance to the Riverland. It's a simple enough affair. A large picture window gives us a view of a modest bistro. A handful of wooden tables are scattered in front of a long mahogany bar. The black-and-white pattern on the tile floor is similar to Glacier's (and a few barber shops I've frequented). A simple white door leads inside. As we pass the picture window, Mike and I glance in. Ella Jones is easy enough to spot. She's at a table near the bar and is the only former TV star in the place. (Unless, of course, Gabe Kaplan is in the can.) But her status and her location are not what gets our attention. It's the fact she's not alone.

"Who the fuck is that?" Mike asks, pressing his face to the glass.

The guy in question has his back to us. His long gray hair is tied into a ponytail and he's wearing a faded jean jacket. He rocks back and forth in the chair and talking with his hands.

"Nobody you recognize?" I say.

"No. Ella doesn't know anyone in town except me and *The Night Hawk* people."

The guy could be a fan imposing on Ella. But she seems to genuinely be in conversation with him. Mike's jaw clenches. By turns, he looks jealous and unsure if he should be jealous. Ella seems frightened. Whatever the conversation is about, it isn't friendly. The guy grabs Ella's wrists and pulls her toward him. Her mouth tightens and she gives him a look of defiance. She bites her lip, trying not to cry out.

"Motherfucker," Mike says.

He pushes past me and dives for the door. Great. A fistfight in a wine bar. Yet another proud moment to add to Mike's resume. To his credit, Mike doesn't knock over tables or shove people out of the way. He moves gracefully but purposefully. When he arrives at the table, Mike clamps a hand on the guy's shoulder.

"What the hell is going on?" Mike says, managing to keep his voice down.

The guy looks up at Mike. Wrinkles crisscross his craggy face. Gray stubble sprouts along his cheeks. I'd put the guy in his sixties. He wears a hooded sweatshirt he probably bought at the airport and a pair of tan slacks. (If I had to guess, the guy's more at home with bowling shirts and shorts.) A corner of his mouth rises, but his eyes are cold. He doesn't let go of Ella's wrists.

"Boyfriend of yours?" he says, his voice high-pitched and phlegmy.

Ella keeps her voice level. "He's a friend."

Mike's hand says on the guy's shoulder. "Who the hell is *this?*"

She doesn't say anything. For a moment, nobody moves. It's a weenie Mexican standoff. (Where's Sergio Leone when you need him?) Mike growls at the guy.

"You're going to want to let go of the lady's wrists."

The guy flicks a look at Mike. "Oh, am I?"

Mike tightens his grip (or at least he tries to). "If you want to walk out of here, you will."

"Maybe you'd like to step outside," the guy says.

"Maybe I'd love to step outside," Mike says, needing work on his banter.

The guy releases Ella's wrists and Mike releases the guy's shoulder. He pops to his feet and squares off with Mike. Mike stands an inch or two taller, but that might not make a difference. Ella gives an embarrassed look around.

"Rob, I don't think this is a good idea," she says.

Rob (apparently the guy's name) sneers. "Tell that to your boyfriend here. Or you can tell it to what's left of him." He turns the sneer on Mike. "You ready to go, candy ass?"

"Born ready," Mike says, narrowing his eyes.

And born a candy ass, but I don't add that to the conversation. I can't believe this is happening. I don't know this Rob guy well enough to comment on his behavior. But with Mike, it usually takes a couple whiskeys to reach this level of belligerence. Rob leads the way down a short hallway past the restrooms and through the backdoor. Mike follows him and I follow Mike. There is an alley behind the building. I try to whisper to Mike without breaking stride.

"This is a bad idea," I say, "This guy could be a fifth degree blackbelt in some kind of deadly kung-fu. You need to pump the brakes."

"Fuck that," Mike whispers back, "This guy needs a good ass-kicking."

"I'm not going to argue with you there," I say, "But I think the best you can muster is a mediocre- to below-average ass-kicking."

Mike ignores me. He hunches his shoulders, ready for a fight. I'm left to gently close the door behind us. Ella hasn't followed, apparently wanting nothing to do with the fisticuffs. Can't say I blame her. I guard the door and fight the temptation to give the combatants instructions. ("Okay, no low blows, no rabbit punches, no dignified combat of any kind…") Both men hoist their dukes. Mike doesn't bother to remove his coat. The air is still and no one's coming up the alley. This ought to be good.

"You want some, motherfucker," Mike says, "Come get some."

They circle each other, slowly. Rob jumps forward, causing Mike to retreat. Rob laughs, as if he's got the measure of Mike. He coils his body and throws a looping right at Mike's head.

And misses by an area code.

The punch comes up so short Mike doesn't even move to avoid it. The momentum causes Rob to lurch forward. Mike sidesteps, more out of shock than anything. Rob passes Mike, trips over his own feet and falls to the pavement, winding up against a dumpster. Mike lines up a kick at Rob's head and lets fly.

And misses.

Rob aids the effort by rolling to one side. Mike's foot crashes into the dumpster. Both the impact and Mike's subsequent cries of "Fuck! Mother…fuck!" ring through the alley. Mike limps away. Rob gets to his feet, crouches slightly and charges, aiming to slice Mike in half with a body tackle.

Mike turns in a little half-circle, trying to walk off his injury. The movement causes Rob to fly past him. Rob instead spears a bike chained to a lamppost. The bike goes down, still chained to the post. Rob rolls off the bike, clutching his shoulder.

"This fucking city," he mumbles.

Mike grabs the front of Rob's hoodie and hauls him to his feet. At least, that was the plan. Rob refuses to go and Mike doesn't have the strength to pull him up. The shirt starts ripping and Rob slaps at Mike's hands.

"Hey fucker, lay off," Rob says, practically spitting.

Mike lets go, but not before Rob kicks at his leg. Mike jumps to one side and comes down on his bad foot. He cries out and lurches back the other direction, stepping on Rob's ankle as he does. Rob grabs the ankle and scoots back, hitting his head on the bike's handlebars.

Mike limps back my direction. "How am I doing?"

"Fine," I tell him, "*I'm* getting a little bored, but you're hanging in there."

The time has come for the coup de grace. Rob rolls to one side, holding his head. Mike lines up and kicks Rob really hard in the ass.

Again, Mike has failed to account for his bad wheel. The kick causes him at least as much pain as it causes Rob. Both guys wind up on the ground, holding their injured anatomies and howling in pain. I wonder if I should call the police or TMZ.

"You got him right where you want him, Mikey," I say, with the same enthusiasm one uses when saying *I've got this dentist appointment today.*

Mike holds his injured foot and sucks in air. Rob sees his opening. He goes for a two-finger eye poke. Mike slides the flat of his hand up and blocks it, Stooges-style. He pushes Rob away with his bad foot, causing himself more pain.

Rob tries another desperation lunge. He swings his right arm, intending to hit Mike with a clubbing blow. Mike blocks it, grabbing Rob's fist. Then he sinks his teeth into Rob's forearm.

My language has not been pristine since my teen years. In fact, over time, I've become a connoisseur of filthy words. But even *I'm* impressed by the depth and creativity of the profanity Rob spews while Mike turns his arm into a glorified chew toy. He finally gets his shit together and throws a knee into Mike's stomach. But Mike is locked on, impervious to pain. Rob throws another knee. No effect. He throws one more, this time to the groin. *That* gets Mike to release the lip lock.

Mike curls into a fetal position and mutters unintelligibly. Rob clutches his arm and continues the profanity, albeit at a lower volume. He slowly gets to his feet, contemplating the continuation of the "fight". Given the pain in his head, arm and ankle, he decides it's not worth it. He slicks down one side of his fraying hair.

"Fuck *you*, man," he says before hobbling off.

I let Rob go, figuring there isn't much to be gained by continuing the conflict. Besides, he's probably not going to answer questions from me. Maybe Ella will play ball. I squat down over Mike's carcass. He looks up at me, face red.

"How did I do?" he asks.

"Well, Randy Savage vs Ricky Steamboat's place in history is secure. But you got rid of the guy. If that's what you wanted to do."

"It was. I just wanted to look cool doing it."

I clamp him on the shoulder. "You're batting five hundred. I suggest you take it."

I help him to his feet, and we amble back to the bar proper. Ella has abandoned the place, leaving her wine glass and a tip on the table. Mike drops into the chair formerly occupied by Rob.

"I guess that was a waste of time," he says.

I slide into the other chair. "Oh, I don't know. You've distinguished yourself. That was, without doubt, the worst fight I've ever seen. And I'm including the time Bob Sunde and Rick Weber got into a wrestling match on the playground and they both fell asleep. I think you set violence back a generation."

"You finished?"

"One more. You may have aided the cause of world peace with the complete futility of that brawl."

Mike gets up, slowly, painfully. "I'm going to get a glass of wine."

"Help for the pain?"

"No, I'm going to throw it at you."

I'd be dismayed, but for two things: one, I probably deserve it, and two, judging by his fight with Rob, Mike can't hit anything.

CHAPTER NINE

The frustrating part of drinking is the way sobriety gets the last word.

It's like eating a really delicious chocolate sundae and discovering a cockroach at the bottom. What's your takeaway from that? You were enjoying the chocolate sundae though nearly the entire experience. Will you remember that? No. In all likelihood, you're only going to remember the cockroach.

That, sadly, is how it goes with drinking. You're out having a good time, living it up, warming your hands on the fire of life. There's nothing that matters except that moment and that time and that feeling. Do you remember any of that the next morning? Do you laud yourself for your bit of carpe diem? No. You can only chide yourself for the headache and the nausea and the nagging feeling that you compromised your dignity. It's not fair that you don't remember the good times.

Of course, if push comes to shove, you probably can't *remember the good times, so...*

"I got a message from Alan, the groom," Carol says, cupping her hands around a mug of coffee, "He was checking in, making sure I was okay. Apparently, he's the one who gave me a ride home the night of the bachelorette party."

I fold up a deck chair and set it against the wall. "You've got that mystery solved."

"But it makes me wonder," Carol says, huddling into her suede coat, "Why is Alan calling me? I like him, but we don't know each other well enough for him to call and check on me. And why did *he* give me a ride home? Shouldn't he have given Chris a ride home?"

"You can call him and ask," I say.

"I don't want to. It would be…awkward."

"What would be awkward about it?"

Carol peers into her coffee. "There are…other questions that I have."

"Such as?"

"Such as why I woke up naked the next morning."

I had forgotten about the nudity. Obviously, it's a concern. I'm wondering what might have happened. Also, I'm trying not to picture Carol naked, because that's not going to get us anywhere.

I can't help wondering if my neighbors are catching any of this. Carol and I are on my deck, which is part of an erector set of decks and stairs that are not native to the building. While it occasionally creaks and moans as if it's going to step away from the building and go into business for itself, it's still a kickass place to hang out in the summer. But, alas, summer is over and it's time to put away the deck furniture. As if to underscore this, the day is overcast, and last night's chill remains. Now that the chairs are folded up, I start taking down the Christmas lights crisscrossing the deck.

"The naked thing is definitely a conundrum," I say.

"Exactly. I mean, I could have done it myself. But I keep wondering if I didn't."

I pause with the lights. "Do you have a habit of waking up naked? After drinking?"

"It's happened before," Carol says, "But usually when I'm, y'know, with somebody. I know I should call Alan, but I'm afraid. And Chris hasn't called me lately, so I'm wondering about that." She rests the mug of coffee on the deck rail. "What should I do?"

I wrap the string of lights around my arm. "Look at it this way: if something happened, it happened. It's like when people are afraid to go to the doctor because they don't want to find out they're sick. If they're sick, they're sick. It's not *because* they heard it from a doctor."

That isn't the answer Carol was hoping for. She circles the deck, finishing her coffee. Her nose is red, and she discreetly wipes it with the back of her hand.

"You any closer to figuring out what's going on with Mike?" Carol asks.

"No. But he had a spectacularly bad fight with somebody last night."

I fill her on Mike's session of grabass with the guy talking to Ella Jones. I'm not sure what gets Carol's attention more: Mike getting into a fight or Mike hanging with a former television star.

"What's the deal then?" Carol asks, "Mike's dating this woman now?"

"No, they're just talking. As far as I know."

Carol contemplates this over a sip of coffee. "She's a little old for him, isn't she?"

"I don't know. Probably." I set the coiled lights in a box destined for my storage unit. "But I don't want to be an ageist about the whole thing. Besides, I really don't think they're doing anything."

"Why do you say that?"

"Because Mike's too afraid."

Carol gives that a barking laugh. "Afraid? Since when is Mike afraid of sex?"

I get the plastic cover out from under the grill. "Since his masturbation fantasy came to life."

Carol looks repulsed. I'm not sure if it's the thought of Ella Jones as Mike's masturbation fantasy or Carol no longer occupying that role. Her only comment is: "Gross."

The grill cover makes a snapping sound like a bedsheet. It covers Carol's last remark before it covers the grill. "The important thing," I say, "is finding out who this guy is. All I got is a first name. Rob."

"And Ella didn't tell you anything?" Carol asks.

"No chance to talk to her. She left before we got back from the fight. Mike tried calling her, but she didn't answer."

"And no other way to get ahold of her?"

"Not that I know of."

With the grill covered and everything folded and boxed up, I can (temporarily) halt my work. I need a few minutes to warm up and then I can haul the stuff down to my storage unit in the basement. I lead the way through the backdoor and down to the coffeemaker. Carol sits at the breakfast bar, her coffee cup tucked just under her chin. Judging by the look in her eyes, she's working on an idea, trying it on for size.

"Ella's still in town, right?" Carol asks.

"The cast members are staying for Queen's memorial. Why do you ask?"

"You said Ella rarely leaves the hotel. If this guy's got business with her, he'd have to look for her there. Your best bet would be to hang out at the hotel. Wait for him to show."

That makes perfect sense. On top of the potential benefits to the investigation, a stakeout would also get me out of the house. (Something that would have never seemed like a boon until Mike started hiding out here.)

"Maybe I'll give it a shot," I say.

"Bring your laptop," Carol says, stepping past me to put her coffee cup in the sink, "You can get some work—if you want to call it that—done while you're down there."

That merits less enthusiasm. "I guess so. Might as well put the rest of my life on hold."

Carol stops. "Worried it will get in the way of your social life?"

"It already has," I say.

"That's right," she says, "Made any progress with the great lost love?"

"She is not my great lost love." That title belongs to someone else. "But it's hit-and-miss. Having Mike around makes it a miss."

Carol contemplates this as she puts on her coat. "I don't know why I'm giving you this advice, since I generally don't want to get involved in your love life. But if you're going to do a stakeout, maybe you should bring this Casey."

At first, I'm tempted to dismiss it, but I remember Casey was okay with helping us when Mike was attacked. And I've never asked a girl to a stakeout before. It has the benefit of having never been tried.

"Might be worth a shot," I say.

"Think about it," Carol says, opening the front door, "and don't expect any more relationship advice from me."

"Understood. I'll go to Mike and Lars."

"Yep. Enjoy life as a lonely old man."

With that, Carol disappears out the front door. I give her idea some thought. Maybe bringing a date to a stakeout is a silly idea, but then again, what the hell? The worst Casey's going to tell me is "no". That's the benefit of having embarrassed yourself sexually in front of someone. You have no fear in other situations. I pick up the phone and call Casey.

Joe Davis: International Man of Mystery.

***

The staff of the Ambassador Suites seem have gotten used to me. No one asks about my presence or even bats an eye when I loiter about the place. We find a seat in the hotel's café (seems a better idea than skulking behind pillars in the lobby). I'm glad they don't throw us out. It would embarrass me in front of my guest.

"What are we looking for?" Casey asks, propping an elbow on the little Formica tabletop.

We're doing our best to fit in. I've worn a dress shirt (my second and last dress shirt, which means I need to do a wash) and Casey has a fashionable hooded coat. We look like the kind of people who can afford beverages, but not a room at the hotel. There are only a few other patrons in the café, and they ignore us. I swirl my apple cider.

"We're looking for Ella Jones for one," I say, "Have you ever heard of her?"

"No," Casey says, "She was in *The Night Man*, right?"

"*The Night Hawk*," I say, taking out my phone, "I'll show you a picture."

Nearly all the Google images of Ella Jones are from her days on the TV show. I find one that's more recent and show it to Casey.

"She's pretty," she says.

"She is." I put the phone away. "At any rate, I need to talk to her. Or this guy Rob that got in a fight—and I use that term loosely—with Mike. I'll know Rob if I see him."

I thought about asking the front desk to contact Ella's room, but reconsidered. I'm flying under the hotel staff's radar. No sense jeopardizing that by asking too many questions. Not when a stakeout will do the job. I doubt Rob will show, but you never know. It would be stupid, but he doesn't seem like a Rhodes Scholar. Meantime, I enjoy the company.

"You do this sort of thing a lot?" Casey asks.

"More than I ought to," I say, "I've had a few adventures. Got Mike out of jail. Kept Carol out of jail. Kept my cousin from getting killed. Had a…*situation* with an ex-girlfriend. And another ex-girlfriend." I don't even want to mention the thing with the contract killer.

"Wow," Casey says, sipping her hot chocolate, "I had no idea you were into that sort of thing."

"I don't know if I'm *into it*. Stuff just seems to happen to me."

"Makes life exciting, I guess."

"It has its moments."

Casey slips her hand into mine. I don't know if it's because she's missed me or if she's intrigued by this air of danger around me (if so, she's a lot more intrigued by it than I am). She's more in her element than I would have anticipated. We keep our eyes on the lobby, checking to see if anyone is coming or going. Our hands remain clasped. There's no sign of Ella, but there *is* a couple coming in from some excursion and possibly going to another.

They're a good-looking couple. He's got a metrosexual thing going, save for the stubble (but I get the feeling even that's a design choice). She looks like a former cheerleader who has graduated to an executive position. They spill into each other and laugh. They've probably been imbibing something that helps with the general mirth. They stop behind one of the pillars, thinking they're out of sight. The laughter dies down. They start making out.

"That seems like a good time," Casey says.

"It does at that," I say.

Casey leans across the table and we go into competition with the couple behind the pillar, oblivious to the rest of the café. Until someone taps the table. Casey and I separate, quickly. A woman with a white dress shirt, no makeup and no sense of humor is at our table. Her lips are pursed. It's the barista at the coffee shop.

"Excuse me," she says, her voice officious, "what are you doing?"

I casually wave my hand. "As you see."

The barista is not impressed. "I'd appreciate it if you'd take it to your room."

So much for the customer always being right. "Of course," I say, "Sorry."

The barista turns back toward the counter. Casey fights off the giggles. I take her hand and lead her out of the coffee shop. We slip over to the glass elevators.

"Where are we going?" Casey asks.

"To our room," I say.

"We have a room?"

"No. But Prissy McGhee back there doesn't know that."

We hop in the elevator and precede to the eighth floor, where *The Night Hawk* cast is housed. My plan is to stroll around the floor, see if we bump into Ella. If nothing else, we can let things calm down in the café before we make our return. Casey hugs my arm as we walk.

"It's a shame," she says, "Us not having a room."

Our faces are very close. "You're right. It is."

We kiss and things get *very* friendly again. We part and I kiss Casey's neck. She pulls me close, sliding her hands down my ass. Yes, this is exciting. But it shouldn't go any further, not in this setting. And that, strangely, makes it even more exciting.

Despite the situation, I sneak a peek down the hallway, in case Ella Jones comes out of her room. I don't see Ella, but I *do* see a door opening further on. If I'm remembering right, it's Hal Murdoch's room. Should I let the great man catch me snogging within sight of his room? Turns out to be a nonstarter. Because Hal Murdoch doesn't emerge from his room.

It's a woman about my age, moving a bit catlike, her curly blonde hair obscuring her face. She wears black jeans and a black suede jacket. She looks around but doesn't see us.

"Something's up," I whisper.

Casey glides a hand over the bulge in my crotch. "I know. I wish we had that room."

I pull back, reluctantly, and look down the hallway. "Not that. Well, that, too. But something's going on."

We slip into a corner where the woman can't see us. She looks around, making sure the coast is clear, and eases the door to Murdoch's room closed. I strain to see if she's carrying anything. Another door opens, just down the hallway and Tim Hefflin, wearing a white bathrobe over an A-Frame t-shirt and boxer shorts wanders out, probably looking for the day's first drink. He sways toward the intruder.

"Hey," he shouts, "who the fuck are you?"

The intruder throws a startled look at Hefflin. For a moment, she's frozen. Maybe she's got a legitimate reason for being in Hal Murdoch's room. (The fact I can't think of one that doesn't involve prostitution says more about me than it does her.) Her hand rests on the doorknob, as if she's playing it cool. Then she takes off running.

So, not playing it cool.

The intruder runs around the corner and speeds toward the staircase, located in the corner. Casey and I are in pursuit. The intruder isn't fast, but she beats us to the staircase. She whips open the door and disappears down the stairs. I get there a second later, hoping I don't fall ass-over-teakettle in pursuit.

We keep the intruder in sight as we run down the stairs. We gain a little, moving from a full staircase away to only half a staircase by the time we reach the lobby. The intruder throws open the door and disappears for a moment.

I leap to the bottom of the stairs and follow. The intruder runs across the lobby. I want to shout for someone to stop her. But no one is available. She's getting away.

Then Sergeant Pike appears.

If Jabba The Hut had materialized in the lobby of the Ambassador Suites, I couldn't be more surprised (and repulsed). Pike wears his usual rumpled suit and his hands are thrust in the pockets of his overcoat. The intruder looks back to see where I'm at. She crashes into Pike. He doesn't move when she slams into him. The intruder bounces off and stumbles to one side. The fountain is just a few feet away. She doesn't regain her balance before crashing into the water.

Pike stands there and watches the intruder flounder. He sees me coming and rolls his eyes. Somehow, he knew I'd be involved in this.

One of these times, I hope my arrival will actually make somebody's day.

CHAPTER TEN

Much as I joke about my weenie bit of celebrity, I'm very comfortable with it. If all it gets me is the occasional, "Hey, aren't you…" or maybe a free coffee or beer, I'm completely cool with that. I don't need anything more.

Why? Because for those who fly higher, the fall is that much more precipitous. Then what do you do with your life? It's like those bands that make a big splash with their first album and are has-beens by their second. Where do you go from there? You're twenty-four years old and, at an age where your dreams should be starting, you've been and gone. How do you live a life after that?

I'll stick with my free coffee and beer, thank you very much.

We can add "unexpected intruders" to the list of celebrity headaches.

I catch up to Pike just as the intruder hits the water. Pike doesn't look any worse for wear. Yes, his tie is askew, but that's a permanent situation. He nods toward the fountain.

"Friend of yours?" he asks.

Before I can answer, the intruder pops up, throwing water in all directions. Her curly blonde hair is plastered to her round face. Her clothes are dripping. Her brown eyes stare daggers at Pike.

"Why don't you fucking watch where you're going!" she says, spitting water.

Pike ignores her, keeping his eyes on me. "Care to explain?"

"We caught her breaking into Hal Murdoch's room," I say

Casey joins us as the intruder sloshes her way out of the fountain, slipping on the tile floor. The intruder shoves the soggy hair out of her face.

"My name is Kelly Smart," she says, "I work for *The Edge.*"

Judging by the look on her face, she expects us to know what that is. She's half right. I've heard of *The Edge*. It's a shitty website designed to spew gossip about celebrities. The tactics used in coming up with said gossip are reprehensible; a combination of spying, digging through trash, bothering friends and relatives, and good old-fashioned ambushes. The sort of stuff that would make the paparazzi sick. So, of course, it's wildly popular. *The Edge* has expanded from a website and into their own TV show and YouTube series. Sweeping the country with a muckrake. Hedda Hopper would be so proud.

Pike doesn't seem to care. "Nice to meet you, Kelly Smart," he says, "Can I ask why you were breaking into Hal Murdoch's room?"

"I wasn't breaking in," she says, her voice slightly pouty, "I had the key."

"Uh-huh," Pike says, and it's nice to watch him turn his cop glare on somebody else, "How did you *get* the key?"

The air goes out of Smart. "I don't have to—"

"If it explains you being in Hal Murdoch's room," Pike says, "you *do* have to." Smart looks down, water still dripping off her. She doesn't seem inclined to answer. Pike takes her arm and says, "Come with me." He looks back at me. "You, too. Your friend can stay here."

Casey looks miffed. I hold up a hand, calming her. I can tell her about my familiarity—and various misadventures—with Sergeant Pike later. In the meantime, she can work under the impression he's a jerk. It's not exactly a misconception.

We tramp across the lobby and past the sunken area containing the cafe. There is a hallway with a string of conference rooms on the other side. Pike has just grabbed the doorknob for one of the rooms when a hotel security guy, self-important crew cut and all, blocks our path.

"Excuse me, sir," the security guy says, working to put some bass in his voice, "Those rooms are for hotel guests only." Pike reaches into his coat and produces his badge. The security guy backs away. "Have a good day, sir."

We slip into the conference room. It's long and white with a mahogany table running the length of it. There's video equipment on the far end and a white screen near the entrance. Various prints line both walls. Pike points us into chairs at the conference table. Smart drops into a chair to Pike's right and I take one to his left. Pike stands at the head of the table. I try not to fidget (Pike always brings that out in me). He thrusts his hands into his pockets.

"You didn't break into Murdoch's room," he says, staring at Kelly Smart over the top of his wire rim frames, "Was Mr. Murdoch in the room at the time?"

Smart looks away. "No."

"Can I assume Mr. Murdoch didn't give you permission to be in there?"

"Correct," Smart says, her lips tight.

"Did anyone related to Mr. Murdoch give you permission to be in there?"

"Not…precisely."

Pike props his fists on the table and towers over Smart. "How did you break into Mr. Murdoch's room?"

Smart looks up at Pike, annoyed. "I got the key from Murdoch's assistant."

"She gave it to you?" Pike asks.

"Not…willingly."

Pike sits at the table. He takes off his glasses and rubs the bridge of his nose. I'm right there with him, mentally at least. Pike replaces the glasses and stares at Smart without blinking.

"Suppose you cut the shit and tell me what you're up to," he says.

Smart crosses her arms. "I should probably get a lawyer."

Son of a bitch. The old *I want to talk to my lawyer* defense. Stupid legal system. (Then again, the Republican Party is doing its best to get rid of *that*.) Pike crosses his legs.

"Depending on what you did," Pike says, keeping a reasonable tone, "there's nothing here that needs to involve charges. We can have a chat, get this whole thing straightened out and then you can be on your way. Sound good?"

Smart considers the offer. She's wondering if Pike is laying a trap (not an unreasonable concern). She studies her fingernails.

"I picked the assistant's pocket," Smart says, "I saw her at a cafe. It was great luck. Then again, I'd been following her. Eavesdropping. I guess it wasn't entirely luck."

I'm getting sick to my stomach. From now on, when someone makes a crack about how I use my college degree to write glorified dick jokes, I'll remember that there are worse uses of an education. Pike, who's likely used to this sort of thing, doesn't respond.

"What was the point of breaking into Mr. Murdoch's room?" he asks.

"I needed information," Smart says, "About James Queen and Hal Murdoch."

Pike inclines his head. "Why not talk to Mr. Murdoch directly?"

"He wouldn't do it," she says, "But I heard there was a story. I had to try and find it."

I prop my elbows on the table. "What's the story?"

Smart gives us a triumphant smile. (She obviously enjoys being the center of attention.) "Murdoch's putting together a new *Night Hawk* movie. And he couldn't get James Queen to sign off on it."

"Another *Night Hawk* movie?" I say, "Wasn't the first one a complete bomb?"

"But this is going to be different," Smart says, "Matthew Anderson is attached."

Holy shit. Matthew Anderson is the director of the moment in Hollywood, a guy who parlayed a small independent film into a series of intelligent, literate thrillers. If he's involved with a Night Hawk film, shit just got real.

"Hal Murdoch got Matthew Anderson?" I ask.

"Matthew Anderson came to him. Murdoch won't be producing. He'll be an executive consultant or something. Once word gets around, there are going to be A-list players interested. But I heard James Queen was holding it up. I don't know how."

I do. Queen owned part of *The Night Hawk*. That had to be what the argument between Queen and Murdoch was about. That's probably why Murdoch didn't mention it. Maybe it's innocent. Maybe it's not. Maybe Smart knows something. I turn toward her.

"Did you find out anything else?" I ask.

"Nothing yet," Smart says, "Not for a lack of looking, I'll tell you."

I can't help being doubtful. If Kelly Smart found anything, is she going to spill it to a couple guys she barely knows, one of whom is a cop? Pike doesn't seem impressed with the gossip. He pushes his glasses up, fishes out a business card and offers it to Smart.

"You're free to go," he tells her, "This is my card if you need anything interesting. It goes without saying you shouldn't return to the Ambassador Suites."

Smart snatches the card out of Pike's hand. She holds it at the end of her fingertips, as if it's radioactive. Pike, probably used to this treatment, doesn't react. Smart sticks the card in her pocket and sloshes out of the room. That leaves me and Pike and a question that's been gnawing at me steadily during this little interview.

"Why are you here?" I ask, "You just happen to show up at the Ambassador Suites, where James Queen's old castmates are staying?"

Pike doesn't bat an eyelash (a skill he's probably built up over time). "Yes, I'm here to talk to them. Just a routine inquiry."

"About what?"

Pike taps his foot as he debates answering. "I want to see what they know about Queen using needles."

"Needles? Queen was doing drugs?"

Pike holds up a cautioning hand. "More than likely not. After he died, we found a leather case with some needles in it. And the autopsy showed some track marks and bruising. We're still waiting on toxicology. But we tested the contents of the unused needles. It's some kind of vitamin compound. I thought I'd ask his old co-workers if they knew anything about it."

"When I talked to you about this the first time, you didn't mention this at all."

"We were still gathering information," Pike says, annoyed that I would call him on the carpet, "We didn't know if the needles were significant."

"Even though someone is after Mike and I told you James Queen was murdered?"

Pike ticks off points on his fingers. "Okay, first off, the needles don't prove murder. They would, at best, prove an overdose, which is not murder. Second, the needles don't prove an overdose, because we tested the contents of the unused needles and there was no narcotic in them. Just some kind of vitamin compound. I want to see if anyone in the cast can confirm that."

Crap. Just when I thought Pike was coming around to my side. "One of the needles in the case was used? Were there any fingerprints on it?"

Pike's brow furrows. "None at all."

"You don't think that's strange."

"I *do* think that's strange. That's another reason I want to talk to Mr. Queen's co-workers. Tie up a loose end."

"But you're still not treating it as a murder?" I ask.

"Nothing to indicate I should. If you'll excuse me."

Pike gets up from the table and strides out the door. I slouch after him. There is no sign of Smart. The janitor is mopping a trail of water that leads out of the lobby. Looks like Kelly Smart followed Pike's orders. Casey stands at the end of the hall. Pike ignores her as he passes. Casey's eyes are bright, and her face is flushed. I stick my hands in my pockets as I approach.

"I think we're done here," I say, "Sorry about the craziness."

"It's okay. It was exciting." She whispers in my ear. "*Very* exciting."

I'd kiss Casey right here if I didn't think we'd get thrown out of the hotel. Here I was, afraid the whole chase thing would freak her out and kill the evening. I whisper into Casey's ear.

"You want to get out of here?" I ask, "We could go to The Tav, grab a drink, go to my place after?"

"Sounds good," Casey says, "But can we skip all that other shit and just go back to your place?"

"We can do that."

We hold hands and run for the revolving door at the edge of the lobby. I wonder if I should be concerned by a woman whose sexual desires are *intensified* by a brush with danger. I can ponder that other time. Tomorrow, perhaps, or the next day.

Or the Twelfth of Fuck It.

***

It doesn't take long to get back to my place. There are only two dangers involved. One is possibly crashing my car

209

from an excess of haste. The other is Mike being in my apartment. I hope he's out having drinks with Ella Jones.

Casey and I arrive at the apartment safe and sound. We hustle up the erector set of stairs and decks. I fumble with the keys to my backdoor. The sun has set, and I honestly hadn't noticed until we got here. I finally get the damn door open and let Casey in. The cats are in the hallway, giving me their usual *And just where have you been* greeting. They scatter when Casey and I charge through the backdoor. I give her a whirlwind tour. (My apartment has four rooms. *Any* tour would be a whirlwind tour.) It's not that I want Casey to see my humble abode. I want to make sure the coast is clear. The Nookie Gods are with me. Mike is nowhere to be found. I finish the tour with the bedroom, which was where we wanted to go the whole time.

Once in the bedroom, things rapidly go in a very friendly direction, as if we're trying to make up for lost time. Buckles, snaps and hooks are becoming unbuckled, unsnapped and unhooked. Hands fumble under clothing, glide over skin that's warm and smooth. Casey slips out of her sweater and tosses it, bra still inside, on to the nightstand. My long-sleeve tee flies out from under the comforter and (probably) lands somewhere in the vicinity of the dresser. Casey and I are nearing where we want to go. She's down to her panties and sliding my boxer briefs down around my ass.

Then my cell phone rings.

You have *got* to be fucking kidding me.

Casey and I freeze in position. Maybe we just imagined it. Maybe it's one of those oddball things you hear. Like a buzz from the refrigerator or something. Then the damn phone rings again.

"Please tell me it's a wrong number," Casey says.

I slip an arm out from under the covers and fumble to find the phone. It takes a few seconds, but I find the damn thing in the pocket of my jeans. I sit on the bed and look at the caller ID. It's Mike. Son of a bitch. Maybe it's nothing. Or maybe he's in trouble. I consider ignoring it (a thought made more tempting by Casey kissing my shoulder), but I can't take any chances. I answer it.

"What in the blue hell could it possibly be?" is how I answer.

"It's me," Mike says, "You've got to get down to United Hospital. Someone tried to kill Hal Murdoch."

Ah. So, the Nookie Gods are *not* with me…

CHAPTER ELEVEN

Defeat tends to hit us on one (or more) of three levels: emotional, spiritual and practical. Which of these is the most devastating tends to tell us about our individual character.

Let's say you don't get a job you were pining for. You can take the emotional response most seriously ("That job would have made me feel good about myself for the first time since I got to second base with Nancy Lawson at the office Christmas party") or the spiritual ("Everything in the third shakra told me this job was my destiny") or the practical ("Maybe it's time I took the bouncer gig at the strip club off my resume"). Sometimes, it's a combination. ("I won't be able to pay rent next month and I'm floating alone in a godless universe.")

Whatever your response, the challenge is to overcome disappointment. For example, my friend Mike used a combination of all three after his most recent breakup. His response was emotional ("Sure, Fredericka breaking up with me was a disappointment, but in a few years, I'll still be disappointed and I'm pretty sure she'll be fat"), spiritual ("Fredericka and I were not meant to be together, probably because she's destined to be fat"), and practical ("If we had stayed together, I would have eventually had to tell Fredericka she was fat and that wouldn't have gotten us anywhere").

As you can see, our responses truly say a lot about who we are.

Having been victimized by another case of *Mikus Interruptus*, though, I can add one more category to that list: homicidal.

I try not to drop the phone. "Someone attacked Hal Murdoch? When?"

"A little while ago," Mike says. From the sound of the air rushing around, he's walking. "Can you get down here?"

"Is he okay?" I ask.

"I think so. He's under observation. You should get down here."

Motherfucker. Mike's right. I *should* get down there. If this is related to whoever killed James Queen and is going after Mike (and it would be a hell of a coincidence if it *weren't*), I need to get some details. And I shouldn't delay. No matter how much I'd like to.

"United?" I ask.

"Emergency room entrance. I can meet you."

"I'll be there in twenty minutes," I say, barely able to get the words out.

I ring off and set the phone on the nightstand. Casey lays her head against my shoulder blade. She's caught enough of the conversation to know we won't be proceeding with the evening's planned program.

"What happened?" she asks.

"Apparently, us chasing an intruder through the lobby of the Ambassador Suites *wasn't* the most exciting thing to happen tonight."

I tell her Hal Murdoch is in the hospital. Casey lays against the headboard and pulls the comforter over herself, a gesture that makes me sadder with each passing inch.

"Then you should probably get going," Casey says, "So should I."

I'm hit with a moment of inspiration. "Why don't you hang out here? I'm not sure how long I'll be at the hospital, but…I'll be back." The last part sounds pitiful, even to me.

"I have to work the opening shift," she says, a sad tone in her voice, "I need to get up early. I should go back to my place."

My heart drops through the bottom of my feet, giving my penis a wave on the way down. I try to put on a brave face. "I get it," I say.

I'm certain *I have to get up early* is an excuse. (It's a classic, right?) But in this case, she's got a point. Even if I get back here at a decent hour, the odds are Mike will be with me. Casey and I rummage around the room, finding various articles of clothing, going through the disappointing process of getting dressed again. The cats peek in, as if to ask, "What the hell is going on around here?" When Casey and I are dressed, we step into the hallway.

"I need to give you a ride home," I say.

"It's okay," Casey says, "You need to get downtown. I'll take a Lyft."

"You're sure?" I say, sounding more desperate than I'd like.

"I'll wait down in the foyer." She pats me on the arm. "You should get going."

Confession: I've always hated when a girl tells me I need to get going. There's something so dismissive in that simple sentence. But I'm resigned to it. I let Casey out the front door and direct her toward the foyer at the bottom of the stairs.

"Raincheck?" I ask, "Again?"

Casey's voice has less enthusiasm than it might. "Sure." A moment goes by, then she says, "I'll see you later."

She disappears down the stairs. I close and lock the door behind her. I walk down the hallway, toward the backdoor and the path to my car. I'm not sure why someone would attack Hal Murdoch.

Right now, I'd kind of like to do it myself.

***

My foul mood lasts the entire drive down to United Hospital. Thankfully, it isn't a long drive. United Hospital is a sprawling complex, right at the bottom of Ramsey Hill. Under less urgent circumstances, it would be walking distance from my apartment. I find a spot in the parking ramp (parking garage to you out of towners) and hustle across Smith Avenue to the emergency room entrance. Mike is waiting for me.

"Thanks for coming," he says, then clears my entrance with the emergency room staff. That's either a testimony to Hal Murdoch's celebrity or mine. (All right, it's a testimony to *his*.) Mike leads the way to Hal Murdoch's room. His hair is piled higher than normal, probably from running his hands through it. He notices the look on my face.

"You okay?" he asks.

"I was mere seconds away from another shot with Casey when you called," I say.

A smirk creases Mike's face. "*Mere seconds* is what you usually do when you get a shot with Casey."

"Dick—excuse me, *Richard*—you want to put the smartassery in dry dock and let me know what's going on?"

Mike stops before we get to Hal Murdoch's room. "All right, Ella gave me a call, asking to get together. I thought maybe I could ask her some questions about this Rob guy. She was even cool with going back to that wine bar.

She told me Mr. Murdoch and Billie were out running errands and they'd probably want to join us."

"Then what happened?"

"Ella and I were waiting at the wine bar. Her phone rang. It was Billie, saying they were going to the hospital. They were on their way to the wine bar and they were run off the road."

"Holy shit," I say.

"Holy shit is right. Billie didn't get a look at the guy or the car. She was more concerned about Mr. Murdoch."

Not a hell of a lot to go on. Then again, that's not the kind of situation where you take in a lot of detail.

"Is Murdoch okay?" I ask.

"I think he's just shook up. But he banged his head and at one point, he was grabbing his chest and having some problems breathing. They're keeping him overnight for observation." Mike lowers his voice. "Billie said Mr. Murdoch got a threatening phone call. Earlier. He hung up on whoever it was."

"Threatening how?"

"She didn't say."

We arrive at Hal Murdoch's room. It's small and antiseptic, not much more than a bed, some monitoring equipment and a few chairs. Hal Murdoch is in the bed, propped up by several pillows. There's a bruise on his forehead and he's hooked to a heart monitor. The beeping of the monitor and the hum of the equipment are the only sounds in the room.

Billie and Ella are on either side of the bed. Ella's face is lined with worry. As soon as we enter, she walks over to Mike and stands next to him. Murdoch runs a hand over his head, straightening his hair.

"I didn't realize I was so popular," he says, weakly.

Billie starts to say something, likely to ward us off. Murdoch stops her. There's a rip in Billie's black shirt and some hair comes loose from her ponytail. The bruise on her right cheek is small, but visible. She doesn't seem happy about Murdoch's command, but she backs off. I approach Murdoch's bed.

"What happened?" I ask.

"Someone tried negotiating with me," Murdoch says, "It seems they play hardball."

"I heard you got a call," I say, "before you got run off the road. Any idea who it was?"

"No," Murdoch says, "Just a voice on the telephone."

"Male or female?" I ask.

Murdoch fumbles with his bedsheets. "Male, from the sound of it. But it was strange."

Mike is next to me. "Like the person was disguising his voice?"

"Exactly," Murdoch says, pointing a knobby finger toward Mike, "Or it's the reception on that damn cell phone. Makes everything hard to understand."

"What did the caller say?" I ask.

Murdoch shifts himself into another position. Billie puts a hand on his shoulder, trying to calm him. He ignores her. "They said they wanted James Queen's rights," Murdoch says, staring at the ceiling, "to *The Night Hawk Rising*."

"*The Night Haw...*" Then it hits me. "The new movie? The one Matthew Anderson is doing?"

A small buzz goes through the room. *I* understand the significance of James Queen's rights to *The Night Hawk Rising*. Billie understands it as well. Mike is clueless. If Ella is aware, she's doing a masterful job of covering. Murdoch's head lolls my direction.

"I didn't realize the word had gotten out," he says.

"Just in certain circles," I say, "Someone from *The Edge* broke into your hotel room. I caught them. Me and a couple friends. One friend, really. And a cop."

Murdoch tries to follow my ramblings. "It's true. Matthew Anderson came to me with the idea for the movie. He's a fan of the comic books. Just like I was. He wants to do The Night Hawk right." He closes his eyes, briefly. "This time we'll do it right."

"A new movie?" Ella says to Murdoch, "You didn't say anything."

"It's in the early stages," he says, apologetic, "I didn't want to say anything yet."

Probably not until he talked to James Queen. Speaking of which... "Is that what the argument with James Queen was about?" I ask, "Was he holding up the movie?"

The blips on the heart monitor pick up. Billie moves closer to the bed. Murdoch doesn't look at her.

"Just like last time," he says, "He wanted to be The Night Hawk."

Even Mike scoffs. "The Night Hawk? At his age?"

"Jimmy couldn't accept anyone else playing the part. His own damn ego, out of control. I told him we were going ahead without him. He threatened to sue. We left it at that."

"And you have *no* idea who called you? Who attacked you?"

"No idea," Murdoch says.

The heart monitor spikes then steadies. Billie moves closer to the bed. She straightens her glasses.

"I think we need to let Mr. Murdoch rest," she says.

I back away from the bed. Ella gives Murdoch's hand a squeeze. We wish Murdoch well and Billie ushers the three of us out of the room. She accompanies us toward the lobby. I glance back toward Murdoch's room as we walk.

"Has he been threatened before?" I ask.

"No," Billie says, "This was completely out of the blue. I have no idea who would do this." Her voice gets thick. "Especially to Mr. Murdoch."

Billie's face is determined, even as her lip is quivering. Ella asks, "Are *you* okay?"

"I'm fine," Billie says, a bit too quickly.

We're quiet the rest of the way to the lobby. Once there, we go through the usual awkward silence that envelopes a group of relative strangers in an emotionally charged situation. Ella gives Billie a hug, which Billie receives in the same stiff manner of a Lutheran congregation told to exchange handshakes. Ella makes arrangements to pick up Murdoch and Billie when Murdoch is released tomorrow. We say our goodbyes to Billie and go our separate ways. Mike, Ella and I walk to our cars in silence. Ella slips a look at me.

"It was nice of you to come down," she tells me, "Mike needed moral support."

Ah. *That's* the cover story Mike came up with. I didn't think to ask beforehand. "That's the case," I say, "Mike's morals need a lot of support."

Ella hesitates, then asks, "Are you going to put this in your article? The one you're writing about James?"

Speaking of cover stories.... "I don't think it has to go in the article," I say, "We'll see what develops."

That's good enough for Ella. "I hope we didn't drag you away from anything important."

Mike smirks. "Nothing that was going to take him very long."

I glower at Mike, but he ignores me. Someone remind me why I'm trying to keep this guy alive?

***

The Minnesota History Center is within walking distance of my place. It's on John Ireland Boulevard, between the St. Paul Cathedral and the State Capitol and overlooking downtown. The interior is all marble floor and tall windows. As a history junkie, I've been here many times. But those visits have been more enjoyable than this one.

"The wedding's going to be there," Carol says, listlessly gesturing down the marble hallway on the second floor.

It's a spectacular view. A giant arched window perfectly frames the State Capitol Building. You can easily picture the happy couple silhouetted by the view. Standing next to Carol, who's in full Gloomy Gus mode, it's hard to appreciate anything, though.

"So, have we gotten past the, uh…vomiting incident?" I ask.

Carol's frown threatens to implode her face. "Let's not speak of it and leave it at that."

222

"Roger-dodger." I hasten to find another topic of conversation. "Have you talked to the bride yet?"

"Chris? I tried. She gave me the cold shoulder."

"The cold shoulder? Why?"

Carol huddles into her dark coat. "No idea. But I get the sinking feeling it's about the bachelorette party."

I glance down the hall. The rest of the bridal party hasn't shown, but we don't want them sneaking up on us while we're talking about this. Assuming they aren't already privy to Carol's darkest secrets.

"Have you gotten any further on remembering what happened?" I ask.

Carol shakes her head. "I'm going to talk with Shannon. The one who sent me the text message. Maybe she knows."

"I hope things go smoothly," I say.

"For you, too," Carol says, looking toward the stairs.

The stairs lead to the lobby and the entrance to the History Center's auditorium. It's where James Queen's memorial will be held. Just as Carol's here for a wedding rehearsal, I'm here for a walk through of the memorial.

"Lars is on a roll," I say, "I'll give him that."

"You think it will last?"

"Does it ever?"

We're interrupted by a voice hailing Carol. A woman is approaching us. Her strawberry blonde hair flows to her shoulders and her bright eyes and big smile are visible from fifty yards. Carol turns to me and mouths, "Shannon." She greets Carol with a hug and grins at me, though I'm sure she has no idea who the hell I am. She turns to Carol.

"Ready to do this?" Shannon asks.

"I guess so." She leans toward Shannon. "Do you have a minute? I want to talk to you about something."

Shannon looks confused. "Sure. Go ahead."

Carol draws Shannon to one side. The acoustics are such that I can hear every word. "I wanted to ask about the bachelorette party," Carol says.

Shannon lets out a cackling laugh that's audible to the Iowa border. She puts a hand over her mouth. "Hell of a night, wasn't it?"

"Sure was," Carol says, twirling some hair around her finger, "I got your text. *Way to Go.* I'm wondering what it meant."

Shannon gives that a flip of her hand. "Just that you were the life of the party. You were the greatest."

Carol winces. "I'm wondering *how* I was the greatest."

Shannon opens her mouth to respond, then stops. "You don't remember, do you?" Carol's head drops. Shannon puts a hand on Carol's shoulder. "You don't have to be embarrassed."

Carol sneaks a look at me, and I pretend to be oblivious. She turns back to Shannon. "Can you tell me what I did?"

Shannon puts a finger to her cheek as she thinks. "Well, there was that guy you told off."

Carol hesitates. "What guy?"

"Some guy we ran into at one of the clubs. He tried hitting on all of us, wouldn't leave us alone no matter how many times we told him to get lost. One of those types. Then he tried hitting on you. *That* was a big mistake. You started cutting this guy down. Everybody in the place was watching you. The DJ even turned down the music. I don't remember everything you said. *Limp dick shit gibbon* sticks out. The guy finally ran out of the place. I don't think he wanted people to see him crying." She holds up a finger. "Then there was the homophobe."

Carol looks sick. "What happened?"

"We were crossing First Avenue and some jackass started yelling at us, saying something about how Chris looked like a man and we were a bunch of lesbians and blah, blah, blah. Then, you went over and put him in his place."

"Another telling off?"

"Yep. And the roundhouse right."

Carol flexes her fingers. I guess this explains a mystery pain in Carol's hand after the party. It probably took her a while to notice, given the various other aches and pains she dealt with. Carol tucks the hand into her arm pit.

"Was the guy hurt?" Carol asks.

"We didn't hang around to find out. But I think the guy was unconscious when he hit the sidewalk, so…almost certainly."

Carol puts a hand to her face. "Is there anything else you remember?"

Shannon opens her mouth, then closes it to think (I get the feeling that's habitual). "My memory's a little hazy, too. I was pretty wasted. I remember you dancing with a male stripper. And shotgunning some malt liquor. And hitting on a cop. And trying to get us all to streak the Government Center Plaza." Shannon bobs her head. "I think that's it."

Carol's foot paws at the marble floor. "I don't suppose you remember anything at the end of the evening? Something with Alan?"

"With the groom? No, I don't. I remember him being there at the end. I think there was some kind of kerfuffle. But I don't remember what it was about."

Carol clenches a fist. (So close and yet, so far.) She brightens, for Shannon's sake. "Thanks a lot. I just…wanted to put a few things together."

Shannon pats Carol's shoulder. "I hope you had a good time."

"It was a blast," Carol says, almost able to keep the sarcasm out of her voice.

Carol thanks Shannon again and says she'll see her at the rehearsal. Shannon strolls down the hall. Carol stalks my direction. She keeps her voice low and level.

"How much of that did you hear?" Carol asks.

"Bits and pieces."

"By which you mean…"

"All of it."

Carol's tone gets icy. "And this will be another thing we never speak of. Am I correct?"

"Yes, ma'am." Because no other response will keep me safe.

Carol walks down the hall to join Shannon and wait for the rest of the wedding party. I glide down the marble stairs to the lobby. I cross the lobby and go into the auditorium. The place is large and functional. Rows of padded tan seats descend toward a large stage. Lars comes up the side stairs to greet me. He starts off at a bound then reduces his speed to a dignified stroll.

"Thanks for coming," he says, tugging at the cuffs of his tan suitcoat, "This will be very informal. Just a walk through for the memorial. You don't have to do your speech."

That's good, since I haven't written it yet. Or thought too terribly much about it. I gaze around the theater. The stage is bare of decoration. A lectern is positioned on the left side of the stage and four chairs extend away from it. On the floor in front of the stage, Ella Jones chats with Bobby Vitality. Her arms are folded, and she keeps her distance, as if ready to run right out of the conversation. (Oh, good. I'm not the only one Mr. Vitality has that effect on.) Tim Hefflin is slumped in a seat in the front row, his hands over his eyes. Hopefully, there's a barf bag in the vicinity. I turn to Lars.

"No Hal Murdoch?" I say.

"Not today," Lars says, "He's out of the hospital, but his assistant, Billie, wants him to rest. He'll be at the memorial."

That's good to hear. All four major news stations and both newspapers have reported the attack on Murdoch. It's not front-page news, but it's not getting buried. Luckily for Murdoch, there's been no mention of *The Night Hawk Rising* as a motive for the attack.

I'm feeling agitated and the source is not the case nor the attack on Hal Murdoch. It's the blown opportunity with Casey. Things were weird when we parted last night, and she hasn't returned the text message I sent her this morning. The whole thing makes me uneasy.

Lars senses something is wrong. "Nervous about the speech?"

"No, I'll be fine," I say.

"You sure? Sounds like a crisis of confidence. You might want to consult Mr. Vitality."

And for my next trick, I'll run my ball sack over a cheese grater. "Is Mr. Vitality going to be part of the memorial?"

"Not directly," Lars says, "But he's my advisor. I don't want to try a thing like this without his advice and consent."

At this point, I doubt Lars would contemplate a trip to the restroom without Mr. Vitality's advice and consent. "I hope it's doing you good," I say.

"It is," Lars says, "In fact, I'm thinking of moving in with Mr. Vitality."

My head swings toward Lars. "Moving in? Are you going to be his butler?"

"No, no, no," Lars says, "Unless he asks me, of course. I'm not moving into Mr. Vitality's personal residence. He has a building."

"A building?"

"A series of buildings. Located together. A campus. Or a compound." Lars starts to wave a hand, then draws it back. "You see, Mr. Vitality has a number of employees and clients and interns. To say nothing of volunteers. The closer he keeps them, the better for business."

"Will he charge you rent? Because you have a sweet deal on your apartment."

"No, I'll be working for my rent."

"What kind of wage are you getting?"

"Oh, I don't get a wage. The experience is my wage."

Okay, I'm not wealthy and I frequently remind everyone just how happy I am with that arrangement. But even *I* have my venal side.

"You're not making any money at all?" I ask.

Lars holds up a finger "But I'm not losing any either. As long as I'm part of Mr. Vitality's organization, all my needs will be taken care of."

"His organization," I say.

"You might even call it his family. Mr. Vitality encourages us to think that way."

I never had a great feeling about this guy, but now it's turned up to eleven. Lars gets a signal from Mr. Vitality. He moves toward the stairs without acknowledging me. Mr. Vitality briefly speaks to Lars and then it's time to get rehearsal started.

It's as brief as Lars indicated it would be. He lays out the order in which each of us will speak and situates us on the stage. Lars, as the MC, gets the chair closest to the lectern. I'm next to him, as the second speaker. Ella sits next to me, then Hefflin and a currently open chair for Mr. Murdoch. Lars will make the opening statement, then introduce each of the speakers. There will be a video review of James Queen's career at the beginning and end of the speeches. (Lars assures us it will be tasteful and leave not a dry eye in the house.) And that will be it. Once the explanation is over, Lars asks if there are any questions. Since none present themselves, we're free to go. Hefflin, wearing a sweatshirt I saw in the hotel gift shop, drags himself off the stage and drops into a chair in the front row. Lars makes a beeline to Mr. Vitality, looking to get his approval.

Ella and I stand. She wears the same clothes from last night. Her hair is a bit mussed and most of her makeup is gone. Normally, this would signal something of the *walk of shame* variety, but Mike was at my place last night. Unless Ella had other company. I'm now cursing myself for thinking such a thing.

I haven't had a chance to ask Ella about this Rob guy from the other night. Mike was hoping to take care of that last night, but the situation with Hal Murdoch distracted us.

Certainly, it wouldn't have been appropriate to bring it up at the hospital. But there's nothing stopping me now, is there?

"Excuse me," I say, choking a bit on the words, "do you have a minute?"

Ella looks surprised. "I suppose." She faces me. "What's on your mind?"

I had hoped we could go somewhere and have a little privacy. But Ella doesn't seem inclined to go anywhere. However, Lars is wrapped up in conversation with Mr. Vitality and Hefflin is more concerned with his own misery than anything else.

"I wanted to ask you about something," I say, "and someone."

"Oh?" Ella says, "Who and what?"

She isn't making it easy on me. I'll give her that. "The guy you were with at the wine bar the other night."

Ella's face is impassive. "The one Mike beat up?"

Beat up. That's cute. Mike beat this guy up in the same way I won the state hockey championship for my old high school because I happened to be in the building when it occurred. Still, I won't remove Ella's delusion.

"Yeah, that guy," I say, "I'm wondering who he was."

Ella debates answering. The wait gives me flop sweats. But Ella plays ball.

"His name is Rob," she says, "He is—*was*—a friend of James."

"Rob," I say, "Does Rob have a last name?"

I've got Ella on her guard (assuming she wasn't already). "Is this going in your article?"

Interesting question. I'm still not sure what said article, if it ever gets written, will look like. But that matters less than giving Ella the answer she wants to hear.

"It depends on how relevant this Rob person is to James Queen's story."

Ella's eyes slide away from me. "He's not. Trust me."

Uh-huh. Trust the person who didn't tell me about Rob's existence, the fact she asked James Queen for help right before his murder or that she was hanging out with my friend Mike on the sly. (Although, I'm pinning that last one on Mike.)

"Is he in town for the memorial?" I ask.

There's a glimmer of something in Ella's face. Hard to quantify, but if I had to guess, she finds something amusing. She quickly extinguishes it.

"I don't know," she says, "I just know he's in town. He wanted to talk to me, see how I was doing. That's it."

Ella folds her arms. Normally, this would seem like a challenging gesture or one of self-defense. This has a different quality. It's as if Ella's hugging herself; hanging on. To what, though, I have no idea.

"Just before we got to the table," I say, "Rob grabbed you. It looked like he was getting aggressive. That's why Mike asked him to step outside."

Ella gives that a flip of her hand. "It was nothing. He had been drinking, he was trying to make a point about something—something that happened a hundred years ago—and he got a little, um, *exuberant.* Mike was very sweet, but fighting Rob wasn't necessary."

I'm not sure fighting (if that's what you want to call it) in an alley qualifies as *sweet*, but I won't argue. Ella's dancing around something bigger. But I've got no way of calling her out on it. I switch tacks.

"The day James Queen died," I say, "you asked for his help. Can you tell me what that was about?"

Ella flashes me a look, then drops her eyes again. "How did you hear about that?"

"Hal Murdoch mentioned it," I say, "Just in passing."

"It wasn't a big deal," Ella says, "I needed a little favor." She gives me a cold look. "Nothing your readers would be interested in."

Yep, dangling by a thread here. Any second now, Ella will stalk away, possibly giving me the finger as she goes. I'm desperate to get something out of her.

"Did this Rob guy have anything to do with the favor?" I ask.

"No," Ella says, turning away from me.

Tim Hefflin pops out of whatever reverie he was in and sits up in his seat. "Rob Quince?"

Ella shoots him a panicked look. "No, Tim. That's not what we're talking about." But she's already given the game away.

Hefflin doesn't look convinced. I must not, either, because Ella takes one look at me and gathers up her purse and coat. Her face flushes.

"I have to go," she says, "Good luck with your article. I'm sorry I can't be more help."

Ella walks off, her heels clacking against the stage. I watch her go, feeling like an ass. Hefflin's hands are folded in his lap. Something is on his mind. I hop off the stage and approach him.

"Excuse me," I say, "do you know this Rob Quince guy?"

Hefflin stands but doesn't take his eyes off the floor. "No, I don't know him." After a second, he adds, "Excuse me" and heads up the stairs.

That leaves me with only Lars and Bobby Vitality for company. Sadly, they both make their over to me. I don't have an excuse to run for it.

"Mr. Vitality was hoping to talk to you," Lars says.

I look past him to the smiling visage of Mr. Vitality. He wears a white shirt, open at the collar, and tan slacks. (Doesn't he know it's after Labor Day?) I wait for him to start talking. He doesn't. You ever had one of those dreams where you're in front of a class and you're supposed to talk about something, and you have no idea what to say? It's a lot like that.

I speak to Lars. "Is he going to say something?"

"Of course," Lars says, "You open to hearing him?"

I try to keep my voice level. "I'm here, aren't I?"

Lars stands aside. Mr. Vitality opens his hands.

"I'm very much looking forward to your speech," he says, "It's going to be a great part of the memorial. And on a very auspicious day."

"I'm sure it's going to be a great memorial," I say, putting about half my heart into it.

There's a slight tremor in Mr. Vitality's cheek. "Yes, the memorial should be wonderful. But there are other events happening that day. Big events."

It dawns on me. "*The* big event, right? The one Lars was talking about?"

Mr. Vitality's head slowly rotates toward Lars. "You spoke to him of the Big Event?"

Lars looks down, chastened. "Just in passing. I didn't give him any details."

Probably because Lars didn't *have* any details. But Mr. Vitality is satisfied with Lars's explanation. He turns to me.

"Yes, that was the Big Event I was speaking of," Mr. Vitality says, "I'm hoping you can be a part of it."

I shuffle my feet. I hate being put on the spot. (More accurately, I hate being put on the spot when asked to do something I don't want to do.) "It depends. What's happening at this Big Event?"

"I'm afraid I can't tell you that," Mr. Vitality says, "But it's going to be big."

"I gathered that from the title *Big Event*," I say.

"Can we count on you to be part of it?"

"I'm not much of a joiner," I say. Truer words…

Mr. Vitality looks at me without blinking, that thing I find so disconcerting. "You *are* a loner. Gregarious and social, certainly. But on the inside, you're very alone." His eyes narrow, as if he's looking deeper. "You prefer it that way. But you're starting to question it."

I find myself staring at him, drawn in against my will. "I'm not sure…"

"We can offer you connection and purpose," he says, "Things you're beginning to crave."

I break eye contact with Mr. Vitality. It feels like a survival mechanism. I spin toward the stairs.

"Hey, this has been great," I say, "I've got to get going. Things to see. People to do. Catch you later."

I flee up the stairs to the back of the theater. Mr. Vitality watches me go. I'll give him credit: he has a few insights about me. Problem is, he doesn't know everything about me. After all, I get annoyed when my friends know too much about what makes me tick.

You realize how annoying it is when a *stranger* figures these things out?

CHAPTER TWELVE

I think sometimes that the loss of personal freedom that has come with the digital age is experienced along generational lines. Here's what I mean…

When the internet came along, I was barely old enough to remember a time before it. Yes, I'm schooled in pop culture and history and everything that came before. But I don't have a strong memory of life without the internet and the tracking capabilities that come with it.

My parents, on the other hand, have vivid memories of such. A time when your interests and hobbies were known to only you and whoever you chose to share these things with. When advertisers hawked their tawdry wares without using your Google search metrics. When you could use an assumed name and a fake ID. (Fake as in one you made up, not one you "borrowed" from the rightful owner.) Those were the days when someone could be run to earth and not be heard from again. Or at least for several years. Now, you'd have to literally run to the earth—find a damn hole in the ground—to maintain relative anonymity.

As I said, the perception of this is generational. My parents can't believe there's no longer a time when someone could disappear without a trace. I can't believe there was ever a time when such a thing was possible. John Dillinger wouldn't stand a chance in today's climate. (Of course, he'd probably be a computer hacker instead of a bank robber, so…)

I won't object to today's pervasive atmosphere. Not if it helps me find Rob Quince.

"You think that's it?" Mike says, pointing past me to the computer screen.

I swivel in my desk chair and sip my beer. It's rare that Mike and I look at the computer together, unless it's videos of pro wrestling botches or bikini chicks. But here we are, perched in the corner, staring at Facebook. We've been going through a variety of Rob Quinces and have found a few that will admit to living in Los Angeles. Now, it's a matter of finding which one might be in our fair city.

"I think it's this guy," I say, moving the mouse toward my suspect.

"No, I'm positive it's this guy," Mike says, sticking his finger on my computer screen, "I remember him from the fight."

The picture isn't clear, so I click on the profile. Most of the photos show the guy in various bars and restaurants. A few show women passing by, the photos framing their asses. (Nice.) Mike again taps the screen.

"That's the guy," he says, "No doubt about it."

I grab a tissue and wipe off the screen. "I'll buy that. We know he's in the Cities. Let's see what we can find."

I look through Rob Quince's profile. No recent status updates. There is, however, a recent photo, posted two days ago. It's a rearview photo of a woman wearing a gray sweatshirt and black tights. She's walking down a sidewalk. There looks to be an overpass ahead. It's hard to tell because the photo focuses on her ass (because of course it does). It's captioned, "Enjoying the local scenery."

I sip my beer. "If nothing else, we know this guy's an ass man."

Mike stares intently at the photo, but not for the reasons you might be thinking (or that I might be thinking). "There's a clue in there."

He starts to point at the screen, but I swat his hand away. "Just tell me what you're looking at," I say.

He gives me a sour look. "There's a business in the background. Can you see the name?"

It's hard to read, but not impossible. I click on the photo, then go to full screen mode. Mike and I look close (great, I'll have to disinfect it now).

"I think it's Ready Wash," I say.

"That looks right," Mike says, "I'm guessing it's a car wash. Look it up."

I open another tab and punch Ready Wash into a search engine. A few seconds later, we find it. Ready Wash is indeed a car wash. It has one location in the Twin Cities. In Bloomington, a first ring suburb that houses both the airport and the Mall of America. Mike takes a hasty sip of his beer, spilling some on the desk. (Goddammit.)

"Look it up on the map," he says, "See if there are any hotels around there."

Wow, *Mike* is beating me to the punch on these things? What the hell is going on? I shake off my sense of displacement and bring up the map. It confirms Ready Wash is in Bloomington, on the border of Edina, a snooty suburb whose high school hockey team best resembles the Cobra Kai. It's on a frontage road near highways 100 and 494 (which would explain the overpass). I zoom in close enough to get a look at some local businesses. Sure enough, there's a hotel right next door. It's a Budgetada, a chain catering to those who just want a clean room, preferably not facing the body floating in the pool

"He's got to be there," Mike says, practically bouncing in place, "We found him."

I'm a little more cautious, but it looks like he's right on this one. I don't see another hotel in the vicinity. In fact, there don't appear to be a lot of businesses. It's not the kind of place one would just happen to choose for a walk. If you're there, you're there for a reason. In all likelihood, Rob Quince's reason is that he's staying at the Budgetada.

"I suppose you want to go after this guy?" I ask Mike

"Damn skippy," Mike says. He starts to sit on the edge of the desk, but I shoo him away. "I want to know what he was talking to Ella about."

I turn the desk chair around to face him. "As opposed to the more expedient method of just asking Ella?"

"I don't think so," Mike says, "I don't know if she'd talk to me about it and I don't want to take advantage of our friendship."

Sure, it's noble, his not wanting to take advantage of a friendship. But he's living here and screwing up my sex life. Apparently, he has no difficulty taking advantage of *all* friendships.

The difficult part is figuring out how Rob Quince fits into this whole thing. According to Ella, he was a friend of James Queen's. Obviously, she knows him. Apparently, so does Tim Hefflin. Beyond that, I don't know who the guy is or why he's here. I don't remember seeing him at the convention, so the possibility of his being involved—at least directly—in James Queen's murder are pretty remote. But I won't know that for sure until I talk to the guy. I down the rest of my beer.

"What do you say?" I ask, "Should we go track this guy down?"

Mike slaps the back of the futon, scattering the cats. (They had been avoiding him up to this point.) "Fuck yeah. Let's do this."

He finishes his beer and sets the bottle on the floor. I pick it up and bring both bottles to the recycling. Mike slips on his black leather jacket and hands my jean jacket to me.

"We don't know this guy's room number," I say.

Mike gives that a flip of his hand. "Leave that to me. Shouldn't be a problem."

I reach for the front door. "I hope you know what you're doing."

"I was going to say the same thing to you."

***

The drive to Bloomington isn't particularly interesting. Take one freeway. Then take another. Enjoy the retail and offices marking the landscape. Add some nerves about the mission we're on and you've got a rather tense atmosphere in the car. Mike decides to break it.

"How are things with Casey?" he asks, "Any progress?"

"Actually, there's been regress," I say, "She hasn't been answering my texts."

"You think the case is scaring her off?"

"No. If that little chase the other night meant anything, it has the opposite effect."

"What about you?" Mike asks, "Does danger have the same effect?"

"I'm a guy," I say, "I don't need an aphrodisiac so much as I need an opportunity."

I pull off Highway 100 and on to the frontage road leading to the hotel. The neighborhood is littered with former restaurants and hotels. Somehow, the Budgetada is still there. Like cockroaches surviving a nuclear holocaust. The tension in the car is palpable. The building itself is two stories and stretches out like a boomerang. It's plain white brick and the entrance is barely noticeable. The parking lot is uneven, with jags of pavement sticking up. Despite the ugliness of the landscape, the parking lot is nearly full. (A reasonable rate and a continental breakfast must go a long way.) I find a parking space near the edge of the lot.

"You got a plan?" I ask.

Mike flips open the passenger door. "Something will come to me."

That doesn't exactly fill me with confidence. We take the cracked sidewalk to the front door. The glass door to the lobby has a long crack in it. Said lobby is larger than the exterior would indicate. There is a raised area where something resembling breakfast is served. Discarded plates, cups and napkins line the scattered tabletops. The pool is visible beyond the front desk. The Budgetada has two floors, bisected by the lobby. The rooms move away from the lobby at odd angles.

Behind the desk, a heavyset Latino girl in her early twenties watches a computer. (I suspect she's not looking over the reservations list.) Mike strolls up to the counter. The clerk gives us a bright smile. Here's the moment of truth.

"Evening," Mike says, propping an arm on the high counter, "I'm looking for someone who might be staying here. I've got his name. I just need his room number."

The clerk's smile fades slightly. "I'm sorry. We can't give that information out."

"No, *I'm* sorry," Mike says, "Clearly, you don't know who we are. My name is John Taggert. This is William Rosewood. Have you heard of the DEA?"

"DEA?" she says, chewing her fingernails, "It's that serious?"

"Maybe," Mike says, "That depends on how cooperative Mr. Quince is. And yourself."

The clerk looks around. There's no manager to consult and she's faced with a big decision. Breach of company policy and all. Mike doesn't blink. I put my hands in my pockets and try to look tough (not exactly my specialty). The clerk grabs the mouse.

"What was the name?" she asks.

"Rob Quince," Mike says, his voice all business, "It might be under the name Robert."

"It's room two-fifty-four," the clerk says, throwing a look over her shoulder, not wanting to get caught. She half-heartedly gestures toward the far end of the lobby. "It's that way."

"Thank you," Mike says, "You did the right thing."

The clerk busies herself with some paperwork. Mike and I make our way across the lobby. Just around the corner, we find a stairway leading to the second floor. Mike leads the way up.

"We're impersonating cops now?" I ask.

"What cops?" Mike says, Mr. Innocent himself, "I just gave her a couple fake names and asked if she had ever heard of the D.E.A. You remember the D.E.A.? Department of Evil Assholes? Robbie and Stoner and me put it together in college."

I had forgotten about that. It was one of a number of fictional organizations we created in college: Department of Evil Assholes, the Gnarly Beaver Protection Society, the University Pricks. The gift that keeps on giving.

We walk down the hall. The place smells vaguely of pot. There are stains on the carpeting and the walls are yellowed. Room two fifty-four is all the way down the hall and around the corner. It's the only room visible.

And the door is ajar.

Mike and I stare at the damn thing. For a couple guys on a mission to confront, we've become shockingly timid. Neither of us move.

"What do we do?" I ask.

"Guess he saved us the trouble of breaking in."

One of us has to do something. Mike seems determined to continue his impression of a pre-lubed Tin Woodsman. (Y'know, that came out sounding filthier than I intended. Sorry.) I step to the door. It's completely quiet. Mike flicks his hands, encouraging me to go into the room. Nice to know the cowardly bastard has my back. I gently tap the door. No response. I push the door open.

And find someone on the floor, unconscious.

At first, I'm not sure if unconscious is all he is. But no pools of blood on the floor. No sign of a massive wound. Mike shoves past me.

"What the hell's going on?" he says. Then he sees the guy on the floor and says, "Oh."

I squat down. "Is that Rob Quince?"

"I think it is," Mike says, "Can't quite see the face, but the rest of him looks familiar."

"What should we do?"

"Call the cops?"

That *would* be the right thing to do. If Mike wasn't impersonating one at the moment. And we'd also have to tell them how the hell we stumbled across this scene and that might also be problematic.

All concerns about call the police, though, go out the window when someone hits Mike from behind.

CHAPTER THIRTEEN

The first question we ask ourselves when the Fickle Finger of Fate gives us a wet willie is, "What did I do to deserve this?"

After all, we don't walk around thinking of ourselves as bad people. Certainly not the kind for whom any comeuppance might be due. Sure, we lose our temper from time to time, say a few things we might regret, flip the occasional bird or run some idiot off the road and into a ravine. But who hasn't?

When someone comes at us, though, you mentally play back everything you've done that might have resulted in such a situation. We can only assume this is life being cruel once again.

See? Life is the asshole, not us.

In this case, the asshole is both easy and difficult to spot. Easy in that his attack on Mike is swift. Difficult in the sense the guy wears a disguise.

Mike goes down. I spin around and see the attacker raising an object. He wears the same disguise as before: ski mask, fedora, overcoat, gloves. I'm not sure if the thing in his hand is a billy club or a Maglite or a tire iron. And I'm not going to try to figure it out.

I throw myself backward, avoiding a swing from the attacker. The object hits the floor with a thud. I stay on my feet. The attacker stands in the doorway. I'm trapped. The only two guys who could help me are on the floor. I'll have to fight my way out of this.

In other words, I'm completely fucked.

I back further into the room, taking care not to trip over Rob Quince's carcass. The room is just a few beds, a bathroom and a small desk. The only way out is through the window. Given I'd have to throw the desk through it, then follow it and drop from the second story without getting injured, all before the attacker takes it upon himself to cave in my head, well, I don't like my chances.

I retreat toward the bathroom, wondering if there's anything in there I can use as a weapon. The attacker keeps coming, waving the nightstick. My eyes slip toward the desk. The desk chair is light and might work as a weapon. I've got the angle, but I've got to move quick.

I jump toward the chair. The attacker follows my movement. He's going to get to me before I can get the chair. I stop. The nightstick swishes past me and cracks against the chair. I grab the chair and hoist it up.

The attacker backs up, keeping his distance from the chair. He feints with the nightstick, testing my willingness to use the chair. A groan comes from the floor. My eyes drop toward it. That's all it takes for the attacker to make a move.

The nightstick comes at me. I bring the chair around in time to block it. The nightstick cracks against the chair. The vibration from the impact stings my hands. I keep hold of the chair.

I turn the legs toward the attacker and drive the chair at him. It pushes the attacker back toward the desk. I've got a clear path out of the room. I drop the chair and make a break for it.

And realize Mike is still lying there.

It's one of those *a thousand thoughts at once* moments. If I run, the attacker will probably kill Mike. If I don't run, he'll probably kill *me*. But I've given up my one weapon. I've got to figure something out. And have no time to think about it.

I kneel next to Mike. The attacker comes at us. Mike stirs. I don't know how ambulatory he is. I don't think I can carry him out of the hotel (or out of this room, for that matter). No idea what to do next. I'm completely out of time.

Then the attacker trips over Rob Quince.

In the attacker's defense, it's not as if Quince is still a lump on the floor. He's gotten up on all fours. The attacker goes right over Quince and crashes to the floor. He keeps ahold of the nightstick. So much for a counterattack. I grab the back of Mike's shirt and haul him to his feet.

"What the fuck?" he asks, slurring.

"Run," is all I tell him.

Mike struggles to his feet. He might not be able to go fast, but he can move his feet. I can provide the speed. I throw an arm around him and yank him out of the room.

We run down the hallway, gangly and awkward, but getting the job done. It reminds me of the time my brother Owen and I won the three-legged race at the Fourth of July celebration. (Owen will be flattered to know my dying thoughts were of me hauling his ass to victory, even though he'll insist it was the other way around.) The attacker comes after us, again moving surprisingly fast for a guy his size. I doubt we'll make the lobby. Mike likely comes to the same conclusion. He raps on the nearest door.

"Fire!" he shouts.

There might be questions about morality here. But it's survival of the sneakiest. I follow Mike's lead, knocking on doors, informing the guests of the impending inferno. (Although, a fire could gut this entire place and cause upwards of about eleven dollars damage.)

Unfortunately, a crappy hotel in a first-ring suburb doesn't draw a huge crowd on a weeknight in the fall. Most of the rooms are empty. Still, the effort crosses up the attacker.

He slows, as if unsure whether to continue pursuit. It gives Mike and I the separation we need to get to the stairs ahead of him.

Mike's recovered and can do the stairs without me hauling him around. My feet touch the stairs maybe twice. A final burst of speed gets us to the lobby. The clerk is on her phone. She takes it away from her ear as soon as she sees us. I throw myself at the counter.

"You need to call the police," I say, gesturing frantically toward the hallway.

The clerk drops her phone. "Aren't you the police?"

Shazbot. In my panic, I lost the cover story. Mike, though, keeps his wits about him. He pushes past me.

"We need to call in backup," he says, "Just call 9-1-1. Tell them someone is attacking guests. Don't mention us."

The clerk pauses after picking up the hotel phone. "Why not?"

"We're undercover," Mike says.

I will never cease to be amazed and horrified by the way Mike can do stuff off the top of his head. Even when he's had a blow to said head. The clerk buys the story and dials the police. I wonder when we're going to see the attacker. But there's no sign of him.

"Stay here," I tell Mike.

"Up yours," is his response.

Since Mike's probably taxed his aching head, what with the chase and the clerk, I'm not going to argue with him. We run to the edge of the lobby and peek down the hallway. No sign of the attacker. We run up to the second floor. Still nothing. I look over the railing.

"There's a side door at the bottom of the stairs," I say, "He could have gone out there. Or he could have gone back to the room."

"Checking the parking lot isn't going to get us anywhere," Mike says, "The guy would be long gone. Let's go back to the room."

"What if he's waiting on us?" I say.

"Then we'll see how he does when he attacks us from the _front_," Mike says.

Before I can stop him, Mike powerwalks down the hall. I don't like this idea. The attacker's got a nightstick. A straight on attack will still result in him doing severe damage to home and hearth. The only hope is that if the attacker is waiting on us, we can hold him off until the police get there.

Our attempt to raise a false fire alarm doesn't appear to have had any effect on the second floor. Everyone is either absent or stoned. We peek around the corner leading to Quince's room. The door is open and there's no sign of movement. We slide up to the entrance and look inside.

The place is completely empty. No sign even of Rob Quince.

I stand in the doorway. "Should we…"

"Search the room before the cops get here? Abso-fucking-lutely."

There's no stopping Mike when he's like this. We do a search, but there isn't much to find. The bed hasn't been made and there are some discarded beer cans and pizza boxes. No cell phone or wallet visible. Quince probably had those things on him when he got clobbered and probably left with them. Mike looks in the closet and steps back.

"Think we got something here," he says.

He reaches into the closet and comes out with a black gym bag. It's leather and contains a copious number of side pockets. Mike holds it between his thumb and forefinger, like he's holding a girlfriend's purse. I point toward the bed.

"Put it down," I say.

Mike complies. I open the bag and rifle through the contents. There are clothes and towels. (The towels look suspiciously like the ones hanging in the bathroom.) There are toiletries in a side compartment, including condoms (gross). I open the other side compartment. There are some spare socks. And a package. I take it out of the bag.

It catches Mike's attention. "What you got?"

"Not sure," I say, "Look in the hallway. See if anyone's coming."

He isn't happy being relegated to errand boy, but he does the job anyway. The package is wrapped in brown paper and feels stuffed with something. I pick at the masking tape, pull it loose and open the package. Tissues have been stuffed in to provide cushioning. I dig through and find something made of hard plastic on the inside. I pull it loose. And find myself holding a VHS tape.

Son of a bitch. These are still a thing?

Mike pops back into the room. "It's all clear." He sees what's in my hand. "Is that a video tape?"

"Looks like it."

"Son of a bitch. Those are still a thing?"

There's a bustle in the hallway. It sounds like the police have arrived. I stuff the package, absent the tape, back into the gym bag. I throw the bag under the bed. Mike and I still have the tape.

"Do something with that damn thing!" he says.

So, I toss it to Mike. He catches it out of self-defense. He looks around, as if inspiration will strike. Voices can be heard in the hallway. Mike finally hoists his shirt and jacket and stuffs the tape down his pants.

I'm not sure how we're going to play it. Since I'll have to burn it now.

***

Yes, I know coffee is supposed to contribute to anxiety and nerves and such. But I generally find trips to a coffee shop relaxing. A bit of writing, a bit of people watching. Some relaxing music and the hum of conversation. Throw in a book and I'm very much in my happy place.

So, it's no fun being nervous in a coffee shop. Unnatural, you might say.

It's a nice enough day. Sunny, though there's a chilly breeze. Leaves blow off the trees and I'm reminded they will be barren in a month. I duck into Jitters and find Casey behind the counter, reading a book. She wears a flowered dress over a white long sleeve tee and her hair is pulled back. She looks up and sees me approaching. She doesn't react. Not the greeting I was hoping for. She sets the book aside as I arrive at the counter.

"Hi, stranger," she says.

"I was going to say the same thing to you," I say, sitting at the counter.

Casey hesitates. There's a sadness in her eyes. Then she says, "Large dark roast?"

I agree and Casey slides away from the counter to pour the coffee. It's a sleepy afternoon. Just a few study groups. I wait for Casey to say something, but she doesn't. I pick at a napkin.

"Hope it's okay that I dropped by," I say.

"Of course," Casey says, over her shoulder. She seems to mean it.

"It's just that you, uh, haven't returned any of my texts," I say.

I'm faltering. It occurs to me that my thinking may be all wrong on this. I haven't been able to figure out why Casey has been avoiding me. Why would my having to rush off and deal with the case make her angry? After all, wasn't she turned on by the danger? It's just occurred to me that I might not be the only one upset by getting revved up and then shut down. Sexist of me, I know. Throw in the creepiness of dropping in unannounced on Casey while she's at work and I realize I'm making a mistake. However, Casey's face softens as she sets the mug of coffee in front of me.

"I'm sorry," she says, "I haven't been avoiding you. I'm trying to figure things out and…well, if you don't know what to say, it's best to say nothing."

I'm not sure how to take that. *Trying to figure things* out never seems like a harbinger of good things. Casey comes around the counter and sits on the stool next to me.

"I *have* missed you," she says.

"I'm glad to hear that," I say.

"I've just been thinking…" Casey runs a hand through her hair. "I don't know…maybe we're cursed."

That's a thing I'd forgotten about Casey (or chose not to remember): she's got a superstitious side; the belief that the Fickle Finger of Fate is giving us *that* finger. I've never had much use for superstition.

"I don't believe that," I say.

"How do you explain it?" Casey asks.

"Bad luck."

That isn't any more convincing than Casey's *cursed* explanation. She props her chin in her hand, looking torn. I put a hand on her back.

"We're making too big a deal out of this," I say.

"Too big a deal?"

"I don't mean…look, I just think we shouldn't read too much into it. I've got this goofy situation with Mike and it's getting in our way. It's annoying, but nothing more."

"I'd like to believe that…"

"And I'd like you to." I move my head so I can get in Casey's line of sight. "Look, do you want to, uh…"

Casey's nostrils flare slightly. "Yes. I really do."

"Good. That's…that's good. We can build on that. Find another time to get together."

"I get off in twenty minutes."

Son of a... There's nothing I'd rather do than take Casey back to my place and spend the afternoon proving what a fluke that afternoon in college was. And I certainly don't want to reinforce Casey's feeling we're cursed. But I can't take her up on the offer.

"I'm sorry, I can't," I say.

Casey's head drops. "Why not?"

"It's, uh, it's the thing with Mike. Again."

I give her the story of what happened at the hotel, including Mike telling the police we were looking in on a friend and the hotel clerk was probably smoking pot and imagined we were with the DEA. (And yes, he came up with all that off the top of his head.) Despite Mike's obvious immorality, telling Casey the story turns out to be a good idea. She listens, rapt.

"Wow," she says, "Mike does good work."

"He was at his bullshitting finest."

Casey slips back behind the counter and pours herself a refill. She talks to me over her shoulder. "What are you guys going to do with the tape?"

"Play it," I say, "That's what's going on back at my place." Casey tops off my dark roast. I wrap my hands around the mug. "See, Mike and I were able to sneak the tape out of the hotel without the cops catching us. There was just one little problem. Neither of us owns a VCR."

"Who the hell does anymore?"

"And when one thinks of useless junk no one would own anymore, one turns to my friend Lars."

And that's what we did. We struck paydirt, of sorts. Lars owns a VCR, but it's in storage. Given his schedule, he won't be able to get it until this afternoon. Mike decided to play hooky from his temp job and is holed up in my place. Lars will be home in half-an-hour and our viewing party, so to speak, is scheduled for then.

"What do you think is on the tape?" Casey asks.

"Not sure," I say, "We're not going to know until we play the thing."

"You'll let me know when you find out?"

"I think that's the least I could do."

She rests on the counter. "And just when do you think that will be?"

I slide my hand into hers. "Not nearly soon enough." Our faces are very close. "I'm going to get this thing with Mike settled. ASAP. Then I'll throw him out and invite you over and nothing will interrupt us."

Casey smiles. "I'd like that."

It's probably not a good idea to kiss her while she's still on the clock. But, on the other hand, fuck it. I slide my hand up Casey's cheek, into her hair and try to gently bring her face to mine. I say *try* because the second my fingers reach Casey's hair, she grabs my face and pulls *me* to her. It's intense. It's wonderful. And it lasts about two seconds.

Some dude farther down the counter ostentatiously clears his throat. "Excuse me, miss? If you could tear yourself away from your boyfriend for a second…"

Casey pulls away. She has a *Whoops, busted* kind of look. But the uncertainty is back in her eyes. She gives me a peck on the cheek and moves down the counter. I sip my coffee and contemplate the murder of Casey's latest customer.

That one I could probably solve.

***

"I'm not sure I even remember how to hook one of these damn things up," I say, looking at the mess of cables, equipment and wires on my coffee table.

Lars, of course, is unflappable. "It's easy. Just hook the coaxial cable into the outlet on the TV, set your TV to *Cable* and turn the VCR on. Then we're in business."

It all comes back to me. When growing up, I was responsible for all technology in the house. My mom was clueless, and my dad thought such things were the devil's work. (I'm convinced my father was a codger before he was a toddler.) It was my job to hook up VCRs, DVD players, computers, laptops, cell phones and such. I tried to use this knowledge to negotiate a later curfew, but my parents reminded me they still provided food, shelter and warmth.

Such things dwarfed technological tchotchkes. Snake eyes for AV Club Boy.

Now, I'm not even AV Club Boy.

Lars expertly hooks up the VCR. Mike and I sit at the breakfast bar. Mike holds the tape, turning it over his hands.

"You think this is a good idea?" he says.

"If it's related to James Queen getting killed," I say, "yes, it is."

I can't figure out Mike's reluctance to play this tape. Before I can ask him about it, Lars glides away from the TV.

"I believe we are ready, gentlemen," he says.

Mike and I move to the futon. There's enough room for all three of us, but I keep my distance, parking it on the arm of the futon. Lars wields the remote control.

"Here we go," he says.

The VCR roars to life. (And *roars* is an apt description. I've gotten too used to the soft hum of a DVD or Blu-Ray player.) After a few seconds of static, the picture comes up. We see a bedroom. The decorations are homey, and there is a poster bed front and center. The footage appears to be shot by a cheap video camera. There's a buzz of conversation.

"I'm enjoying the mise-en-scene," Lars says, steepling his fingers, "I like the way the bed sits a little off-center. The space gives you a feeling of suspense. Makes you wonder who might be coming in."

I took one film class in college, but I vaguely remember that mise-en-scene relates to telling a story through shot composition. (I think. I spent a lot of the lectures staring at Amy Whittaker, who sat one row below me in the lecture hall and tended to wear low cut t-shirts.) Regardless, I'm not certain the bed is off-center due to any artistic choice.

Finally, someone enters the frame. It's a woman in her thirties, wearing a loose-fitting blue dress. Her face isn't immediately visible. She sits on the bed, wraps her arms around one of the posters and looks toward the camera. The image comes into focus. We all recoil, like we're watching a horror movie.

"Ah shit," Mike says, "that's Ella."

Ella Jones is recognizable at any age. That isn't normally a drawback, but when appearing in a bootleg video, it can be problematic. Mike squirms.

"We should turn this off," he says, reaching for the remote.

But the remote is in Lars's hand. He looks over at me and I shake my head. Lars holds his hand out, keeping the remote out of Mike's reach.

"Sorry, brother," Lars says, "no can do."

Mike spins toward me. "What the fuck?"

"We have to see what's on the tape," I say.

"You can't figure it out?" Mike says, his eyes flashing.

I can, of course, but I need to know for sure. I ignore Mike. He sits back and crosses his arms. On the video, Ella smiles, but there's something vacant in her eyes. At least it looks that way on the low-quality video. She weaves, nearly losing her balance and falling off the bed. She speaks to someone just out of the frame.

"I don't know, Jimmy," she says, slurring, "I don't know if…if I want to do this."

A cultured, familiar voice comes from off-camera. "It's just some fun, baby."

Ella slumps against the poster and looks at the person off-camera (and it *has* to be James Queen). Someone else enters the frame, sliding on to the bed behind Ella. It's a guy in his mid-thirties with feathered blonde hair and a wispy mustache. He's stripped down to his black BVDs, showing off a physique that's more pale skin than muscle. He kisses Ella on the neck. She recoils, then relents. The guy slips his hands down Ella's legs and takes hold of the hem of her dress. A moment later, he slips the dress over Ella's head and tosses it someplace out of the frame.

That's all Mike needs to see. He stalks out of the room, taking refuge in the kitchen. "Enjoy the show, assholes."

Lars and I continue to watch, though I'm not happy about it. On screen, Ella makes a feeble attempt to cover herself. She wears a matching black lace bra and panties. The guy kisses her neck again. She looks off-camera, then relaxes.

The guy comes up for air and encourages someone off-camera to approach. Another woman enters the frame. She's your standard operational southern California beach bimbo. The Silicone Express. She's stripped down to her matching underwear. The bimbo also begins kissing Ella's neck. Ella closes her eyes, though it's not clear if there's any pleasure in it. The bimbo's hands glide over Ella's breasts while the dude reaches behind Ella and unclasps her bra. It's about to slide away from Ella's chest when the tape comes to a halt.

Because I've stopped it.

"Okay," I say, "*now* we know what's on the tape."

Lars spins toward me, looking as if he's going to make a lunge for the remote control I've commandeered. Instead, he crosses his legs and folds his hands over them. I tap the remote against my chin.

"I'm guessing this thing hasn't found its way to the internet yet," I say.

"If it had, I'd know about it," Mike says, "So would every fanboy geek at that convention. Ella never would have shown her face."

I set the remote on the coffee table, keeping it out of Lars's reach. "This was in Rob Quince's possession. Safe to say this is what he was talking to Ella about. And what she needed James Queen's help with."

Mike walks over to the VCR and pops out the tape. He hefts it in his hand. "Do you think Ella is the one who attacked Quince?"

"She'd have plenty of motive," I say, "And there's the possibility she was in disguise."

"You think?" Mike asks.

"The attacker was disguising their voice. We've both heard that. With the costume and everything, it's possible it was her."

Mike bobs his head, debating the matter. "You think she's strong enough?"

"If you have a nightstick and you're pissed, how strong do you need to be?" I say.

He holds up his hands, conceding the point. I pace the living room, thinking. Lars takes the tape from Mike and looks it over. (He must realize I'll never let him take it home.)

"The next step seems easy," Lars says, loosening his tie, "You need to talk to Ella Jones."

Mike scowls. "Do we have to?"

I slip the tape out of Lars's hand. "Yeah, we do," I say, "We need to know what was going on. And with this, we can get some answers."

Mike glares at me. "You're going to browbeat her with that shit?"

"I'm going to ask some questions," I say, "Let her know what I know. And see what she has to say."

Mike's jaw tightens. "You're going to humiliate her."

Alright, now I'm getting pissed off. I'm doing this to keep his sorry ass out of the morgue and he has the nerve to get a case of the red ass with *me*? I fold my arms, keeping the tape against my chest.

"Are you worried she's going to know I saw the tape?" I ask, "Or are you worried she'll know *you've* seen it?"

Mike looks like he's going to take a swing at me. I set the tape down and clench my fists, even though I probably won't do anything with them. Mike takes in a few breaths through his nose, then turns toward the door.

"Do what you gotta do," he says, "If you can still sleep at night."

With that, he stalks out of the apartment, slamming the door behind him. For a few seconds, the place seems frighteningly quiet. I pick up the tape and sit at the breakfast bar. Lars drops a hand on my shoulder.

"I'm sorry that happened, brother," he says, "It's always rough having a falling out with a friend. All because of a simple thing like that tape. I should do something to help."

"You going to talk to Mike?" I ask.

Lars strokes his beard. "I could do that. I was also thinking I could take that tape off your hands. Guard it for safe keeping. It's only logical."

On the one hand, it's irritating to have Lars insult my intelligence. On the other hand, it's nice to know the old Lars still lurks around. I tuck the tape under my arm.

"I'll hold on to it, thank you very much," I say.

Lars raises a hand, as if he's going to argue. He relents and backs toward the front door. "I trust you completely. I'll just be downstairs. In my apartment. If you need me. Just, uh…make sure you knock."

Lars slips out the door before he can see the disgusted look on my face. I set the tape on the breakfast bar and push it away from me. I have faith that Mike will eventually get over his disgust with me.

The bigger question: will I get over my disgust with myself?

CHAPTER FOURTEEN

I'm pretty close with my father. It's anathema, of course, to suggest my dad would favor any one of his sons over the others. The man has a scrupulous sense of fair play (and a particular skill with the sly bon mot.) But Dad and I have always had a strong connection.

And yet, my dad and I haven't had many heart-to-heart talks. So, I remember the few we've had with clarity. There was, for example, the time we had a few beers and chatted about my upbringing. Maybe it was the beer, but I was more interested in hearing about his perspectives than in sharing my own. I asked him about the hardest part of bringing up me and my brothers.

"Realizing I had to give you up to the world," he said, staring into his beer, "It made me afraid. Not of the horrible stuff, necessarily. Just all the casual cruelties. A girl breaks your heart. You don't get something you really want. You fall out with a friend. That sort of thing." His voice got quiet. "Those were the worst. Because I couldn't protect you from them. And I shouldn't want to. Even though I do."

It almost made me forget this was the guy who grounded me for spray-painting a smiley face on the side of the garage. Almost.

It's the *falling out with a friend* thing I'm dealing with right now.

Carol sips her latte and contemplates the matter. "It's unique. But it's not the worst thing I've ever heard. You guys will be fine."

If only I had her faith. It's been less than a day, but Mike has shown no signs of wanting anything to do with me. He even stopped staying at my place and moved down Lars's. (We'll have to see how long that lasts.)

I have one friend, at least, who isn't pissed at me. We're at a small table on the sidewalk outside of Glacier's. The day is warm, but we're the only customers outside. Not too many days of *al fresco* dining left. Carol has a to-go latte in front of her, reminding me she's a busy person and could get called away at any time. But at least she's given me *this* time, so I can't complain. I shove my mug of dark roast aside.

"Mike was pretty pissed," I say.

Carol flits a hand. "Mike gets pretty pissed at everything. He gets over it. Believe me."

If there's one person who knows that to be true, it's Carol. Still, this isn't a one-sided deal. "I'm a little pissed at him myself," I say, "Everything I'm doing is to help him. And this is the thanks I get?"

The irritation kept me up a lot of the night. It only got worse this morning when I realized it so consumed me, I didn't think to invite Casey over, with the apartment empty and all. I'm not sure if there's such a thing as retroactive blue balls, but I think I've got them.

"The tough part is figuring out how it all fits together," I say, "But at least, I know how Queen was killed."

Carol holds her coffee under her chin. "Poison?"

"Exactly. Someone poisoned one of Queen's vitamin shots. The only people who could have done it were the people from *The Night Hawk*. They were all backstage. They all hated James Queen. They all had motive. Hefflin was getting sued. Queen was getting in the way of Murdoch making the new movie. Ella needed his help with the tape. And Queen was involved with that tape. They all have holes in their alibis. And I'm assuming they all knew about the vitamin shots. The tough part is figuring out what Mike could have seen, and which one is after him. And figuring out how the other stuff fits in."

"Like what?" Carol asks.

"Someone attacked Murdoch, threatening him about the movie rights. Rob Quince was attacked. I'd guess it was the same person. But I don't know who or why."

Carol twists her mouth to one side. "I don't think it could be Hal Murdoch. No offense, but the man is old and in poor health."

"Good point. I mean, he could have poisoned Queen. I guess. But the other stuff is out of his league. Besides, if the murderer attacked Murdoch, the murderer couldn't be him."

"Unless the two aren't related," Carol says.

I rub my forehead. "The whole thing gives me a headache."

Carol runs a finger around the rim of her cup. "What's your next step?"

"We're going to talk to Ella. I don't know if Mike's going with me. Lars is setting it up. After looking at the tape, he suddenly doesn't mind being in touch with Ella."

Carol winces. "I wish you wouldn't put *Lars, touch* and *Ella* in the same sentence."

My phone buzzes. I pick it up from the table. It's a text message from Lars. I read it and set the phone back on the table. Carol waits for information.

"I meet Ella in half-an-hour," I say, "In her room at the Ambassador Suites."

"Will Lars be there?"

"He volunteered to go," I say, "I'm going to turn him down. The conversation is going to be uncomfortable enough without him drooling over Ella."

She glances at her phone. "I'd go with you, but I've got a meeting."

My coffee stops just short of my lips. "It's late afternoon. You got a dinner meeting?"

"It's not a business meeting. I'm meeting Alan. The groom."

She looks away, trying to cover the red spreading across her cheeks. I can't help being amused. And confused. I prop my forearms on the little table.

"You're meeting the groom?" I say, "About what?"

"I wish I knew," Carol says, "He called me, said there was something he wanted to talk about. Asked if I'd meet him. I wasn't sure it was a good idea—I'm still not—but he sounded kind of...I don't know, desperate. I said I'd meet him someplace public."

"What if the bride finds out?"

"She won't," Carol says, "Besides, Alan and I are not doing anything wrong. It's as innocent as what we're doing here."

"Oh," I say, "Then this would be a bad time to declare my undying love for you?"

Carol snaps a look at me. She doesn't laugh. She doesn't even smile. I lift one corner of my mouth. It takes her a second to realize I'm joking. She forces a laugh, grabs her purse and tosses her cup into a nearby trashcan.

"I'll see you," she says, "Let me know how the meeting with Ella goes."

"Will do. Let me know how the meeting with the groom goes."

Carol shivers slightly. "Wish me luck."

"Luck."

She turns on her heel and takes off. I watch her walk down the sidewalk. I feel for Carol. Heading into an unknown situation, fraught with complication, knowing a friendship may very well be on the line.

Gee, I wonder why *that* sounds familiar?

***

Despite his, um, abundant enthusiasm, I decline Lars's offer to join me on the Ella Jones visit. He finally lets it go (though he does ask again about borrowing the tape). I fly solo on the trip to the Ambassador Suites. A warm afternoon has turned into a chilly evening. I briefly think of calling or texting Mike. But on the other hand, fuck him. I've tried contacting him umpteen times already. Let him get off his high horse on his own.

I ditch the Saturn in the parking lot and walk through the lobby. As expected, the staff pays no attention to me. I take a glass elevator to the eighth floor. I think about the situation with Mike. I should just tell him to save his own sorry ass. I want no part of it.

Except I know better.

Mike and I will not always be mad at each other. In fact, as two (relatively) grown men, we shouldn't even be mad at each other now. Mike is welcomed to disagree with my tactics involving the tape, but he doesn't have turn it into World War III. Again, the natural order of things has been violated. Usually when Mike and I are at odds, it's because *he* has done something to violate *my* code of ethics. I'm not sure how much of this topsy-turvy stuff I can take. I've built my life on a solid foundation of routine. Only so much change can be tolerated at one time. I make my way to Ella Jones's room, steady myself and knock.

It takes Ella only a few seconds to answer. She's dressed casually in a red sweater and jeans. She says. "Come on in. Join the party."

She closes the door behind me. The living room is neat as a pin. No sign that anyone is living there (the sort of thing I can admire). A bottle of wine is open on the coffee table, next to a couple of plastic tumblers and a cheese plate. Mike sits on the sofa. He seems right at home (which has me wondering) and makes a point of not looking at me.

"Joseph," he says.

"Michael," I say.

Ella hasn't known us all that long, but she can see something is wrong. She positions herself between us and asks, "Is everything okay?"

That gets Mike and I to look at each other. We might be pissed, but the telekinesis we share from sixteen years of stupid acquaintance is intact. One of us has to transition into the uncomfortable part of the conversation. One look from Mike and I know this is my show. There is also an implicit warning: go easy on her.

"There's, uh, there's something I need to talk to you about," I say, trying to find a comfortable pose. And failing.

Ella looks confused. "Is something wrong?"

"That depends," I say, "It's, uh, it's about the tape."

She looks stricken but catches herself. "Tape?"

"The one you wanted back from Rob Quince," I say.

But Ella isn't playing ball. "I don't know what you're talking about."

"I think you do," I say, "It's a tape Quince had in his possession. It shows you with, uh…some people. Intimately."

To my relief, I don't have to go any farther. Ella sinks down next to Mike. Her face reddens. Her hands drop into her lap.

"You saw the tape?" she asks.

"Part of it," I say.

Ella sneaks a look at Mike. "You, too?"

He looks away. "Just a few seconds. Nothing…you wouldn't have wanted me to see."

I sit in the chair across from her. "We turned it off pretty quickly. We didn't see much."

Ella doesn't seem comforted. She bites her lower lip. After a few moments, she looks toward me. "Do you have the tape?"

"It's back at my place. I've got it in hiding."

"What are you going to do with it?" Ella asks.

"Let's not worry about that right now," I say, "I'd like to talk to you about Rob Quince."

Mike glowers at me. I hold my hands out, trying to let him know I have no choice. It doesn't get through to him. The look softens, though, as he turns to Ella and puts a hand on her back. She turns to me.

"What do you want to know?" she asks.

I try to keep from fidgeting. "Rob Quince was a friend of James's. Am I right?"

"He was," she says, "They met after *The Night Hawk* went off the air. They became drinking buddies. It…wasn't the best time for James. Rob latched on to him right away."

"Was Rob an actor?" Mike asks.

That draws a rueful laugh from Ella. "Rob wasn't anything. He was a professional hanger-on. The only thing he could do was drink, do drugs and run errands."

"What kind of errands?" I ask.

"Mainly, buying booze and scoring drugs."

"Ah."

Ella runs her hands along her legs. "I never liked Rob. He fed James's addictions and did nothing, but leech off him. Off us. But I could never get James to see that. Rob was his right-hand man. Even after James cleaned himself up."

"Except for vitamin shots?" I say.

"A policeman asked me the same thing," Ella says, "He said something about track marks on James's arms. I told him about the vitamin shots, and he seemed satisfied with that." She sighs. "A nutritionist told James it would keep him young. The guy was a real quack. But James bought every word of it. He would inject this ridiculous vitamin concoction into his arm. I tried to tell him it wouldn't do anything, but he wouldn't listen."

Ella knew about the vitamin shots. What about the others? "Did everyone know James took vitamin shots?"

"I'm not sure," she says, "Why?"

"Just trying to get some information," I say, "About Rob Quince..."

Ella looks at her hands again. "He had the tape. We made it years ago. We were doing a lot of drinking and...other stuff."

Mike puts a hand on Ella's forearm. "You don't have to talk about this," he says.

"It's okay," Ella says, "We would have parties all the time. When we still had the big house. We'd call whatever friends we had and then, when we discovered we didn't have as many friends, we'd invite whoever was willing to get wrecked." She crosses her legs. "The parties got wilder and wilder. What you saw on the tape, that was rock bottom. For me, anyway."

"Sounds like it was for the best," I say.

"But it was the beginning of the end with James," Ella says, "I pulled away from him."

"Did you know what happened to the tape?" I ask.

"I didn't," she says, "We had a few tapes hanging around. *I* starred in the one. James put them someplace. To be honest, I was so focused on getting out, I didn't even think about them. By the time I left, I'd completely forgotten about the tapes."

"How do you think Quince got ahold of it?" I ask.

"I have a theory." She turns to Mike. "Should I tell him?"

Mike looks surprised. Judging by the vacant look on his face, he doesn't know any more about Ella's theory than I do. But he plays along.

"It's up to you," he says.

It's quiet for a few seconds while Ella thinks it over. She gets up and paces the living room, near the French doors leading to the patio.

"Rob let me know that he had the tape," she says, "He called me and said he was going to put it out on the internet. Make some money with it. He wouldn't listen to anything I said. He said it was too good to just throw away."

"Great guy," I say.

"Glad I kicked his ass," Mike says.

Ella's eyes drop toward the floor. "I thought the only way I could get through to him was by talking to James. Rob would do anything he said."

"That's what you talked to James about?" I say, "That was the favor you asked?"

"It was."

"And he wouldn't do it?" I ask.

"No, he would," Ella says, "For a price."

It's a fine example of purple prose to say a chill filled the room. But that's the closest description to the feeling that sweeps over us. Even if Mike is in denial, even he has seen enough of James Queen to know what he's capable of. I'm afraid to ask, but I need to anyway.

"What kind of price?" I ask.

Ella runs a hand along her cheek. When she speaks, her voice is subdued. "It was about Ashley."

"The actress?" Mike says, "The one from your class?"

"Yes," Ella says, "James wanted to spend time with her. And her to be…extra friendly."

Mike's head drops. If he had any lingering naivete about James Queen, it's officially gone. Asking Ella to pimp out a young actress so that an old sex tape—one that he shot—won't be released to the public? Quite a piece of work, our James Queen.

"What did you tell him?" I ask.

"I told him I wouldn't do it," Ella says, "At first. He said he'd let Rob release the tape. I told him…" She looks down. "I told him he could have me. If that was the price. All he said was, 'Been there, done that.' It was Ashley or nothing."

Revulsion slithers through my gut. I'm the worst person in the world, putting Ella through all this. No, second worst. Wait, James Queen is dead. *I'm* the worst.

"And that's when you left his dressing room?" I ask.

"Yes," Ella says, "I had tried to reason with him, but he wouldn't have it. I was…very upset." She grabs the wine off the table. "You know the worst part? I actually considered it. Just for a minute."

"Would Ashley have done it?" I ask.

"She would have," Ella says. She takes a large sip of wine. "For me, she would have. But I couldn't ask her to. I could never have faced her again."

We're quiet. I try to swallow down the bile. Maybe the attacker was right. Maybe James Queen *did* get what he deserved. But amidst all the disgust, a thought occurs to me.

"You said you had a theory about how Rob got the tape," I say.

"I think James gave it to him," Ella says, "I think James being with Ashley was the whole idea." She sits on the sofa again. "There's no money to be made releasing a video like that. No real money, anyway. The plan the whole time was to blackmail me into giving him Ashley. Once James told me his price for the tape, I knew that was the reason."

She's probably right on that one. Sex tapes are worth their weight in publicity, but there's not a lot of monetary value in them. Particularly when they involve television stars who were only famous for a minute-and-a-half. There had to be an ulterior motive. If not for Rob Quince, then certainly for James Queen.

"When we saw you and Rob at the wine bar," I say, "what were you talking about?"

Ella refills her wine glass. "That was a different negotiation. Rob still had the tape. He said he was planning on releasing it. Unless I paid him."

Mike refills his own glass. "Great. The blackmail train rolls on."

"He wanted a fortune," Ella says, "I told him I don't have that kind of money. He said I was going to get James's money. He knew that. He said I could pay him out of that. I tried to reason with him, but he wasn't having it."

"Why did he grab you?" Mike asks.

"I threatened to go to the police," Ella says, "I said I would tell them the whole thing. Then the conversation got a little…heated. I wasn't even thinking about what I was saying. I think I said, 'James got what he deserved.' Then he grabbed me and you two showed up."

And the ridiculous fight between Mike and Rob Quince commenced. But I don't want to talk to her about that. Speaking of ass-kickings…

"Someone assaulted Rob Quince the other night," I say, "They attacked him in his hotel room, out in Bloomington. Did you hear anything about that?"

Ella's eyes slide toward the table. "I didn't. Was Rob hurt?"

"Didn't seem like it," I say, "He was knocked out for a minute. He came around and then he disappeared."

Ella looks from me to Mike and back again. "You two were there? Did you…?"

"I kicked his ass once already," Mike says.

I try to ignore Mike's delusion. "At any rate…that's how I got the tape."

We fall silent again. I look down. Mike taps the arm of the sofa. Ella's eyes are large and liquid.

"What are you going to do with it?" she asks.

That's the Sixty-Four Thousand Dollar Question (and other TV shows that went off the air before I was born). If Ella Jones killed James Queen, the tape establishes motive. In which case, everything blows up in Ella's face. She kills James Queen because she's being blackmailed about the tape. The tape is used as evidence in court. Boom. To the general public, Ella Jones is now *both* a murderer and a pervert.

Mike's glare is toned down a few notches. He doesn't seem to care that the woman he's defending could very well be the one who's trying to kill him. My path is clear.

"I'm going to destroy the tape," I say.

Ella's head drops, more out of relief than anything. It's as if whatever tension was holding her up has been released. Mike looks stunned. He didn't think I was going this direction. (Jeez, have I really been *that* ruthless?) Ella stands and gives me a hug.

"Thank you," she says, "Just…thank you."

I give her a reassuring nod when we part. I need to get out of here. I'm not good in these situations. How the hell do you transition out of *I'll destroy the sex tape you're starring in?* to *You guys want to hit happy hour?* Best to run for the hills.

"I'm going to go," I say, "I'll destroy the tape as soon as I get home."

"Thank you," Ella says, "Again."

I go to the door. Mike and Ella are on the sofa, holding hands. Mike mouths to me, "Thank you." I leave. I guess Mike and I are just like peas and carrots again.

That's not going to stop me from asking what's going on with he and Ella Jones the first chance I get.

***

Despite my many jokes about sleeping until noon, the truth is my morning tends to go in shifts. The cats wake me up early, usually around seven or eight, in order to be fed. (I could ignore them, but between Squiggy threatening to bat my water glass off the nightstand and Lenny sitting on my face, I really have no choice but to comply.) After feeding the two adorable assholes, I have a choice: go back to bed or stay awake. The decision depends on either the activities of the night before or my general attitude on being up and about.

This morning, I'd rather go back to bed. But I stay awake. The events of the night before—of the last several days, really—have given me a touch of insomnia. The apartment is cold, and the morning is overcast. (Welcome to the roller coaster that is Minnesota weather.) I pull on a pair of socks and a red Porter's Bay High School hoodie my mom sent me. I get a pot of coffee started and sit at the breakfast bar to wait.

I could have called Casey last night, after I got back from the hotel. We would have finally had the apartment to ourselves. But after everything I'd discovered with Ella, sex wasn't the foremost thing on my mind. Or other parts of my anatomy. It's a regret now. I imagine waking up with Casey and getting some coffee and then going back to bed for…ah, thinking like that isn't going to get me anywhere.

I'm not sure where Mike spent the night. He didn't come back to my place. He might have gone to Lars's or he simply might have gone home. Or…he was in Ella Jones's room when last I saw him. And he seemed awfully comfortable. I'm not sure I want to think about it.

I pour myself a cup of coffee and go into the living room. I'm about to drop on to the futon when there's a knock at the front door. Goddammit. I know who it is and I'm in no mood to see him. But I get the feeling he'll keep knocking until I either answer or throw myself out the window. Decisions, decisions. I answer the door.

Lars is chipper in the morning. (He was like that before taking up with Mr. Vitality.) He wears a suitcoat over a collared shirt and slacks. (That he did *not* do before taking up with Mr. Vitality.) He's pleasantly surprised to find me awake. "Morning, brother. Thought I'd stop in, say hello."

I let him into the apartment. He goes to the kitchen and helps himself to some coffee. He has the mug down from the cupboard before he stops to ask permission. I gesture toward the coffeemaker, letting him know it's okay.

"I was hoping you'd be able to meet with Mr. Vitality today," he says, pouring a cup, "He's anxious to see you again. Maybe get you involved with the Big Event."

I stretch out on the couch, coffee perched next to my hip. "Sorry, I'm busy."

"With what?"

Dammit. I hate when people call for proof. Can't they just trust I'm busy and am in no way attempting to bullshit them? Squiggy hops on my chest; his butler-like way of asking, "Sir? Sir? Should I show him to the door?" I scratch his ears and he settles on my chest; quiet but ever vigilant.

"I'm working on the thing with Mike," I say.

I give him the rundown on the conversation with Ella Jones. Lars listens intently. He flinches slightly when I talk about destroying the tape.

"The tape is gone?" he asks.

"It is," I say, "Soon as I got home last night, I drove over it with my car. Repeatedly."

"Is there anything left?"

"Doubtful."

Lars tries to assume a casual air. "I don't suppose you remember what you did with the remains of the tape?"

"I'm not going to tell you that."

He starts to slap the counter, then stops himself. He sets the hand down gently. I know he's suffering and probably won't agree I've saved him hours of fruitless labor trying to put the tape back together. Then again, Lars is actually accomplishing things these days. Maybe he *could* put the thing back together. But I won't have to find out.

Lars sits on the arm of the futon. "I still think you should talk to Mr. Vitality," he says, "He could consult you on this. For a favor."

"Favor?" I ask. After hearing about Ella's meeting with James Queen, that word has a sour ring to it. "What kind of favor?"

"Help with the Big Event. Writing some press releases. Copywriting, I think they call it. We could use the publicity and the professionalism. Mr. Vitality thinks you have real potential."

I try not to make eye contact with Lars. He has, consciously or unconsciously, picked up Mr. Vitality's habit of talking to me without blinking. Maybe it's time to tell Lars that Mr. Vitality's organization is complete and utter hooey. I face Lars, ready to lower the boom.

Then my phone rings. Saved by the bell, as it were.

I get up from the futon, dislodging Squiggy, who dashes away without looking, lest I see his expression of resentment. (Lenny makes no such effort when disturbed.) I grab the phone off the breakfast bar. Lars watches me. The voice on the other end is babbling. I mumble a few responses, then ring off and drop on to one of the stools. Lars hops up from the futon.

"What's up, brother?" he asks.

"That was Mike," I say, "He's going to see Tim Hefflin."

"Tim Hefflin? About what?"

"Apparently, Hefflin tried to kill Rob Quince."

CHAPTER FIFTEEN

Okay, guilty confession: I've never seen the movie Rebel Without A Cause. *Yes, I know. Mr. Pop Culture Commentator, the guy who's immersed himself in way too many TV shows and movies, has never seen a piece of low-hanging cinematic fruit; a classic with legends like James Dean, Natalie Wood and the guy who played Mr. Howell on* Gilligan's Island. *I may not have seen* Rebel Without A Cause, *but I've known a few.*

Some of you probably think I'm talking about my friend Mike. However, Mike doesn't fall into this category. There's usually a purpose behind his activities. The purpose is generally self-interest. These are the actions of a sneaky S.O.B. rather than a rebel. I'm surprised Mike never went into espionage.

No, the variety of rebel I speak of is someone who does stuff for no purpose other than to rile things up. Your classic shit-stirrer. Beans Madden, a classmate of mine in high school, fell into this category. Where wise men fear to tread, Beans liked to jump in and see what was going to happen. He got kicked off the school newspaper for insulting the principal, started his own underground paper, set off stink bombs at the homecoming parade, claimed to have nude photos of Miss Kidder, the science teacher (sadly, this was never substantiated), tried to bring a mule to the spring formal and set the Porter's Bay High School record in Getting Thrown Out of Class.

The thing I always wondered about Beans (beyond how he managed to obtain the mule) was: what's the purpose behind all this? But slowly, over time, I began to realize there was no purpose to it. Or rather, the acts themselves were the purpose. Maybe, in the words of Alfred the butler in The Dark Knight, *"Some people just like to watch the world burn."*

These days, Beans sells insurance. Clearly, that lack of a moral compass guided him toward his future career.

I'm reminded of Beans when I look at the actions of Tim Hefflin. Random destruction serving no purpose beyond destruction itself. If there's a difference with Hefflin, it's that *self*-destruction might be the purpose. Apparently, though, he's going to take Rob Quince with him.

Mike doesn't give me any details on Hefflin's attack. He just asks me to meet them at Pete's Grill. It's a glorified lunch counter in downtown St. Paul, not far from the Xcel Energy Center. I throw on a pair of jeans, grab my pea coat and dash out the backdoor. Lars decides to join me. (At least I'm keeping him from Mr. Vitality's office.) We hop into my Saturn and run downtown.

Pete's Grill isn't much to look at, but if you're in the market for a good breakfast, it's the place to go. Yes, the plates tend to be chipped, the Formica tabletops should have been changed out years ago and the staff constantly looks as if they're dreaming of doing something else. But the food is great, and the portions are the kind your mother might give you if you haven't visited in a while and she thinks you're looking too skinny. (I once ordered their Three Egg Everything Omelet and discovered I had breakfast for the better part of a week.) As soon as Lars and I walk in, Mike waves us over to a corner booth. He wears the same clothes from last night. We slip through the morning bustle and discover him sitting with Tim Hefflin and Ella Jones. Lars and I slide into either side of the semi-circular booth. Ella addresses us.

"Thank you for coming," she says, "Sorry if we got you up early."

"No worries," I say, "We were up already."

"My mentor, Mr. Vitality, has a saying," Lars adds, "*The early bird catches the worm.*"

Ella looks confused. "I think that's an old saying."

"His wisdom certainly has a timeless quality," Lars says, giving her a clueless smile.

Hefflin wears shades, but there's discoloration around the outside that tells me they're hiding a black eye. His hair is mussed and he's sporting a growth of beard. In other words, same old, same old. He stares at us and tries to remember who the hell we are.

"Who the fuck are you guys?" he says.

I could be disappointed that Hefflin doesn't remember me, even though he's met me a couple times now. Given his usual state, though, it doesn't come as a surprise. Ella clamps a hand on Hefflin's shoulder.

"These are friends of mine," she says, her teeth clenched, "They're going to help."

Hefflin's cowed but doesn't look convinced. "You guys lawyers?"

Lars does the snorting for the rest of us. "Hardly."

"Private dicks?"

"No," Lars says, folding his hands on the table, "we're very public dicks. Especially my friend here."

I know he meant it as a compliment but, as per usual with Lars, it comes out sideways. I look at Hefflin.

"We're friends of Ella's," I say, "We're looking into what happened with James Queen. And with Rob Quince."

A defiant sneer curls Hefflin's lip. It fades the second he gets a look at Ella. He picks up the coffee in front of him. "What do you want to know?" he asks.

"Simple," I say, "What happened with Rob Quince last night?"

Hefflin slips off his shades, revealing his bloodshot eyes and the black-and-blue mark around his right eye. "All right, Rob and I have known each other for a while. We met when I was doing that fucking *Night Hawk* movie. He and James were friends. Rob was his hookup. Drugs and stuff. I wasn't into that, but Rob made a decent drinking buddy. He and I would go out from time to time." He sips his coffee, his hands shaking. "I heard about the tape. I was pissed."

"How did you find out?" I ask.

Ella raises her hand, tentatively. "I told him."

Hefflin lurches forward, his stomach bumping against the table. "I dragged it out of her. As soon as I heard someone mention Rob Quince, I knew the fucker was up to no good. I asked Ella about it." He sighs. "I shouldn't have been surprised. I called Rob. Figured I'd meet with him, see if I could get the tape back. I met him at his hotel room. He kept playing dumb, saying he didn't have the tape, that some asshole stole it. I wasn't buying it. Then I went after him."

"What did you do?" I ask.

"It's hard to say. I'd had a few. Thought it, uh, thought it might help this damn cold." He adds a loud sniffle. "I remember I shoved him. He shoved me back. I went for a tackle and missed. I wound up in the bathroom with the towel rack in my hands. Must have grabbed it when I fell.

Rob was walking away. He probably thought I was out. Then I got up and went after him with the towel rack."

Everyone winces. "What kind of damage did you do?" Mike asks.

"Aw, the towel rack's all bent to hell," Hefflin says, "They'll never be able to use that thing again."

I pinch the bridge of my nose. "What kind of damage did you do to Rob Quince?"

"He had some knots on his head," Hefflin says, "And I might have hurt his ribs. Although, I think he did that on his own, after he crashed into the desk."

I look to Mike and Ella, who are separately rolling their eyes. (And again, when someone can make *Mike* roll his eyes…) I look at Hefflin again.

"What happened after the, uh, the attack?" I ask.

"Rob started running," Hefflin says, "I wanted to go after him, but I'd gotten my bell rung. I let him go. I tried to find the tape. No luck." He turns to Ella. "Sorry."

A silence descends. Hefflin's intentions were good, but his execution left something to be desired. And that's not even the worst part. Ella puts a hand on his arm.

"I appreciate you standing up for me, Tim," she says, "But it wasn't necessary."

"No, don't give me that *I can fight my own battles* stuff," he says, "This guy's a shark. He's dangerous to you as long as he's got that tape."

I turn over my coffee cup, signaling to the server. "Then it's probably good he doesn't have it anymore. We got the tape from Quince and I destroyed it last night."

Hefflin's body sags. "When Quince said he didn't have the tape…"

"He was telling you the truth," I say.

Again, the table goes silent. Hefflin mutters, "Motherfucker." He looks toward Ella. "I wanted to let you know what happened. That's why I asked to meet you. I didn't know you were going to bring…" He waves a hand toward us. "Them."

Sure, I could be offended. But that's not going to get us anywhere. The server pours me a cup of coffee and takes our orders. I'm not hungry, but the others partake. Hefflin orders the Three Egg Everything Omelet and I don't think it's going to take *him* several days to finish it. Everyone takes some coffee and settles in.

"It's kind of strange," I say, "You being friends with Rob Quince. Him being friends with James Queen. And you and Queen hating each other. That wasn't awkward?"

"We didn't talk much about James," Hefflin says, "We'd just drink and bullshit. From time to time, Rob would let something slip about James and I'd pretend like I cared."

"When was the last time you saw Rob?" I ask, "Before last night?"

"Couple weeks ago," Hefflin says, "We bumped into each other at Cuttings, a little watering hole we both like. Closed the place down."

"What did you talk about?" I ask.

"The usual. He told me about the new movie and that was it. Nothing much."

I snap a look at him. It gets Mike's and Ella's attention as well. Lars sips his coffee, blissfully ignorant. I push my coffee aside.

"You knew about the new movie?" I ask, "*The Night Hawk Rising?*"

Hefflin pauses in sipping his coffee. "Yeah. No one else did?"

Ella fumbles with a napkin. "I didn't know."

"Oh." Hefflin goes back to his coffee. "I was hoping I could get a role in it. Not anything big. Just a cameo. Maybe it could lead to something bigger. You know how John Travolta was nowhere until Tarantino put him in *Pulp Fiction?* Same thing could happen here. Sometimes they just need to see you to remember they like you. That could be me."

It's a cute idea, Hefflin using a brief cameo to launch an A-list career. Such is the power of hope. It's not my place to take it away. I stir some sugar into my coffee.

"Did you talk to anyone about it?" I ask.

"Hal Murdoch," Hefflin says, "Backstage at the convention. He said he'd put in a good word for me. Hal's a good guy. I knew he'd look out for me."

"Did you know James Queen was holding up the movie?" I say.

"I wasn't surprised. James was never going to let anyone else play The Night Hawk. Motherfucker."

Interesting. Hefflin knew about *The Night Hawk Rising*. He had ambitions toward the movie, and they were being obstructed by James Queen. Hefflin knew about the tape. He had his own ancient grudge against Queen. Motive piling on motive. There is, of course, the question of means.

"Did you know Queen took vitamin shots?" I ask.

Hefflin scratches the stubble on his chin. "I think I remember that. Rob said something about it. James was always into shit like that. He was afraid of growing old and dying. Like it was something that was supposed to happen to someone else. Dipshit."

"You didn't see him doing the shots before the convention?" I ask.

"Nope," Hefflin says, "I imagine he did them, though. It's just how he worked."

"You didn't see where he kept them?"

"I didn't. I didn't have any interest, either."

The food arrives, interrupting the conversation. We eat largely in silence, making a little chit-chat about the weather (a requirement when in Minnesota). When we're done, Hefflin announces that he has to get back to the hotel and sleep off his "cold." Ella escorts him. When we get to the sidewalk, we say our goodbyes. Ella exchanges an awkward handshake with Mike and joins Hefflin in strolling toward the Ambassador Suites. Mike, Lars and I walk toward my car.

Mike speaks without looking at me. "Sorry I got mad at you. I know you were trying to help. I get a little protective of Ella. She's been through a lot. You know how it is." I'm tempted to ask about the nature of his relationship with Ella, but Mike can volunteer the information if he feels like it. He turns to Lars. "I'll get my stuff when we get back."

"Sounds proper," Lars says.

I look at Mike. "Finally moving back home?"

"No," he says.

"Moving in with Ella?"

Mike looks like I just urinated on the sidewalk. "Are you kidding me? Why the fuck would I do a thing like that?"

"Sorry," I say, "Where *are* you going?"

He looks as if it should be obvious. "Your place."

I try not to sound like the weight of the world is on my shoulders, "The futon is yours."

Mike claps a hand on my shoulder. "Good to be back."

We reach the car. Mike goes around to the passenger side and gets in. Lars hangs back and lowers his voice.

"Glad you could take over there, brother," he says, "I don't know if you realize this, but Mike can be a pain in the derriere."

He slips past me and into the back seat. Since I'm alone for a moment, I plunk an arm on the roof and lay my head on it. Okay, Mike's back and I've got to find out who's trying to kill him. Then I can get rid of him, and Casey and I can have the place to ourselves.

Just when I thought I was out…

***

As often stated, I obsessively clean my apartment. I very much subscribe to the notion *orderly space, orderly mind*. In order to write dick jokes for a living, I need my place to remain as clean as an operating room in order to focus. I also clean when I need to think. I used to get ideas while driving around in the car (still a good source), but now I get an equal number while cleaning. In that regard, it's good to have Mike around the house. He's nothing if not a constant source of filth. Plenty of time to clean and think. Such as dreaming up ways to kill Mike.

"There's no way this is going to last, is there?" Carol asks, watching from a safe distance while I wipe down the breakfast bar.

"The irony, of course," I say, working hard to eliminate a coffee ring Mike left, "is that he's here because I'm trying to keep him alive. And he might not survive the experience."

"At least you're getting along again."

"If you want to call it that. I'm starting to think of our tiff as the good old days."

Carol sits in the comfy chair with Squiggy curled up on her black skirt. She scratches his head. "You don't know where Mike spent last night?"

"Nope. He wasn't here and he wasn't at Lars's. I doubt he went home. That just leaves…Ella Jones's hotel room?"

"I see," she says, drawing out her words, "you think Mike is sleeping with this old lady?"

That stops my cleaning. "I don't know if he's sleeping with her. But I do know she's not an old lady."

"She's over fifty," Carol says, working to keep the edge out of her voice, "that doesn't make her old?"

"No. It makes her…older."

Carol snorts. "Ah yes. The *er* makes all the difference."

I got back to my cleaning, making the place glow even if the day remains stubbornly overcast. (Dust mites wouldn't *dare* appear in this air.) Experience has taught me there's no winning this argument with Carol. It bears repeating. I love Carol. I love Mike. But there is an entity known as *Carol and Mike.* Since they were dating and for some time after, *Carol and Mike* have been nothing but a source of irritation. The only thing I can do is change the subject.

"This stuff with Tim Hefflin is interesting," I say, "The guy clearly has a violent streak. And he drinks enough to be unpredictable."

"Don't remind me," Carol says.

"Sorry. And he had plenty of motive. It all comes back to what Mike saw. And he doesn't remember seeing anything odd."

Carol gets up from the comfy chair (and dislodges Squiggy). "When does Mike get home from his temp job?"

"He didn't go in," I say, finally winning the battle of the coffee ring, "He called in sick. Said he felt like taking the day off."

"Then where is he?" Carol asks.

"He ran an errand to his storage unit."

"In his building? I thought he was avoiding that place."

"He is," I say, returning the Lysol to the cabinet and tossing the used sponge in with the laundry, "He rented a new storage unit. On Marshall. That strip between Snelling and Hamline? His stuff is pretty safe there."

Carol turns back toward the living room, stepping gently on her high heels. She doesn't want me to see the look of concern on her face. She might get annoyed by Mike, but that doesn't mean she wants any harm to come to him. Old habits die hard, I guess.

I pour a cup of coffee. "Speaking of killing and maiming, how did your meeting with the groom go?"

Carol spins around, her ponytail whipping behind her. Squiggy, alive to any discomfort in the room, sits up on the back of the futon. Lenny lazily looks up from his perch on the radiator shelf. Seeing there's no food or affection involved, he lays back down and goes back to sleep. Carol shudders and joins me at the breakfast bar.

"It did not go well," she says. She looks toward the door, as if someone might burst in. "Can we keep this between the two of us?"

"Of course," I say.

"No telling Mike or Lars?"

"Absolutely not. It'll just be between you, me and the billboard I'll put up on I-35."

Carol clenches her fist. "Joe…"

"You can trust me," I say, "You know that."

She steadies herself. "All right, Alan wanted to get together. We were supposed to go to a bar, but he changed his mind at the last minute. He said he was afraid someone would see us together and get the wrong idea."

My coffee cup stops short of my lips. "There's a wrong idea to get?"

"I wondered the same thing," Carol says, "But I went along with it. Maybe Alan knew something about the night of the bachelorette party, something I needed to know. I agreed to meet him where he wanted."

"And that was…"

Carol picks at the lapel of her navy-blue blazer. "The honeymoon suite at the Ambassador."

Ah cripes. "I can't see how anyone would get the wrong impression from *that*."

"I know, I know," Carol says, "It was a stupid idea. But I was desperate. And Alan is a decent guy. I thought it would be all right."

"And…?"

Carol grimaces. "I met Alan up there and he offered me a drink. I wanted one, but I turned him down. I was already getting a weird feeling. Normally, Alan's really laid back and cool. This time, he was jumpy. And I think he'd already had a drink. Maybe two. We tried to make small talk, but it was pretty obvious he had something on his mind. I thought we should get it over with. So, I asked him what was on his mind." She taps the side of her coffee cup. "Alan said he couldn't stop thinking about the night of the bachelorette party. I asked him what happened. He went into the story." Carol leans on the breakfast bar. "There was a lot I already knew. He showed up at the last bar we were at. He was going to give Chris a ride home. But she got mad at him."

"About what?" I ask.

"Alan didn't know. It was some conversation Chris had while we were barhopping. Something about a woman's role and being subordinate. She wasn't making a lot of sense. Alan tried to talk to her, but the more he tried to calm her down, the more pissed she got. Then they started arguing. And I tried to break it up. I guess there was a lot of shouting and stuff. Finally, Chris stalked off and got a ride with someone else. I was going to call a Lyft, but Alan offered to take me home. I agreed. Gladly, I'm told."

"By Alan?" I ask.

"By him. He offered to walk me to my door. Apparently, though, I was already on my way to the apartment by the time he got the offer out."

"Like you do."

"Yeah," Carol says. She draws the word out. "According to Alan, I, uh, started to undress on the walk up."

I suddenly find my coffee very interesting. "Like, uh…like you…do."

"The only good part is that I had a head start on him," Carol says, "Alan was busy picking up my clothes while he followed me. By the time he got into my apartment, I was already under the covers in bed. But I was still awake. I guess Alan got me a glass of water and some ibuprofen. Then we sat up and talked."

"About what?"

She strokes her cheek. "According to Alan, he had his doubts about the marriage. *Has* his doubts about the marriage. He needed someone to talk to. I don't remember anything he said. Hell, I don't remember the conversation. Anyway, then he kissed me."

Danger, Will Robinson. "He kissed you?"

"That's what he said. You have to remember, I'm just a spectator here. I only know what I'm told."

"How, uh, how far did it go?"

"Not far. Alan had his doubts and I was fading. I offered him a place in my bed. Alan told me he was tempted. But he decided not to take advantage. Which was good because that's exactly what it would have been. Then he left. But he's been thinking about me."

Wow. On the one hand, I can understand Alan's temptation. Hard to see someone strip down and climb into bed and invite you to join them and then get *that* out of your head. The part I struggle with is the doubt about the marriage. Don't get me wrong. I've had my doubts about plenty of relationships. (Nearly all of them, if I'm going to be honest.) But how you let it get as far as marriage (or close to it) and not fully commit is beyond me. Although, to be fair, getting as far as *marriage* is beyond me, so maybe I'm not the right source on this.

"At least you know now what happened," I say.

Carol isn't comforted. "Yeah. I know *all* of it."

There's something in Carol's voice I don't like. It gives the impression there's more to the story. I move closer to her.

"Did something else happen?" I ask.

Carol looks toward the window. "I, uh, I may have made out with Chris as well."

I nearly spit out my coffee. "Chris? Chris the bride Chris? That Chris?"

"The same," she says, hanging her head, "When Alan talked about kissing me, the whole thing came back to me. It happened in a hallway outside the ladies' room, at one of the last clubs we went to. We were talking about when we used to date and suddenly, we were making out. Not passionately, I think. Just more of a 'Hey, let's try this' sort of thing."

"I see." Or at least I'm picturing it.

"We were drunk. It only lasted until someone came out of the men's room. I remember Chris giving me a look. It was hard to read. Kind of sad and confused. I don't know. I wasn't in any condition to figure it out. Then she argued with Alan and we haven't really talked since."

Wow. I knew Carol could loosen up when she's had a few, but I didn't realize she could be quite so wanton. I'm intrigued. More intrigued than I ought to be.

"So, you're saying you kissed a girl…and you liked it."

Carol wanders around the living room. "I don't know what to think. I used to date Chris. There's always been an attraction. But now she's a woman. And I'm fine with that. It's great. This is who Chris is and she's happy. But I'm still attracted to her. I'm not gay. And I don't think she is. But we had this thing once and now it's a totally different thing. But it really isn't." She rubs her temples. "If it's this confusing when I'm stone cold sober, can you imagine how confusing it was when I was drunk off my ass?"

"I can."

"You *aren't* going to tell anyone, right?" she says.

"Of course not. First, I'm a man of my word. Second, Mike can't handle the notion his teenage crush is reciprocating his feelings. I throw something like this at him and his head's liable to explode."

Carol sits on the arm of the comfy chair. "At least I know why Chris is pissed at me. I got involved in the argument. Then she probably saw me leaving with Alan. Chris asked Alan about it and he told her nothing happened. He doesn't think she believes him."

"Question is," I say, "is Chris jealous about Alan or jealous about you?"

Carol throws up her hands. "I can't even think about that. I've just got to get through this wedding and then forget it ever happened."

"You realize forgetting what happened was the thing that was bothering you before?"

"The good old days," Carol mumbles.

I go to the kitchen to get myself another cup of coffee, leaving Carol to her thoughts and her sexual confusion. I'm passing the breakfast bar when my phone rings. According to the caller ID, it's Mike. Nuts. I have to take this.

I scoop up the phone and answer with, "Cannibal Café, you friend 'em, we rend 'em. How may I help you?"

Mike skips completely past my hilarious greeting. "Joe, I need you to get down here. My storage unit's been broken into."

CHAPTER SIXTEEN

When I was in college, I did a few shows in the theatre department and became friends with some of the actors. The best part of doing the shows (beyond the drinking at the cast parties) was striking the set (theatre terminology for dismantling the set once the show is over). Everyone was required to participate, and the theatre department sprang for pizza. A group of us would usually spirit away one of the pizzas and eat it amongst ourselves in the theatre's lounge. Then we'd put the empty box in a space above one of the ceiling tiles. I'm told the tradition continued after I graduated. I heard they did some remodeling on the building a few years back. I can only imagine the reaction after the construction guys removed that tile and brought fifteen years' worth of pizza boxes down on their heads.

The point is not my gluttonous youth, but rather the dangers of accumulating stuff. We hold on to things of sentimental value, but of absolutely no practical use. By the time I reached my teen years, I had a vast collection of comic books, pro wrestling magazines and Hardy Boys books. Once I moved to the Cities, my parents ordered me to figure out what to do with the stuff. (My belief they would keep my room intact as a shrine to my time there was grossly mistaken.) Since I couldn't afford a storage unit and had no desire to haul all that crap from place to place, I skimmed it down to only the stuff I might look at. Since then, I've lived by a strict rule: don't accumulate stuff.

A rule Mike absolutely does not live by.

It's not a long drive to the storage unit, only about five minutes. The facility is called St. Paul Storage (props beaucoups for the creative name, folks). It's in a strip of storage units along Marshall Avenue between Snelling Avenue and Hamline Avenue, running parallel to Highway 94. It's a flat, square building, two stories high and completely white. It sits back from the road and is surrounded by a chain link fence. Mike waits outside the gate, huddled into his leather jacket. As soon as he sees us, he punches a code into the small box next to the gate. That done, he hops into the backseat of my Saturn.

"Just pull in," Mike says, "I'll show you where it's at."

Carol speaks to him over the seat. "What was stolen?"

Mike chews his goatee. "Actually, nothing."

I take my foot off the gas. "Nothing was stolen? Then why am I here?"

"Because someone's after me and now they're after my stuff," he says, slapping the back of the seat, "I need to find out what's going on."

Carol turns forward again. Mike directs us to the second floor. The place is sterile, all cement floors and walls, storage units made of sheet metal. Mike's storage unit looks like every other unit. Mike gets agitated as we pull up.

"This is my place," he says, "It's been violated."

I'm tempted to remind him this is a faceless storage unit placed among other faceless storage units in a faceless complex set among other faceless complexes on a faceless stretch of road and should not, therefore, be confused with home and hearth. But loyalty to his stuff is the only loyalty Mike has ever shown. Girlfriends, family and friends have never made the cut. (I have no doubt Mike would gladly lay down my life for his.) I'll grant him this indulgence.

We hop out of the car. The building might not be much to look at it, but at least it's heated. There are no signs of a break-in to the storage unit, but Mike stands there, mournful, as if watching the last vestiges of a fire that's destroyed his ancestral home.

"They picked the lock," Mike says, "Did a good job, too. I had no idea someone had been in here until I opened the door."

If anyone would know about lock-picking, it's Mike. He had a sideline business as a cat burglar when we were in college. He wasn't exactly John Dillinger. He only swiped small ticket items when he was short of cash and couldn't hit up his parents for money. I like to think he left all that behind him, but I've had need of his skills in recent months and let's just say Mike hasn't seemed rusty.

"Open it up," I say, "Let's get a look."

Mike undoes the lock and hoists the door. The interior looks like a real dick of a tornado hit the place. Boxes tossed in all directions. Bins overturned. Comic books and toys intermingled in the wreckage. Complete chaos. In short, completely indistinguishable from Mike's apartment.

I'm tempted to go through the stuff, but where would I begin? "You sure they didn't take anything?"

"Absolutely," Mike says, "I went through it."

Carol levels a look at him. "And yet you did nothing to clean up the mess."

Mike throws his hands out. "There was a break-in and all my stuff had been thrown around. Who could think of cleaning at a time like that?"

"Or in your case," Carol says, "any time."

I attempt to stop George and Gracie over there. "Okay, getting back to the point. How did they get in?"

"Excuse me?" Mike says.

"Whoever broke into the unit," I say, "It's not like they can strongarm their way into the building. They'd need your code to get in. How did they get it?"

Mike doesn't have an answer for that. Who knows him well enough to get something like that? Me, Carol and Lars, but it's not like we're going to break in here. Possibly Ella, but I'm not going to bring that up. Carol put her hand on her chin.

"Excellent question," she says, glancing toward Mike, "Any theories?"

"Nope," Mike says, "Nobody has access to that info except me."

So much for that. My mind flicks from *who* to *why*. I look over the unit. I'm tempted to go through it, see if the intruder left something behind, but that would be pointless. If anything were missing, Mike would know it. I stand in the entrance to the unit. Carol joins me.

"What are you thinking?" she asks.

"Mike has something," I say, quietly.

"Like an STD?" Carol says.

"No," I say, "Although, we can't rule anything out."

Mike has the *Who farted* face firmly etched on his visage. "Hey, this is fucking hilarious. You want to tell me what the hell you're talking about?"

"The guy who attacked you," I say, "This whole time we thought he was after you because you knew something. Maybe it's because you *have* something."

He doesn't look convinced. "I don't have anything."

Carol gestures toward the storage unit. "I beg to differ."

"So do I," I say, "You might not *know* you have something, but I'll bet you do. The intruder didn't find it."

Carol looks into the unit. "I don't think we're going to have any more luck."

"Not necessarily," I say, pushing off from the entryway, "If it's related to James Queen's death, the intruder wouldn't be looking through *all* of Mike's stuff. He'd only be interested in the stuff Mike brought to the convention. Did that stuff get taken?"

"No," Mike says, "I have a hiding place for that."

Wow. Even in his storage bunker, Mike felt the need for extra security. Paranoia has its advantages. He goes over to a large chest marked *80's Iron Man* and pulls it free of the wreckage. He runs his hands over the bottom and, after several seconds of toying around, pulls it loose. A chest with a false bottom. Who would have thought Mike had it in him? He pulls out the backpack with the memorabilia.

"Everything is in here," Mike says, "I went through it. None of it is missing."

In less than a minute, Mike has systematically removed everything and laid it out on the hood of my car. Carol, who also knows Mike's slobby ways, can only shake her head.

"He can find all this, and he still managed to lose my class ring," she says.

"That's what you get for spending a year of your life being defiled by Oscar Madison," I tell her.

"Hi, guys," Mike says, "Sorry to interrupt. Thought I might remind you I'm *right fucking here*."

"I know," I say.

They're the same things I saw in James Queen's dressing room: Night Hawk action figure, Night Hawk fan magazine, toy Nightmobile, mini version of the Night Cave, etc. All of it bearing James Queen's signature. None of it is interesting. Sure, I would have loved it when I was twelve, but it doesn't hold a lot of interest for me now. (Okay, maybe the mini-Night Cave. And the toy Nightmobile.)

"And it's all still intact?" I ask.

"Yep," Mike says, "everything in mint or near mint condition."

I pick up the toy Nightmobile and examine it from all angles. It's pristine, bearing only James Queen's signature on the driver's door. Something about it looks different, but I can't quite figure it out. It's difficult to study because Mike is hovering about like I'm holding the last copy of the Magna Carta. (Assuming Mike knows what the Magna Carta is. And he almost certainly does not.)

"Go easy with that," he says, "that one's special."

"I know, I know," I say, tapping James Queen's signature.

Mike takes the toy Nightmobile from me and holds it with a tenderness I guarantee you he will never show his first child. "This one's got secret compartments with all of The Night Hawk's weapons: grappling hook, Nightarang, pontoons, laser, oil slick."

"Oil slick?" Carol asks, "How does it do that?"

"It throws out little black discs that are supposed to be puddles of oil," Mike says.

"It's cooler than it sounds," I say. "Actually, it's *exactly* as cool as it sounds."

Mike runs a hand over the toy car. "And the pièce de résistance—"

I turn to Carol. "Which is French for *piece of resistance*."

Mike ignores me. "The Night Flyer."

Carol, probably against her better judgment, asks: "What is the Night Flyer?"

He gives her a pitying look. "The Nightmobile is capable of becoming a low altitude aircraft. All you have to do is release the car's undercarriage, spread the wings and boom, you're airborne. Allow me to demonstrate."

He holds up the toy Nightmobile like he's revealing the next Lion King. The index fingers of both hands slide to barely visible buttons below either door of the Nightmobile.

After the required dramatic pause, he hits both buttons simultaneously.

And nothing happens.

"Wow," Carol says, "I'd certainly trade my vacation money for a thing like that."

Mike looks over the toy, dismayed. "What the hell? This thing was working fine before." He gives it a light shake. "Something's rattling around in there."

"Must be a broken part," I say.

Mike starts to turn green. He pushes the buttons on the side of the car. "These still want to go in. Something's blocking them."

He uses his fingernails to try and work the top free. Mike's loathe to risk the health of the car. The top finally comes loose with a pop. Mike stumbles back, a piece of the car now in each hand. Something falls to the floor. Carol and I stand over it.

"It's a syringe," Carol says.

Mike puts the toy Nightmobile back together. "A syringe? What's a syringe doing in there?"

Carol bends to pick it up. I throw a hand out, stopping her. "Don't touch it," I say, "Do you have a Kleenex in your purse?"

She gives me a confused look before running to the car to search her purse. Mike finishes putting the toy car back together and waits for an explanation. Carol rummages through makeup, slips of paper, gum, breath mints, Amelia Erhardt, what have you. Finally, she comes up with a Kleenex and brings it over to me. I use it to gently pick up the syringe.

"We need something to put it in," I say. I look toward Mike's stuff. "Give me one of those mylar bags."

Mike doesn't move. "Those are for protecting my comic books."

I speak through gritted teeth. "You can double bag a few books. Just get me the damn thing."

He doesn't look happy about it, but he complies. He slaps the bag into my hand. I slip the syringe inside.

"Why is this so important?" Mike asks.

"Because this is what the intruder was after," I say. I hold the bag up slightly as Mike and Carol gather round. "This is the murder weapon."

***

It's not a clever turn of phrase, but my father was fond of it. He'd say, "There's never a cop around when you need one. But there's always a cop around when you *don't* need one." When it comes to Sergeant Frank Pike, I'm inclined to agree. When I'm looking into idiot stuff that really shouldn't concern me, Pike pops up like a rash. But when *I'm* looking for *him*, he's nowhere to be found.

I try calling Pike's number but get no response. I leave a couple messages, but he doesn't get back to me. I get through to St. Paul Homicide, only to be told Pike is off-duty, and do I have his card? Ah, the joys of dealing with a bureaucracy. It's like rinsing your papercuts in lemon juice. Only less enjoyable.

I do a hard-target search online, call a couple of contacts (believe it or not, I *do* have them) and manage to track down Pike's address. Not surprisingly, he lives in a crappy neighborhood off Maryland Avenue, bordering the east side of St. Paul. The building looks like a converted house. Probably no more than eight to ten apartments. Cozy enough, I suppose. There's no buzzer at the front and no way to get inside. I go around to the side of the building. A tiny parking lot borders an alley. There's a door around the side and it's ajar. Bingo. I head up the side stairs and follow the apartment numbers. The building is clean enough, though the carpeting is threadbare. Noise is audible from the other apartments. (Thin walls. My worst nightmare.) Pike's apartment, apartment ten, is at the top of the stairs, on the left. I knock on the door.

Several seconds go by without an answer. I knock a second time and hear movement in the apartment. And what might be swearing. The peephole darkens.

"Joe Davis?" Pike asks, behind the door.

"It's me."

"What do you want?"

One of these days I'll show up at someone's door and they'll be glad to see me. ("Joe Davis? It's been forever! Come on in! The hookers and blow are in the next room! Help yourself!") But that won't be today. And never will be with this guy. I produce the mylar bag with the syringe.

"I found something," I say, "It's related to James Queen's death."

Pike's sigh is audible through the door. He's likely debating between opening the door and giving into this foolishness or telling me to get my skinny ass off his (rented) property. Finally, he undoes the lock and opens the door a crack. He's situated so I can only see his face. What's left of his hair is standing up and his glasses are askew.

"What do you think you have?" he asks.

"James Queen was poisoned," I say, tapping the mylar bag, "This needle is the proof. You want to let me in?"

There's something strange in Pike's eyes. Doubt? Fear? It's weird. Normally, Pike just tries to stare a hole right through me. He's not as decisive this time.

Before he can decide on my request for entry, a female voice comes from inside. "Frank? Hey Frank, who's there?"

The voice is vaguely familiar. Pike throws a panicked look back. As he does, he absentmindedly lets the door open a little further. I get a look into the apartment. All I see is a bit of the living room and a corner of what passes for the dining room. I also get a better look at the occupants. Pike wears a pair of plaid boxer shorts and a white A-frame t-shirt. Behind him, in a small hallway that must lead to a bedroom, is Kelly Smart of *The Edge*. Her hair is mussed in what experts refer to as "fuck hair" and she's wearing a blue STPD t-shirt. And only a blue STPD t-shirt.

For crying out loud, is *everybody* in this town getting laid except me?

CHAPTER SEVENTEEN

Save for a handful of perverts (good band name, by the way), nobody likes getting caught in flagrante delicto. *It's tough to maintain your dignity when you've been caught (literally) with your pants down. And I've never understood why that is.*

There was the time I was at a house party and engaged in a ferocious near-naked make out session with a girl named Amy. We were engaged in said activity in a tool room in the basement when the door unexpectedly opened, and my friends Robbie and T.J. walked in on us. (Turned out, they were looking for the keg in the garage and got lost. Which, coincidentally, was the first thing I ordered them to do.)

For a few days, I would bump into T.J. and Robbie and we'd make awkward conversation. Our buddy Stoner, the wisest and most corrupt of us, finally asked what was going on. I told him the story. He got a confused look on his face and asked, "You're supposed to feel bad about getting laid?"

And there it was, from out of the mouths of borderline criminal babes. I was embarrassed that Robbie and T.J. had caught me (somewhat) in the act. If they had seen nothing and I told them later what happened with Amy, they would have congratulated me and bought me a beer. Instead, because they saw me doing some dirty sinful business, it became a Thing That Must Not Be Named. Unless it involves personal experience, sex is a thing best enjoyed in theory.

Although, that doesn't exactly explain the porn industry.

Now, I'm on the other end of the equation. And neither Pike nor I are happy about it. He starts into the hallway, then realizes he's in his underwear. Then he realizes Smart is in his apartment. He must choose the lesser of two evils. He joins me in the hall. Smart moves toward the door.

"Frank, why don't you let me—"

That's all she gets out before Pike closes the door on her. I can't help being amused by Pike's discomfort. He turns toward me.

"What the hell are you doing here?" he asks.

"I had *Largely unattractive cop in his underwear* in the scavenger hunt, so…"

"You want to quit fucking around?"

I cut my eyes toward the door. "You sure you want to accuse *me* of that?"

He lowers his voice. "Pretend you didn't see that."

"I'd love to," I say, "You got some bleach I can put in my eyes?"

Pike runs a hand over his face. "It's just a fling."

"Last time I saw you two, she was thinking about the best way to scatter your corpse."

"I gave her my card, she called me," Pike says, "She wanted to get together for a drink. I went along with it. Then we got together and…well…"

I try to put this delicately. "You realize she's just using you for information."

"I know," he says.

"She doesn't care about you at all," I say.

"I know."

"You're just a piece of meat."

"I know. A piece of meat grinning from ear to fucking ear."

I'll give him that. I move away from the door, hoping for a little more privacy. I gently hold up the mylar bag.

"This is the murder weapon."

"For which murder?"

I square him with a look. "Come on."

I hand the mylar bag over to Pike. He takes it from me, reluctantly, and he studies it.

"Alright, how is this supposed to be the murder weapon?" he asks.

"You know James Queen did vitamin shots. Someone got into his dressing room and switched his vitamin shot syringe with a poisoned one."

"Why didn't we find this in Queen's dressing room?" he asks.

"Because the murderer went back later and switched the syringes again."

Pike holds up the bag. "And where did you find this?"

"In a toy car belonging to my friend Mike."

There's a risk, of course, that he'll think Mike is involved in the murder. Pike's never gotten over someone so shady being innocent of murdering his neighbor. Mike is the great whale. Pike studies the toy car.

"Suppose you give me your theory?" he says.

"Queen had the vitamin shot syringes in a leather case," I say, "The murderer switched out one of the syringes for a poisoned one, probably while Queen was out of the dressing room. The murderer was able to switch them back and stashed the poisoned syringe in the toy car. Mike had to go back to Queen's dressing room and get some stuff he'd forgotten. The toy car was part of that. When Mike grabbed his stuff, he left with the weapon, not realizing what he had. The murderer knew Mike had the murder weapon and had to get it back. He wanted Queen's death to be thought of as a stroke or a heart attack."

"And who *is* the murderer?"

"That I don't know. It had to be someone from *The Night Hawk*, but any of them could have gotten in there."

Pike looks over the mylar bag again. His brow furrows as he thinks. "Interesting."

"How so?" I ask.

"The toxicology report came back. There was a trace of something in Queen's system. Barely there, but there."

"What was it?" I ask.

"They aren't sure. They're running some more tests. I'll give them this, see if it helps."

"You're treating it as a murder?"

Pike speaks slowly. "I'm going to give them this and see what they say."

I shake off the frustration. Pike isn't lazy and looking for a reason not to investigate. If he and I have bumped heads in the past, it's because he proceeds strictly from facts and doesn't have the luxury of wild theories. And he doesn't want a moron like me to be right. There is professional pride to consider. He finally looks up from the bag.

"Who else has touched this?" he asks.

"As far as I know, just James Queen and the murderer."

"Not even you?"

"I used a Kleenex to get it into the bag. Made sure no one else touched it."

Pike mutters, "Good boy." He draws in a breath. "All right, I'll have this looked at, see if there's anything worth finding. While I do that, you stay the hell out of it."

"What about Mike?" I ask, "Whoever killed Queen is still coming after him."

I shouldn't have wasted my breath. I already know what Pike will do. He'll proceed by the book and expect me to stay out of it. Pike folds his arms, the bag dangling from his hand.

"We don't know that there *is* a threat to your friend," Pike says, "But if you want to know for sure, then leave this—" He shakes the bag for emphasis, "to the people who know what they're doing. Understand?"

"Understood," I say. This is what I should have done in the first place. It's how I've always handled people who give me orders. I nod, smile politely, then do whatever the hell I want.

Pike studies me, wondering if he can trust me, knowing almost certainly he can't. If he has any intention of debating me, it goes out the window when he realizes he's still standing in the hallway of his apartment building in his undies. He starts to open the door. It bumps into something. There's movement inside. Pike frowns, uncomfortable. I hang my head.

"That's right, we'll keep the circle of knowledge small," I say, "Just you, me and the niche group that uses the internet."

Pike peers over the rims of his wireframe glasses, giving me a warning look. I hustle down the stairs. The door to Pike's apartment closes. I have no idea how much Kelly Smart heard. But I'm sure she'll be, uh, pumping Pike for information. I shake away the thought.

For the first time in my adult life, I'm beginning to think sex is overrated.

***

"I hope you realize the sacrifice I'm making for you," Mike says.

One of the advantages I had growing up—something I didn't appreciate at the time—is that guilt was not one of the weapons in my parents' arsenal. They used a delicate blend of threatening and cajoling to keep me and my brothers in line. Sure, there was the occasional "I'm not angry, I'm just disappointed" which, depending on the level of sincerity, could be interpreted as a form of guilt. But my upbringing was largely free of that form of manipulation.

"I appreciate it," I say, standing over the stove.

Mike sips a beer. "When I was staying at Lars's place, I didn't feel safe at all. People come and go all the time. And most of them are weirdos from that Bobby Vitality thing."

I stir the spaghetti sauce. Everything's proceeding apace. Sauce simmering in the frying pan. Water about to boil in the stock pot. Oven preheating, waiting for a loaf of Italian bread. Mike will soon abandon my apartment and stay at Lars's for the evening. Casey is on her way over. God's in His Heaven and I'm going to get laid.

I check on the water. "Are the weirdos threatening?"

Mike slouches at the breakfast bar. "Not really. But they all act like they're radio-controlled. It's creepy."

I go to the liquor shelf for a bottle of reasonably priced wine. "For what it's worth, I appreciate the sacrifice."

He greets that with silence, continuing his impression of the Incredible Sulk. I shake off my own sense of foreboding. The weather outside is not helping, what with the chill in the air and the breeze rattling the windows. I may have finally convinced Pike that James Queen was murdered. But the murderer is still out there. And there are questions still picking at me. Who broke into Mike's storage unit? Who got his code? Who could have arranged the poison? How premeditated was the murder? And, of course, who committed it?

Weirdly, knowing the murder was after Mike because he *had* something rather than he *saw* something makes things more difficult. It renders everything Mike saw backstage as useless. Someone stashed the syringe in Mike's toy car. Why?

Did Mike surprise them? Was there another reason? It feels like we're back at square one.

"I know we've done this already," I say, "But tell me what happened when you went backstage. Maybe there's something we're missing."

Mike stares at his ratty sweatshirt as he thinks. "I got past Chuck and went backstage. I saw James Queen chewing out Lars. I went into the dressing room—"

"Did you see anything out of place?" I ask.

"I had been in there once and spent most of the time looking at James Queen. I wouldn't know what was *in* place."

"Understood."

"I figured I had to get in and out as fast as possible," Mike says, "The backpack was sitting next to the little table. The toy Nightmobile was on the table. I grabbed it and got the hell out. Ran past the curtain and out into the convention."

"And you didn't see anything?"

"Nothing."

Mike walks over to the desk and picks up the toy Nightmobile. He cradles it under his arm. I wouldn't be surprised if he started petting it. I set the bottle of wine on the breakfast bar.

"You sure you want to hold on to that?" I say, "Shouldn't it be in a safe or an indestructible glass case?"

"No way," he says, petting it (I knew it), "I'm not letting this thing out of my sight. If someone wants this, they'll have to kill me for it."

"With all due respect, I think that's the general idea."

Mike gives me the stinkface. I study the car while setting two glasses on the breakfast bar. James Queen's signature, in silver pen, right on the door. My Spidey Sense is tingling for some reason. Have I missed something? Since it's not readily apparent, I let it go, even if it's a bit disquieting.

Speaking of disquieting, Lars knocks at the door. Since I'm preoccupied with opening the bottle of wine, I look at Mike and nod toward the door. He sighs, ever put upon, and answers it. Lars glides in, wearing his work clothes, sans tie. He looks tired and moves slower than normal. He peeks into the kitchen.

"Everything shipshape, brother?" he asks.

"Indeed," I say, "The ship is truly taking shape."

Lars slaps the breakfast bar. "Good to hear. Just don't let it distract you from tomorrow."

Ah yes, tomorrow. James Queen's memorial down at the History Center. I'd like to tell you I've been working tirelessly on my speech, but it would be an utter lie. It's not from laziness or distraction. For a somewhat meticulous writer, I don't like being too prepared for a speech. Takes away the spontaneity. Much like the lie I'm about to tell Lars.

"I'm ready to go," I say, "Stirring speech I've put together."

Lars gives me a thumbs up. "I have complete faith in you, brother." He takes a whiff of my spaghetti sauce. "Looks like preparations are going well on this front?" He waggles his eyebrows, then stops and folds his hands in front of himself. I go to the stove and check on the spaghetti.

"They're fronting to beat hell," I say.

Lars gives me a thumbs up and starts toward the door. He stops and spins on his heel. "You know the Big Event is tomorrow," he says, "Mr. Vitality will be there. Do you think you could take a minute to talk to him?"

Truthfully, I'd rather take a corkscrew to my nasal cavity. But refusing Lars would be risking bad karma. After everything that's gone down with me and Casey, I can't risk any more of that. I swallow my pride (and my bile).

"I think I can make that work," I say.

Lars claps his hands, then resumes a dignified pose. "I knew I could depend on you."

He glides toward the front door. Mike picks up the duffle bag containing his clothes and follows. Lars gives me a little bow.

"Have a good night, my friend," he says, "I hope you enjoy yourself. Thoroughly."

"And don't be too loud," Mike says as he leaves.

I do a happy dance as the door closes. Alone again. Thankfully.

I look over the apartment. It's spotless. The cats are sleeping in their individual kitty beds in the corner. They know something's up and they will likely be kicked out of their usual sleeping spots next to me. Sorry, fellas. A man has got to have priorities.

I make quick work of getting the meal ready. I drain the spaghetti, return it to the stock pot and add the sauce. Ever the anal-retentive chef, I rinse out the frying pan and set it in the sink. I don't have a proper dining room table (or a proper dining room), but if I dress up the breakfast bar, it works to good effect. I set out two plates, put the silverware on red folded cloth napkins and the wine glasses next to the plates. Next, I slide a votive candle between the two plates. I put Van Morrison on Spotify and, voila, the scene is set.

Joe Davis: Gangster of Love.

I'm hunting around for a lighter when there's a knock at the backdoor. Casey's here. Dear Lord, please don't let me fuck this up. I check my look in the hall mirror. Black dress shirt and black slacks are wrinkle free. Hair is coiffed just so. I've gotten the cologne balance just right. Good to go. I stroll down the hall and open the backdoor with a flourish. And somebody clubs me upside the head.

I really need to stop answering the backdoor.

CHAPTER EIGHTEEN

On the bright side, the blow isn't particularly hard, no harder than the playful swipes my brother Kevin used to give me. (Actually, he found them playful. I found them irritating.) I stumble back and bump into the wall. The guy who delivered the blow lurches into the room after me. It takes a few seconds to recognize him.

"Rob Quince?" I say, clutching the side of my head. Interesting relationship I've got with this guy. Three times I've met him, and every occasion has involved violence.

Quince has seen better days. His hair is disheveled, bruises are prominent on his face, and one eye is partly closed. He still wears the hoodie he probably bought at the airport. From the look and smell of it, he hasn't bathed recently. There's a stiffness to his movement, probably the result of some internal injury. I'll give Tim Hefflin credit. He did a number on Rob Quince.

He lurches toward me. "Where's the fucking tape?"

"What tape?"

Playing dumb only buys you a few seconds. Quince clenches his fist. "The fucking tape!" he says.

"Oh, the *fucking* tape," I say, "You mean the tape of the fucking."

Quince reaches for me, but I sidestep him. His hand bumps against the wall and he winces. "Quit fucking around," he says, "I know you stole the tape. I want it back."

When I was in high school, my friend Sam ran afoul of some football players. As a threat level went, we were torn. On the one hand, these guys were bigger and faster than Sam. On the other hand, we'd seen them play football. It was the most incompetent play since a squirrel invaded the pitch at the Puppy Bowl. Just how much did Sam have to fear?

I face a similar situation here. Rob Quince is sincere in wanting to beat the hell out of me, but I question his ability to get the job done. Do I want to put this to the test? I back farther into the apartment. Quince comes at me, moving stiffly.

"You hear me?" he says, as if volume is the issue, "Give me the tape or I will kill you!"

Quince lunges at me. But he trips over the small table in the hall and crashes to the floor. A few framed photos of my parents hit the deck. (I *just* set those damn things back up a few months ago. The last time my place was invaded by a murderous intruder.)

Quince makes another lunge. I avoid him and he lands on the futon. I look around for a weapon, something that might bring this idiocy to an end. But the only thing I own is an old tennis racket and that's in the closet. If these home invasions continue, I should probably buy a gun. (Not the bullets. Just the gun.)

Quince gets up from the futon, gritting his teeth. He sets himself to make another pass. For reasons passing understanding, I try to negotiate a peaceful solution.

"I don't have the tape," I tell him.

"Bullshit."

"I bullshit not. I don't have the tape."

"Then where is it?" Quince says.

"It doesn't exist. Not anymore."

Quince gets a stricken look, like I told him there's no Santa Claus. "What do you mean?"

"I destroyed it. I drove over it with my car and threw what was left of it in the trash."

He puts a hand out, trying to stop himself from collapsing on to the futon. Quince is devastated. Not only is there no Santa Claus, but if Mr. Claus *does* turn up, he's wanted by the federal government for tax evasion.

"Why would you do that?" he asks.

"Because it's the decent thing to do."

He flinches like a mosquito's buzzing around him. "You realize how much money that thing is worth?"

"Now? Yes. Nothing." A thought occurs. "I take it there isn't another copy?"

"No," Quince says, "I just found the damn thing. I don't know anything about uploading shit and I didn't want to take a chance on giving it to someone. They'd take off with the damn thing. Use it for themselves."

"People, huh?" I say, "What a bunch of bastards."

The truth is I'm relieved. Even in destroying the tape, I wondered if there was another copy out there. This isn't 1992. If something is viral worthy, it's on every platform in less time than it takes to set up a porn site. Now that I know I've destroyed the only available copy, Ella Jones is well and truly safe from public humiliation. Assuming, of course, she didn't kill James Queen. (I can't save her from *that* humiliation.)

Quince glowers. "You cost me a fucking fortune."

"I cost you a quick buck," I say, "Or fifteen minutes of fame. Neither of which you earned and neither of which you deserve. I don't feel too bad."

"Fuck you!"

Quince comes at me again. I backpedal toward the front door. My cell phone is on the desk. Maybe I can call the police while playing rope-a-dope. Quince throws a kick at me.

I leap to one side. He crashes, leg-first, into the wall and winds up on the floor, holding his knee. His carcass is between me and the desk. Figuring the shortest distance between two points is a straight line (the only geometry I've ever found useful), I leap over Rob Quince.

Who chooses that moment to try to get to his feet.

Anyone who has ever tried and failed to leap a hurdle will know what the next few seconds are like. My legs are taken out from under me and my trajectory is altered. I tumble in the air and land shoulder-first, my head under the desk. I don't think anything's broken (either on me or in the apartment) but the Russian judge will take away style points.

A second later, Quince is on top of me, determined to strangle the life out of me. Well, that's his determination. His execution leaves a lot to be desired. His hands are not actually on my windpipe. I hold his wrists, keeping them away. I kick my legs but realize I'm not strong enough to get him off me. We've got a stalemate. All I can do is wait several hours for Quince to get drowsy and fall asleep.

It doesn't take that long. Several seconds into the stalemate, there's a loud *clang* and Quince goes cross-eyed. He falls away from me. Casey holds the dripping frying pan, fresh out of the sink.

"Is this part of the date?" she asks, her eyes flashing.

"It is now," I say.

***

A few minutes later, we've brought Rob Quince
around. He sits on my futon, with four of us standing guard.
Lars and Mike have been recruited to help (since they were
useless during the fight). They stand on either side of the
futon. Casey sits at the breakfast bar, rocking a bit on the
stool. The frying pan is next to her on the bar. There are a
few bits of spaghetti sauce on the floor and the furniture, but
I'll forgive her for it. Quince looks up at me.

"You gonna call the cops?" he asks.

"Maybe," I say, "Let's chat first."

"About what?"

I sit on the arm of the comfy chair. "You and James
Queen were using the tape so he could…" I pause, looking
for a way to phrase this delicately.

"Bang one of Ella's students," Quince says.

Sure, it lacks discretion, but it gets to the point in a
big, big hurry. I look to Casey, the one most likely to be
offended by Quince's phrasing. She simply runs her hands up
and down her black skirt. The frying pan is still handy, so
Quince best be careful.

"That's what he wanted," I say, "but it didn't work."

"Because he was killed," Lars says, stroking his beard.

Quince mumbles, "Of all the fucking luck."

I run a hand over the bruise that's forming on my jaw. "What did you want from Ella?"

He gives us a defiant sneer. "You guys cops?"

"No," I say, "But they're only a phone call away."

Quince deflates. He realizes how much less comfortable this conversation will be with the police. He has probably had a few of those in his time. He lets out a sigh.

"She's going to get a piece of the movie," he says, "The new one. *Night Hawk Rinsing.*"

"*Rising,*" Mike says.

"Yeah, that," Quince says, "Jimmy's leaving it to her. His cut of *The Night Hawk*. I think he figured it wasn't going to be worth anything. Then the new movie came up. He, uh, he got killed before he could change his will."

Mike clenches his fists. "So, you figured you'd change it for him."

Quince flips his hands out, not showing a hell of a lot of regret. "That was the play. I had something to work with. I had to use it. That's how you make money."

I'll have to take his word on that, since I make *my* money by (marginally) more respectable means. Mike looks like he wants another go at Quince. I can't allow that.

"Why did Queen leave his portion of *The Night Hawk* to Ella?" I ask.

"Got me," Quince says, "He probably had some sentimental thing for her. Don't know why. Jimmy hated the people from *The Night Hawk*. He loved laughing at them behind their backs. Like when he came to this thing. He told me he was going to give everyone a signed toy car from him. Like they were getting a present from the real star. He knew it would piss them off. That's the only reason he did it."

Mike's head drops. His disillusionment of James Queen continues unabated. I focus on Quince.

"You were blackmailing Ella to get part of *Night Hawk Rising*," I say, "Is that also why you attacked Hal Murdoch?"

Quince gets a blank look. "Why I what-the-what?"

"Attacked Hal Murdoch," I say, less sure of myself, "You called him up and threatened him. Then you ran his car off the road."

Quince looks as if I'm about to reveal the whole joke. He lets out a hearty laugh. He claps his hands and sits back on the futon.

"Where the hell did you come up with that?" he says.

I look to Mike, who seems thrown off as well. "That's what Hal Murdoch said."

"I wouldn't try a thing like that," Quince says, "Ella was going to own a piece of *The Night Hawk* and a piece is plenty. You can't try for the whole enchilada. That's greedy and it's just going to get you caught."

"He's right on that," Mike says.

"Thank you, Fredo." Then I turn to Quince, "You had nothing to do with Hal Murdoch?"

Quince looks bored with the conversation. "Nope."

That's interesting. Then who attacked Murdoch? If we rule out Ella and, obviously, Murdoch, it could have only been Tim Hefflin. But why? Hefflin has always spoken highly of Murdoch. And Murdoch was willing to get Hefflin a small role in *Night Hawk Rising*, so what motive would Hefflin have in going after him? It doesn't make sense. And there's the issue of Rob Quince.

"Here's the deal," I say, "You're going to leave town. Do not pass 'Go', do not collect two hundred dollars. I never want to see you again. And if I hear you so much as said 'Hi' to Ella Jones, I'll go to the police and let them know you assaulted me and tried to blackmail her. I've got a friend in the St. Paul Police Department."

It's a massive bluff. Pike would rather throw *me* in jail than Rob Quince. But Quince buys it. His mouth tightens. But he's got only one way out. He gets up from the futon and goes to the front door. It looks like he wants to spit on my floor, but he resists. Quince whips open the door and goes down the stairs. A few seconds later, the building shakes with the sound of the front door slamming. It's followed by a howl of pain. Out the front window Quince can be seen limping down the front walk. A wiener to the end. I turn to Lars and Mike.

"Thanks for coming," I say, "Eventually."

Mike starts to say something but casts a look toward Casey and bites it back. He slinks toward the front door, sullen expression in place. Lars follows, escorted by me. When we get to the door, Lars lowers his voice.

"Sorry about not coming sooner," he says, "We didn't know what was going on."

"Seriously?" I ask, "What the hell did you think was happening?"

He flicks his eyes toward Casey. "We, uh, we thought you were…doing incredibly well."

I swallow a response and gently guide Lars out the door. I turn toward Casey. We have an awkward junior high type of moment, broken by a bit of laughter.

"I guess I owe you thanks," I say.

Casey pushes a strand of hair behind her ear. "It was just a reaction. I saw the backdoor open and I saw what was going on. I looked around for a weapon. I saw the frying pan and I grabbed it and there it was. I did it without thinking."

I stick my hands in my pockets. "I'm glad you did."

"Me, too," Casey says, her cheeks flushing beneath her bit of makeup, "It was exciting."

There's a little silence. We look at each other. The air is charged. I'm getting my first good look at Casey tonight. She's wearing a gray t-shirt and a black skirt under her usual jean jacket. She looks amazing. (After the little fight with Quince, I doubt I can say the same.) There is a fluttering in my stomach. I look toward the kitchen.

"I've, uh, I've still got dinner waiting," I say.

"That's nice," Casey says, rubbing her hands on her skirt, "Or, y'know, we could skip dinner and, uh, go into the bedroom."

"Y'know, I was just thinking. We could skip dinner and go into the bedroom."

I pull Casey into an embrace, one that threatens to topple us into the breakfast bar. After several seconds, Casey comes up for air and runs for the bedroom, pulling me along. There's another make out session at the doorway to the bedroom. Then Casey throws off her jean jacket and backs toward the bed.

Things progress quickly. Our clothes wind up on the floor. (A black thong? Yes!) I flip the bedroom door closed, lest the cats get any ideas about interrupting. Casey slides under the covers and pulls me in with her. Time passes pleasantly. Then she pulls me on top of her. Her mouth is close to my ear.

"Just take it slow," she whispers.

I'm kissing Casey's neck. "Of course."

She guides me home. I need to distract myself. This has been a long time coming. We would have gotten to it sooner if not for this case. If not for Mike. For Mike. For…Mike. Wait a minute. That's it. That's it! Holy shit, I figured it out!

Just then, I'm aware of something. Not just the answer to the case, but something…else. Something's happened. Something I didn't intend. My worst fears are confirmed when I hear Casey's voice coming from under me.

"Is that it?"

***

"Again?" Mike say, his cackling laughter floating through the air outside the History Center, "It happened *again?*"

This is so embarrassing. While I haven't exactly erased the memory of 1960s and 1970s Warren Beatty in the dating department, I've done okay. If my relationships have foundered (as all of them eventually have), they've foundered on issues unrelated to what goes on in the boudoir. There, I've had no complaints. Many satisfied customers. Now, I'm the kid from *American Pie*. To Mike's everlasting delight.

"I was thinking about the case," I say, watching the crowd stream in for the James Queen memorial, "and I realized something and I just…got out of hand."

"So to speak."

"So to speak."

Obviously, I'd rather not have this conversation with Mike. But I owe him an explanation if it's related to the case. We're on the walkway outside the History Center, watching the crowd stream in for James Queen's memorial. A different crowd slips past every now and again, heading for the wedding upstairs. The Nightmobile is on display in front of the entrance, gleaming in the sunlight. Manny, the guy in charge of the car, hovers nearby. I should be enjoying this day. The weather's warm and the fall colors are at their most brilliant. But all is not well.

Mike puts his hand over his mouth, trying in vain to contain his mirth. "What happened after? Did you get tongue-tied again?"

"Yes and no," I say, tugging at the cuffs of my suitcoat, "I got tongue-tied, but in a totally different way. Instead of clamming up, I rushed to explain things. But my mouth was moving about a minute ahead of my brain. I was babbling to beat hell. I'm sure Casey thought I was either speaking in tongues or having a series of small strokes."

"Did she say anything?"

"Nope. She just got up, put on her clothes and stormed out. Even the cats looked like they pitied me. Of course, I was standing in the hallway, naked and babbling, so…"

Mike straightens his tie, knocked askew by his body shaking with laughter. "You tried calling her?"

"Not yet," I say, "I'll let her calm down. Give her a decent explanation."

"Good luck with that."

I look down over the parking lot, trying to ignore Mike's glee. My dark suit is getting warm in the sun. Mike scratches his face, the clean-shaven look making him uncomfortable. He hoists his backpack on his shoulder. A crowd gathers on the far side of the lot. They are dressed in white and don't appear to be headed toward the building. I wonder if they're here for James Queen's memorial or the wedding. But they don't seem interested in either.

Speaking of the wedding, Carol approaches, wearing a bridesmaid's dress that may cause a yellow chiffon shortage in North America. On the bright side, the large hat can be used for gardening. She looks as if she's walking the last mile. I hold up a pretend mic and extend a hand toward her.

"Ladies and gentlemen, we're proud to present Miss Grim Death of 1976," I say, doing my best Don Pardo impression (and *best* must be defined rather loosely).

Mike turns toward Carol. Just when I thought his cup of mirth was filled to the brim, it runneth over. He doubles up with a new round of laughter. Carol gives us a very lady-like middle finger.

"Enjoy it, assholes," she says, waving a hand toward the outfit, "I'm having a bonfire later. Bring booze and friends."

Mike wipes tears from his eyes. "This might be the greatest day of my life. Between this dress and Joe's thing with Casey."

I wave my hands in a vain effort to stop Mike. But the feline has been released from the grocery container. Carol's eyes light up.

"What happened with Casey?" she asks, "Don't tell me you guys got interrupted again?"

"No," I say, "I don't want to talk about it."

Carol looks to Mike. He holds his fingers up like a gun and fires, making a little "pew" sound for effect. Carol's head swivels toward me.

"Again?" she says, "Oh my God, it happened *again?*"

I hold up both hands. "I'm sorry, ladies and gentlemen of the press, I won't be taking any further questions at this time."

Carol's body quakes, causing the chiffon to ripple in all the wrong places. "What happened?"

I look toward the heavens. "We were in bed and I was thinking about the case in order to…control myself. Then I realized something and I…*lost* control of myself."

Now Carol is wiping her eyes "What did you realize?"

"Nothing much," I say, "Just who killed James Queen and has been trying to kill Mike."

That, as I hoped, brings all laughter to a halt. Carol's mouth opens slightly. Mike already knows my theory. I remain silent, the international sign I'm serious. Carol grabs my arm.

"Who is it?" she asks.

I look toward the building. "Everyone at the memorial will find out soon enough."

"I won't be *at* the memorial," Carol says, "I'll be upstairs at the wedding."

"If you hadn't played *Let's Mock Joe*, I might be willing to tell you," I say.

Carol gives that a cluck of disgust. Look who's Captain Yuck-It-Up now. She stomps a high heel and puts her hands on her hips. "You have this great theory. And you didn't consider calling the police?"

"I called Sergeant Pike this morning. He's trying to find a match for the prints on the syringe. I told him my theory, but he didn't seem impressed. Not enough to bring somebody in. Proceed from facts. By the book. Blah, blah,

blah." I adjust my tie. "I'll take my chances at the memorial. If it works out, you'll be the first to know." I look toward the crowd filing in. "Or, more accurately, the eight-hundredth."

She taps the backpack on Mike's shoulder. "I'm guessing that has something to do with your theory?"

"It does," I say.

Carol waits for me to explain. I don't. She gives up and fusses with her disaster of a dress. "Have fun. At least one of us will."

"Still no go with the bride and groom?" I ask.

Carol reaches to bite her nails, but realizes they're manicured. "Neither of them is speaking to me." She starts to run a hand through her hair, but realizes it's been styled. "I was in the bridal suite this morning. Tension City."

Mike scoffs. "Look on the bright side: you could be in my place. I might be dead before the day is out."

Carol waves a hand at her dress. "Mike, look at what I'm wearing. You think I'm really clinging to life right now?"

Members of the bridal party walk past, all attired in the same hideous manner. I hope the bride is stunning. At least this bridesmaids' attire would serve a purpose. Carol allows herself to be swept up in the sea of chiffon. She mouths, "Good luck." Mike shakes his head as he watches her go.

"Times like this," he says, "I'm ashamed to say I slept with that woman."

"If it means anything," I say, "I don't think she's doing a lot of bragging about it, either."

He gives me the stinkeye. I lead the way into the building. We walk down the long hallway to the main lobby. Most of the crowd turns left, heading for the theater. Lars stands off to the side, letting the crowd file past. His hair is slicked back, and he wears a dark suit. Sweat seems ready to do damage to both. He pushes off from the wall.

"Good to see you, my friend," he says, "I hope you can help keep me on the straight and narrow today. I'm mighty distracted. Mr. Vitality is handling the Big Event. I wish I were there, but I'm here. Flying solo."

In the recent past, that would not have been a problem for Lars. Judging by his fret level, it's a major problem now. He pulls some now-damp notecards from the interior pocket of his coat and shuffles through them. He drops three of them, then scrambles to pick them up. Lars in full meltdown. This is a new one.

"It's going to be fine," I tell him, "You don't need Mr. Vitality. You've got this."

Lars looks toward the hallway leading outside. "I hope so. I wish Mr. Vitality wasn't so focused on the Big Event. *I* could be helping *him*."

Gee-willickers. The closest thing I've had to a mentor was Mr. Somrock, the faculty advisor on my high school newspaper and the person who gave me my first column. And even he would have gotten creeped out if I had shown him this kind of dogged adoration. (Actually, Mr. Somrock would have wondered just how much pot *was* going through the high school.) I pat Lars on the shoulder.

"You'll be great," I say, "Where is this Big Event taking place?"

"It's outside," he says, "In the parking lot."

Mike looks that direction. "That would explain the people in white out there. What are they doing?"

"I don't know," Lars says, "It was Mr. Vitality's call. You'd have to ask him." He looks over his shoulder at the last of the people trickling into the theater. "We should get inside." He takes a shallow breath. "Good luck to you."

We head into the theater. Lars leads the way to the stage. The place is completely full. The crowd buzzes, respectfully, as they take their seats. A giant picture of James Queen from an old publicity photo dominates the stage. Mike walks behind me. His seat is in the VIP section near the front. He slips the backpack off his shoulder and hands it to me. That done, he slides down a row, into his seat.

Once onstage, Lars greets Ella, Hefflin and Hal Murdoch. He takes his place at the lectern while I find my seat. I set the backpack at my feet. Ella is next to me, wearing a black dress. She looks uncomfortable as the designated widow. Hefflin wears an ill-fitting cheap suit. His hair is combed, and he's shaved, but he looks tired. Murdoch wears a pink carnation in his lapel, showing he's not entirely in mourning. Lars taps his notecards against the lectern, then gestures to the back. The house lights are lowered. The crowd comes to a respectful of silence. Lars approaches the mic.

"Thank you all for coming," he says, fighting to keep a squeak out of his voice, "This is the memorial service for James Queen. An actor. An icon. A hero to millions. Right up until his untimely and partially humiliating death. To honor him, we have prepared a short video. This will be followed by some words from those who knew him best. And Joe Davis."

Thanks for the big buildup, Lars. The video, at least, is very well done. Stirring music, a lovely video montage, clips from Queen's work (focusing more on *The Night Hawk* and less on his aborted singing career and his failed movies). There's not a dry eye in the house. Which is fine. There are plenty on stage. Once the video is done, Lars returns to the lectern.

"Now, I'd like to introduce our first speaker," he says, "He's a moderately popular local columnist for *The Daily Bugle*, revered among a socially awkward niche fanbase. Ladies and gentlemen, Joe Davis."

A respectful applause greets me, which is more than Lars's introduction merits. I take the speech from the inner pocket of my suitcoat and lay it on the lectern. Here goes nothing.

"I first became a fan of James Queen when I was seven years old," I say, reading from the script, "Reruns of *The Night Hawk* were on TV every afternoon when I came home from school. I absolutely fell in love with it. I would imagine myself sliding down a pole, into the Night Cave. Of course, when I tried it myself, I used the laundry chute and destroyed a clothes hamper. So, I don't think my mother was a fan of James Queen."

That gets some polite laughter. It relaxes me. I need it. The next part isn't going to be easy.

"But my mother wasn't the only one who didn't care for James Queen. While Mr. Queen had a large following—as the crowd here will attest—that didn't extend to the people he worked with." A stir in the crowd. Ella, Hefflin and Murdoch exchange looks. I set my notes aside. "Ella Jones was married to James Queen. Not happily. Queen was neglectful, selfish, and unfaithful. Ella had no choice but to divorce him. Queen never forgave her. When Ella needed his help with something, he offered her a humiliating bargain. If that gives you an idea what James Queen was all about."

The stirring grows. The crowd didn't come for this heresy. Ella looks mortified. Hefflin's face darkens. Murdoch grips his cane. If I keep this up, I'm going to get burned in effigy. If not in actuality.

"Tim Hefflin also hated James Queen," I say, "Queen stepped on his co-stars and nobody more than Tim Hefflin. Hefflin wrote a tell-all biography that, viewed from a certain angle, was libel. Mr. Queen definitely viewed it from that angle. He threatened Hefflin with legal action and almost certainly would have followed through."

Hefflin starts to stand but doesn't make it. (Guessing he's had a few today.) He sits heavily in the chair. Ella puts a hand on his shoulder, steadying him. I lean on the lectern.

"Hal Murdoch made James Queen a star," I say, "Mr. Murdoch would tell you he also created a monster. Queen used his leverage to get a piece of *The Night Hawk* franchise. And he tortured Murdoch with that ever since. Queen's ego wouldn't allow anyone else play the role. It resulted in a disastrous movie that ended Hal Murdoch's career. And if something wasn't done, history was going to repeat itself."

Murdoch's knuckles whiten on the cane. If he had a cigar in his mouth, he'd be chewing it. The crowd's discontent threatens to boil over. They ain't seen nothing yet.

"Three of the people on this stage were in town for the convention," I say, "They watched James Queen die. It was a shock to everyone. Except one person. The person who murdered James Queen."

The crowd's reaction to my pronouncement of James Queen's murder draws the reaction a pro wrestling heel dreams of. Screams and cries are hurled at me. Some leap to their feet, Ella Jones among them. Lars smoothly blocks her. She stops but doesn't sit down. I wait for the tumult to die down before I continue.

"You see, James Queen took vitamin shots," I say, "He injected them with needles. Quackery, but he believed in it. The people around him knew about the shots. It was a simple matter of switching one of the regular syringes with a poisoned one. Then switching them back later. The murderer only got it half-right, though. This is what happened."

Despite the audience's rage, they quiet down and listen. It's the same with the group onstage. I fold my hands on the lectern.

"James Queen gave everyone in *The Night Hawk* an autographed toy Nightmobile," I say, "Just like the one my friend Mike asked him to sign." I reach into the backpack and come out with the toy. "See, the fun part of these toys are the secret compartments." I push a few of the buttons, hoping I remember Mike's tutorial. "A perfect hiding place for a needle." The toy Nightmobile comes apart cleanly. I show the interior to the audience. "Both to smuggle a needle into

James Queen's dressing room and to smuggle it out again. The murderer brings the toy car containing the poisoned needle into Queen's dressing room. When Queen steps out, the murderer goes into Queen's dressing room, takes the poisoned needle out of the toy car, switches it out with the regular needle, hiding the regular needle in the toy car. When Queen leaves the dressing room again, the murderer goes back in and switches the needles again. This time, though, the murderer was interrupted when my friend Mike returned to fetch some stuff Queen had signed. They leave the car sitting out, so Mike doesn't notice anything out of place, and they find a hiding spot. Mike, in his haste, grabbed the wrong toy Nightmobile. Instead of his own, he grabbed the car with the poisoned needle inside, never realizing what he had. The needle is now in the hands of the St. Paul Police Department. And they'll soon be coming to the same conclusion I've reached. James Queen was murdered."

A buzz ripples through the crowd. Ella sits heavily, hanging her head. Hefflin looks confused. Murdoch doesn't move. I put the toy car back together. I keep my eyes on a dark spot at the back of the house, ready for the big finale.

"No one will ever accuse my friend Mike of being the most observant soul." I'm sure Mike's glaring at me, but I'm still staring at the back. "If he was, he might have noticed a big difference between the toy car in his possession and the one he actually owned. James Queen personalized the autograph on Mike's car. *To Mike, James Queen.* He did the same for the toy cars he gave to the other people from *The Night Hawk.* Except for one. Am I right?" I turn toward the others. "Hal Murdoch?"

This time, there isn't an explosion from the crowd. In fact, you could hear a pin drop, wave to its carpool, stroll in the front door and say, "Hi, honey, I'm home." Every head in the place turns to Hal Murdoch. He rises slowly, glaring at me. I stand my ground.

"You came to St. Paul prepared," I say, "James Queen was holding up *The Night Hawk Rising.* Your dream project. Your life's work. Maybe you hoped you could talk Queen out of it. Then you argued with Queen and you realized you couldn't. So, you went with Plan B." I put the toy back in the backpack. Murdoch rests on his cane, not moving. "Problem was, my friend Mike made off with the murder weapon," I say, "And you had to get it back. Or get rid of Mike before he realized what he had."

"How could he do that?" Ella asks. The sound of a voice other than mine is a shock to the audience's collective system. "I'm sorry," she says, "but Hal…he's not really going to disguise himself and attack someone, is he? He's…"

Lars raises a hand. "Too old and decrepit?"

Ella concedes the point. Hefflin flicks his head back and forth between me and Murdoch, like he's watching a tennis match. I keep my eyes on Murdoch.

"He didn't have to," I say, "He had someone who could do it for him."

Mike's voice comes from the audience. "Billie?"

"A former bodyguard," I say, "Fully capable of kicking our asses. After Queen died, Murdoch called the shots and Billie did the dirty work." I face Murdoch. "I'm right about that, aren't I?"

Murdoch drops his head. The place has gone completely, eerily quiet. Murdoch silently confesses his defeat. Then he takes my legs out with his cane.

I still got a confession out of him, right?

CHAPTER NINETEEN

When I was a kid, there was a bully in my neighborhood (every neighborhood has one) named Jason Skalsky. (Well, not every neighborhood had Jason. Just ours.) Jason was older than most of the kids he bullied, which was not a coincidence. The older kids would have gladly given Jason a swirlie at any time. Jason avoided them and stayed in his lane, bully-wise.

As we got older, Jason's odiousness extended beyond the neighborhood kids. He began to terrorize any adult he assumed wouldn't fight back. (When my father responded by fetching a Louisville Slugger and contemplating the merits of putting it upside Jason's head, he was left alone.) One of Jason's prime targets was Mr. Johnson, a kindly gentleman who lived at the end of the block. Jason took delight in uprooting Mr. Johnson's vegetables and kicking down the fence around the garden. Mr. Johnson would simply replant the vegetables and put the fence back up and go about his business.

The bridge too far occurred when Jason extended his enterprise to keying Mr. Johnson's Cadillac. While Mr. Johnson was working in the driveway, trying to buff out the scratches, Jason (who was eighteen by this time) stood nearby and confessed to the crime. As Mr. Johnson strolled to the end of the driveway, Jason laughed and made some comment about not needing to take his hands out of his pockets. The neighbors stepped out of their houses. Then, in front of God and country, Mr. Johnson beat the ever-loving snot out of Jason Skalsky. When it was over, Mr. Johnson rolled his sleeves down and went back to work on his car. Jason Skalsky lay in a heap, his days as a neighborhood menace over. (Last I heard, he works at a gas station on the edge of town.)

The observant among us realized the lesson. Don't judge a book by its cover. Don't assume a kindly man has always been a kindly old man. It's entirely possible he was once a Navy boxing champion who could kick your ass if you messed with his car.

I don't know if Hal Murdoch ever boxed. If his work with a cane means anything, he probably played some baseball.

The cane hits me right in the shins. For not the first time in my life, I'm on the floor with no memory of falling. (This might be the first time it's happened when I'm sober.) Warm pain rolls up my legs. I clutch my shins. Air comes in short bursts. Sweat breaks out on my forehead. Someone squats next to me.

"You okay, brother?" Lars whispers, "You need a doctor? An ambulance? Last rites?"

Among my other friends (okay, *all* of them), I would have taken the last bit as sarcasm. But Lars is completely serious, so I cut him some slack.

"Get Murdoch," I say.

"Gonna be a tall order, brother," Lars says, "I don't know where he is."

My eyes clear. Murdoch is nowhere to be found. The auditorium is in chaos, everyone shouting and pointing. Ella and Hefflin are both in shock. Mike has reached the stage. He ignores me and makes sure Ella's okay. (Nice to know the cats aren't the only turncoat bastards in my life.) I look around for Murdoch.

"Where the hell did he go?" I say.

"Up the stairs. He moves fast for a guy with a cane."

Likely another of Murdoch's deceptions. Lars helps me to my feet. I'm not sure my legs will support me, but they hold. The pain in my shins has eased to throbbing level. Lars leads the way toward the back of the auditorium. I limp after him. Mike tears himself away from Ella and joins us. He puts a hand on my shoulder. It's a light touch, but it nearly knocks me down.

"You going to be okay?" he asks.

"Fine," I say, "Nothing an amputation won't solve."

We push through the crowd and get to the main lobby. There's no sign of Murdoch. Come on. The guy might be faster than he looks, but he's still a hundred and seventy-five years old. How far could he have gotten?

We get out of the lobby and look down the long entryway. Murdoch hustles faster than I would have given him credit for, toward the front door. I push Lars and Mike ahead of me.

"Stop him!" I shout, waving at Murdoch's escaping form.

But it's not just Hal Murdoch we're facing. Billie zips out from behind a pillar. She's dressed in black. She's not wearing glasses and her hair is pulled back and braided. She's all business. And if her appearance didn't make that obvious, the hunting knife in her hand certainly conveys it. Mike, Lars and I come to a halt.

Lars holds out a hand. "Billie, you don't want to hurt us. Put the knife down and we'll talk."

Billie holds the knife toward us with a casual flick of her hand. "Fuck you."

"That always works for Mr. Vitality," Lars says, "What am I doing wrong?"

Listening to Mr. Vitality, for one. But we can deal with that problem later. Right now, we're confronting either Murdoch's escape or our own deaths (or both). Billie moves forward, gesturing with the knife.

Before she can get too far, a general ruckus comes from the stairs. Three people are in what looks like a three-way fight. (Actually, it looks more like a gaggle of puppies fighting over a bone.) We recognize one of them.

"Carol?" Mike says, "What the fuck?"

The bride goes after the groom. Carol tries to break them up. The bride also goes after Carol. The groom tries to break *them* up. Complete chaos. The fight comes over to us, like a tornado consuming everything in its path. Even Billie is transfixed. That turns out to be to her detriment. The fracas crashes into her. Carol knocks Billie down. The knife clatters across the floor. Lars makes an awkward slide and corrals it. Billie hops to her feet and takes off after Hal Murdoch.

Carol rises, looking slightly dazed. The hat is gone, and her hairdo is fraying. The chiffon dress is torn at the shoulder. "Thanks," she says, "The wedding, uh, isn't going as planned."

I limp forward. "Neither is the memorial. Now, if you'll excuse me, the fucking murderer's getting away."

I start down the hallway, moving not unlike Jack Nicholson in the last ten minutes of *The Shining*. Mike and Lars fall in behind me. So does Carol.

"You're not going back to the wedding?" Mike asks.

"This is more peaceful," Carol says.

Billie hustles Murdoch through the glass doors and out to the parking lot. A car is visible in the drive. Even with my legs not working properly, I lead the charge. Mike is a lifelong smoker and Lars has the most unathletic run known to man. Carol wears high heels and disheveled formalwear. It's all up to me. I hurl myself through the door.

Billie and Murdoch are in the car, but the car isn't moving. The entire driveway of the History Center is filled with people dressed in white, lying down, their arms reaching toward the sky. Bobby Vitality walks among them. He wears a green robe, holds a book in one hand and a bullhorn in the other. He speaks toward the heavens.

"This is the moment of enlightenment, my children," he says, "We stand at the nexus between two worlds. The visitors will arrive soon. When we see the silver chariot emerging from the sun, we know the hour of consciousness is at hand. Release your spirit and prepare the way."

We watch the scene. The police must be on their way, between one thing and another. They're going to have a fight on their hands when they get here. If not from Hal Murdoch, certainly from Bobby Vitality and his followers. Lars's face goes blank.

"That's, uh, that's the Big Event," he says.

"So it would appear," I say.

Lars loosens his tie. "That's, uh, that's a little…whackadoo."

"It has whackadoo in it," Mike says.

"Prominently featured," Carol adds.

But there's no time to watch the weirdness unfold. We still need to get Hal Murdoch. The Big Event cuts off the easiest escape route. But Billie isn't going to let that stop her. She throws the car into reverse. It backs the length of the building, then spins around and disappears around the corner.

We have no options. My car is on the other side of the lot. I won't get to it in time. I turn to the others.

"Did anyone park close?" I ask.

"I rode with you," Mike says.

"I'm on the other side of the lot," Carol says.

"I walked down here," Lars says.

Son of a bitch. Murdoch's going to get away. Maybe the police will catch him, but maybe they won't. Maybe he comes for me or Mike before they catch him. I can't take the chance. Ella and Hefflin come through the doors, catching up with us. I push past the others.

"Are either of you parked close?" I ask.

They both shake their heads. It's over. We're screwed. Then Ella spins toward Manny, standing near the Nightmobile, Armor All in hand. "Manny, you have the keys, don't you?"

Manny's eyes get wide. "You've got to be kidding."

Ella grabs Manny's arm. "Hal murdered James. We can't let him get away. Give them the keys."

Manny's torn for a moment. Then he slips the arm free and reaches into his coat pocket. He pulls out a set of keys and tosses them to Mike.

"Here," he says, "You can use the car."

I'm not sure if it's my imagination, but the Nightmobile starts gleaming. It's accompanied by the sound of a heavenly choir. (I'm sure *that* is my imagination.) Mike is frozen, unable to believe this one moment of luck in a life otherwise devoid of it. Ella puts her hands on his cheeks.

"Go," she says, "You can't let him get away."

Mike looks toward the Nightmobile and grips the keys tightly. "This is my moment." He turns to me. "Come, my trusty cohort. Let us to The Nightmobile."

It's a childhood fantasy come true. I look to Mike. "Away."

We run to the Nightmobile. Mike grabs the windshield, swings himself over the door and into the driver's seat. I slide across the hood and wind up on my ass on the pavement. I pop back up and leap into the passenger seat, catching my foot on the top of the door and nearly crashing into Mike. He slips the key into the ignition and the car roars to life. I grip the dash.

"Engine powered up," I say, "All systems go."

"Check that," Mike says, slipping on his shades, "Let's roll out."

Mike throws the Nightmobile into gear and mashes the accelerator to the floor. I can hear the build of the theme song in my head. There's a giant roar and we pull out with a squeal of tires. Manny looks like he's going to cry. We follow Billie's path around the building. There's a hole in the fence where Murdoch's car has gone. The Nightmobile charges through it and sails on to Tenth Street. Murdoch's car is visible farther down the street. It's got a lead, but nothing we can't overcome. Mike punches it. The Nightmobile charges forward.

And we discover the damn thing only does forty miles an hour.

Mike taps the speedometer. "Wow. The guys who made *The Night Hawk* did a hell of a job editing the car chase scenes."

I lay my head back against the bucket seat. "We are totally fucked. There's no way we're going to catch him in this thing. We'd stand a better chance if we got out and walked."

"Don't give up, pal," Mike says, "Just watch."

The Nightmobile zips along Tenth, making some progress. Billie doesn't seem willing to go *way* over the speed limit, lest she draw the attention of the police. It gives us a chance to close some ground. For all the good it will do us.

"If they make the freeway," I say, "there's no way we're going to catch them."

Mike grips the wheel. "Then we won't let them make the freeway."

There it is. Why didn't I think of such an obvious plan? Oh yes. Because it's complete bollocks. I'm not going to convince Mike of that, though. Not when he's deep in the Night Hawk fantasy. Besides, he's a considerably better driver than I am. I'll follow his lead.

Murdoch's car races to Cedar Avenue and hooks a right. It speeds to Seventh, one of the major thoroughfares of downtown St. Paul, and whips a left. The Nightmobile stays with it. Traffic is light, but we nearly sideswipe a Prius while going through a red light on Seventh. Surprisingly, we don't get the finger or any horn honking. They're probably trying to figure out why the hell the Nightmobile is prowling the streets of St. Paul. I crane my neck to look ahead.

"They're going to go for Highway 94," I say, "We won't catch them out there."

"Hold tight," Mike says, his voice dropping an octave. taking on a suave tone.

Seventh Street is four lanes. Murdoch's car is in the righthand lane, going east. Mike throws the Nightmobile into the left lane and puts on a burst of speed. The car rattles and shakes. It's not cut out for this level of excitement. We pull up alongside Murdoch's car. Billie has her eyes forward. Murdoch shouts instructions. I turn to Mike.

"What if they run us off the road?" I say, "You think this thing could take a beating?"

Mike beams. "We don't have to worry about that. Murdoch designed this car. He'd kill The Night Hawk, but he'd never hurt the Nightmobile."

Will Murdoch still feel that way if push comes to shove? But Mike's in charge of this chase. Good Lord, what have I stumbled into? And why am I enjoying it so much?

We're side-by-side with Murdoch's car. Up ahead, a Corolla pulls out at the intersection of Seventh and Jackson. Murdoch's car has no place to go. It can either crash into us or crash into the Corolla.

"Holding steady," Mike whispers, "Holding steady."

I picture a three-way crash; one where the Nightmobile recreates the end of *Vanishing Point*. I grip the dash.

A second later, Murdoch's car has disappeared. It cuts across the sidewalk and goes down Jackson. Mike maneuvers the Nightmobile around the Corolla. The Nightmobile doesn't even lose a hubcap. We go down Jackson in pursuit.

"Activate the grappling hook," Mike says, stone-faced.

"Mike, that was a special effect on the TV show. There's no grappling hook in this car."

Mike remains unperturbed. "Then we're going to have to improvise."

Murdoch's car fishtails around the corner at Fifth Street. The Nightmobile is right behind. It's a one-way with two lanes. Cray Plaza looms on the left, in all its depressing glass and cement glory. Mears Park is next. Murdoch's car is in the left lane. Mike throws the Nightmobile into the right lane and speeds past Murdoch's car.

"What are you doing?" I say, "We don't want to pass them."

"We're not passing them, pal," Mike says, "We're gaining leverage."

Mike throws the Nightmobile into the path of Murdoch's car. Billie follows the movement, to avoid hitting the Nightmobile. There's a gap between two parked cars. Billie jumps the curb and sails into Mears Park. Shady dudes scatter in all directions. The homeless denizens merely watch, pleased with the diversion. Murdoch's car hits a cement bench that's bolted to the pavement. It bounces off and crashes into a parked car. There's a crunch of metal and an explosion of glass. Smoke rolls out from under Murdoch's car. Done and done.

"Hope they fastened their seatbelts," Mike says, "They certainly failed to use their left and right turn indicators."

He parks the Nightmobile near the curb and hops out. We cautiously move toward Murdoch's car. Mike approaches the driver's side door while I take the passenger door. There's no movement in the car.

Then the driver's door bursts open, knocking Mike to the ground.

I throw my hands out just in time to stop the passenger door. Murdoch's cane cuts through the air, just missing me. Hal Murdoch slides out the passenger door, surprisingly nimble for a guy with a cane.

Murdoch circles toward me. "You couldn't leave well enough alone, could you? Jimmy was dead and no one was going to miss him. That didn't sound like a win-win deal?"

I hold my hands out, keeping my distance. "You were trying to kill my friend."

"I couldn't let him screw everything up," Murdoch says, his voice dropping to a rasp, "Just like Jimmy, getting in the way." He holds the cane, backing me up. "I just wanted one damn thing in life. A movie that looked like *The Night Hawk* was supposed to look. The network wouldn't let me have it. James Queen wouldn't let me have it. Your friend Mike wouldn't let me have it. So, I took matters into my own hands."

I back up, trying to calculate the distance between Murdoch's cane and my head. "I get that," I say, "But it's not an excuse for murder."

"When you can count the days you have left," Murdoch says, "you'll realize it is."

Mike circles around Billie, who assumes a judo stance. He speaks without looking at me.

"The time has come to end this, pal," he says, "You ready to bring the pain?"

I find myself answering without thinking. "For justice? Born ready."

Murdoch swings the cane. I duck and the cane rings off the car door. I dive forward, driving my shoulder into Murdoch's midsection. He makes an *oof* sound when I hit. We crash into the car. Murdoch raises the cane above his head. I narrowly avoid the swing. Murdoch holds the cane toward me, feinting, trying to get his range. I keep my distance. Murdoch keeps coming.

"Walk away and let this go," Murdoch growls.

I can't do that, of course. But there's no point in telling Murdoch that. He's off the deep end. He draws the cane back.

There's a scream behind us. Murdoch looks back. Billie dives toward Mike. He sidesteps. Billie crashes into the side of the car. She stumbles back, drops to one knee, then gets up. She's out on her feet.

Mike adopts a grim look. "Bang-pow, pal. Bang-pow."

He leaps toward Billie, raises his fist, and…pushes her over with his other hand. She hits the deck and doesn't get up. Murdoch sees Billie's carcass. I make my move.

I hit Hal Murdoch with the best hip check I've got. It isn't much, but it does the job. He's thrown flat against the door. The cane flies out of his hand. He sways for a moment. Then the fight goes out of him. He falls back against the car. Mike circles around the front to join me.

"Good work, pal," he says, "The police can take it from here."

I smack my fist into the palm of my hand. "And then into the Nightmobile."

"And home," Mike says.

Hal Murdoch hangs his head. "I hate that fucking show."

EPILOGUE

It boggles my mind when someone greets the death of a celebrity by saying, "A part of my childhood just died." We delude ourselves about our relationships with celebrities. There's no way the death of a celebrity can kill a childhood. Life takes care of that on its own. The entirety of our relationship with a celebrity is through their work. And the work will live on. We've lost nothing. The artist's work lives on. They've *lost nothing.*

Except their lives. Even celebrity has its drawbacks...

This is among the reasons I'm rarely asked to speak at funerals.

And nothing about the last few days will change that. Regarding celebrities, I'm more than ready to get this collection out of my life and let things get back to normal.

It's a beautiful morning for it. The sun is out. The air is crisp. Outside, anyway. The air in the airport is recycled.

"Going to be glad to see L.A. again," Tim Hefflin says, shuffling along, "Get some peace and quiet."

We walk down a hallway under the concourse, heading for the rental counter. Hefflin drags his luggage behind him. Ella walks with Mike, who is handling her luggage. Carol, Lars and I walk behind them.

Ella looks around, wistfully. "It's hard to believe we're going back without Hal."

Hefflin and Ella look at me, as if it's my fault. Mike jumps in.

"No offense to Mr. Murdoch," he says, "but I'm not singing the blues over here. The guy tried to have me killed."

"I wouldn't have expected that of Billie," Ella says, "I knew she was protective of Hal. But she seemed so…nice."

"That's how it goes sometimes," I say, "Dedication crosses a fine line into blind loyalty."

Hefflin runs a hand through his groomed hair. "The guy's going to spend the rest of his life in prison. All over a fucking movie."

I agree with the sentiment. In the couple days since his arrest, Murdoch has confessed to killing James Queen, but always with the excuse that it was the only way the movie would get done; as if this somehow justifies everything. There's been no comment, as far as I know, from Billie. Everyone from *The Night Hawk* has their names in the press. Again. As Mike pointed out, the show didn't get this much publicity when it was still on the air.

"Poison," Ella says, with a shiver, "How did Hal even get it?"

"It's called Death Camus," I say, "According to Sergeant Pike, it's a plant that grows out in California. If you process it right, you can turn it into poison, and it's hard to detect. Murdoch came to Minnesota prepared. He was going to end negotiations with James Queen. One way or another."

Carol turns toward me. "What about the attack on Hal Murdoch? Somebody wanted his cut of the movie."

"Never happened," I say, "He and Billie faked it. Their way of throwing any suspicion off them. The article I was supposedly writing was making Murdoch nervous."

Lars pats me on the shoulder. "You're lucky they didn't come after you."

"Yeah," I say, "if there's one thing I'm feeling after the last couple days, it's lucky."

Carol tries to contain her mirth, knowing what I'm talking about. She covers it by diverting to something else. "We're lucky no one else got killed."

"Really lucky," I say, "According to Pike, that was Murdoch's next plan. Kill Mike. Kill me. Scorched earth. Blame the whole thing on Rob Quince."

Ella spins toward me. "Rob? Why blame Rob?"

"Convenience," I say, "Rob was nosing around, trying to blackmail you. He had conflicts with me and Mike. If we both turn up dead, who better to frame?"

"It was Billie who attacked Quince in his hotel room," Mike says.

"Yep," I say, "We were just lucky enough to stumble on to it."

That sends another little shiver through the group. Carol twists her mouth to one side.

"One thing I still don't get," she says, "One thing I've *never* gotten. How did they break into Mike's storage unit?"

Mike scratches the back of his head. "I gave it to them. Accidentally."

Carol doesn't look any less confused. "Okay, how did you pull that off?"

"We were hanging out at the hotel with Murdoch, and I mentioned the passcode I use for everything is the same one Diana Rushman would use to get into her secret Nightgirl lair."

I cock my head. "I don't ever remember them revealing that."

"They didn't come right out and say it," Mike says, "But if you followed Diana's fingers on the keyboard, even in a long shot, you could figure it out. I just had to see it a few hundred times when I was a kid. Anyway, Murdoch was the one who came up with the code in the first place. As soon as I mentioned it, he must have known what it was. And he must have had Billie follow me to the storage unit."

"Wow," Carol says, "Great job keeping a secret."

Ella slips her arm through Mike's. "It was an honest mistake." She sighs. "He thought he was among friends."

I could kick Mike for not being more careful. He had to know he was a room full of suspects. Common sense would tell you to keep your cards close to the vest. But common sense has never been Mike's strong suit.

We reach the rental car counter and Ella and Hefflin settle business. The rest of us hang back, standing in a circle. I turn to Lars.

"By the by," I ask, "how is Mr. Bobby Vitality?"

"He's out of jail now," Lars says, "The organization paid the bail."

Carol grimaces. "Please tell me you're not still working for this guy."

"Sadly, I've had to leave Mr. Vitality's organization," Lars says, "I'll always be grateful for the experience. But as with many great visionaries, he became too ambitious. Flew too close to the sun, you might say."

"Like Icarus," I say.

"I'm sorry, I don't know who that is," he says. Before I can educate him on Greek mythology, Lars rambles on. "It got to be too much. The compound, the Big Event, the visitors from space, the fraud, the embezzlement, the allegations of inappropriate sexual conduct. I admire Mr. Vitality, but some things I simply cannot truck."

"There can be no trucking," Mike says.

"A truck-free zone, this is," Lars says, waving a hand at himself, "But I'm grateful to Mr. Vitality and no amount of my turning state's evidence against him can change that." He puts a hand on my shoulder. "By the way, I've been thinking about that movie theater vendor idea of yours. I see some possibilities. We should talk it over with Chuck. What do you think?"

"I think it's a stupid idea," I say.

Lars wags a finger at me. "A lot of the most brilliant ideas were thought to be stupid. It just takes a little stick-to-it-iveness."

I slip his hand off my shoulder. "It's good to have you back."

Ella and Hefflin return from the rental counter. We walk toward the far side of the lobby, to the escalators for the departure gate. Ella leads, a certain lightness in her stride.

"I'm anxious to get home," Ella says, "It will be nice to see my students again. And to know they're going to be okay."

Mike slips her a look. "I'm sure you'll be getting calls from agents and producers. People suddenly remember who Ella Jones is."

"I'm not going down that road again," Ella says, "Besides, *I* know who Ella Jones is. That's enough."

We board the escalator. All eyes turn to Tim Hefflin, silently wondering what *he* is going to do with his newfound notoriety. He fumbles with the bag on his shoulder.

"My agent says there's interest in me writing another book," Hefflin says, "It could be about what happened to James. I, uh, I'm going to do some research for this one."

Ella puts a hand on Hefflin's shoulder. He looks away, so we won't see him blushing. We come off the escalator and turn toward the departure gate. This is as far as we can go with Ella and Hefflin. It's a weird parting. We've been through a lot together and yet, there wasn't the kind of trust that breeds closeness. How do you handle a situation like that? (Social niceties can be a real bitch.) Mike slides Ella's suitcase over to her. There's a moment where their hands touch on the handle. They look at each other, but don't say anything. They part. Ella smiles at the rest of us.

"Take care of yourselves," she says.

"You as well," I say.

Lars bows toward Ella and Hefflin. "I hope you'll return for another convention."

Ella's smile fades slightly. Hefflin mumbles something like, "Fat fucking chance." Ella taps the handle of her luggage.

"I'm certainly willing to consider it," she says, "It's been a very…*interesting* time."

"We aim to please," Lars says.

We exchange a few more pleasantries. Then Ella turns toward Hefflin and gestures toward the departure gate.

"Shall we?" she asks.

Hefflin offers his arm. "Sounds like a plan."

Ella takes Hefflin's arm and they walk to the departure gate. The rest of us turn back to the escalators. Just before we get there, we nearly bump into someone. Turns out to be someone we're familiar with.

"Kelly Smart," I say, "On your way back to L.A.?"

Smart is as thrilled to see us as she would be to get an STD. "Yes," she says, struggling to control an oversized backpack, "Can't wait to get back."

"There's a lot of that going around," I say, "You got enough for your article?"

"I guess," Smart says, "It won't be the greatest I've ever written." She gives me a contemptuous look. "Somebody decided to make all the best information public."

She wants me to feel guilty, but I couldn't care less. "Sorry," I say, without an ounce of sincerity.

"I wouldn't bother reading it if I were you," Smart says, "It won't have too many kind things to say about this city. Or it's police force."

I can't help wincing. I don't like Sergeant Pike, but I don't want to see him held up for ridicule, either. "I guess things didn't work out with Sergeant Pike?" I say.

Smart clucks her tongue, disgusted. "Last time I sleep with someone just to get information. Probably." She looks around, disdainful, and spots something that gets her attention. "Is that Tim Hefflin over there?"

I follow her gaze. Hefflin is digging through his coat, probably looking for his boarding pass. "That's him," I say.

Smart's eyes light up, "He must have an interesting story. With the James Queen thing. We're on the same flight."

"You know that for sure?" I ask.

"Oh, it'll happen," Smart says. Her phone buzzes. She looks at the caller ID and rolls her eyes. "Him again. Decent guy, but clingy as fuck."

She sticks the phone in her pocket and sashays off. I should probably warn Hefflin, but I've gotten involved enough with these people. He'll have to figure this one out on his own.

We ride down the escalator and back toward the parking garage. As we descend, Carol looks at me and nods toward Mike. She wants me to ask him something. I've been nominated Chief Buttinski. (That's okay. I probably would have taken the job myself.)

"Nice to see Ella in such good spirits," I say.

"It is," Mike says.

"I'm going to miss her."

Mike keeps his eyes on the bottom of the escalator. "Me too."

"But I suppose you'll stay in touch with her," I say, "I assume you guys exchanged, uh, contact information."

My voice quavers. I'm on the brink of doing the *Nudge, Nudge, Wink, Wink* sketch from *Monty Python*. Mike steps off the escalator and turns toward us.

"Is there something you want to ask me?" he says.

I'm hoping one of the others jumps in. But there's no sign of that. Ah, this wouldn't be a gathering of friends if I weren't getting hung out to dry.

"I wanted to ask you about Ella," I say.

Mike sticks his hands in his coat pockets. "You want to know if I slept with her."

"I know it's none of my business," I say, fidgeting, "But I can't help wondering what was going on."

Mike lays a hand on my shoulder. "You're right," he says, "It *is* none of your business."

With that, he heads down the concourse. I can't blame Mike. We've swapped enough stories of sexual escapades over the years. He's entitled to keep this one to himself. Even if it's killing me. Speaking of sexual escapades and things that are killing me, Carol turns the spotlight my direction.

"Have you heard from Casey?" she asks.

"Nope," I say, "I tried calling her, but I got her voicemail. I sent her a few texts. Nothing. I thought about stopping by Jitters, but I've lost enough dignity in this deal." I slip my hands in my pockets. "I guess this one's lost to the ages."

I keep my eyes on the floor. I don't want to see the looks of pity. Blowing my second chance with Casey is bad enough. Having everybody know about it (again!) makes it worse. It will take me a while to live this one down.

We pile into the elevator for the parking garage. I hit the button for the top floor. We've got our own special parking space up there. Mike turns to Carol.

"What happened with the wedding?" he asks.

"It's off," Carol says, "Irreconcilable differences."

Lars glides to Carol's side. "What kind of differences?"

"They both like me," she says, "And I don't like them. Like I said, irreconcilable."

I hold up a finger. "Really, it's a three-way irreconcilability."

"Whatever," Carol says, "Alan, the groom, keeps calling me. Chris decided to take the honeymoon on her own. Hopefully, she'll start speaking to me again when she comes home. But she almost certainly won't."

"At least you got out of that hideous dress," I say.

Carol mumbles, "In more ways than one."

Judging by the horrified look on her face, she didn't intend to say that last part out loud. The rest of us look at her, waiting for an explanation. She blows out a sigh.

"The reception was supposed to be at the University Club," she says, "Obviously, the happy couple weren't going to be there, but the rest of the wedding party figured, what the hell? Why let the place go to waste? We went there to get drunk and forget the wedding ever happened. I started talking with Walt, one of the groomsmen. We, uh, we hit it off. *Really* hit it off."

Normally, Mike greets talk of Carol with another guy by issuing a low growling sound. This time, though, he simply asks, "What happened?"

Carol plays with her bangs, pulling some hair over her face. "We went back to his place and things got…friendly. But not for long."

"What do you mean 'not for long'?" I ask.

She levels me with a look. "I mean, 'not for long,' Joe. You of all people should know."

Lars cringes. Mike bites a knuckle to keep from laughing. Carol folds her arms. I stare at my feet.

"That's…awkward," I say.

"No doubt," Carol says, "Walt just sat there, close-mouthed, until I finally got dressed and got the hell out of there. Great night."

"It happens," I say.

Mike snorts. "Not to all of us."

Oh, one of these days…

The elevator doors open on the top level of the parking ramp. We walk down a long row of parking spaces to a private space near the end. A canvas construct screens it from view. Mike leads the way around. We stop to admire the view. The Nightmobile gleams in the autumn sunlight. Mike tosses the keys in the air and snatches them with a flourish.

"Our chariot awaits," he says, gliding to the driver's side door.

Carol follows him. "How long is Manny going to let you borrow this?"

"Until I can get it back to his trailer," he says, hopping over the driver's door.

"And how long will that be?" Lars asks.

Mike frowns. "Probably ten minutes after I drop you guys off. Depending on whether I take one last joyride. His trailer is waiting over by Allianz Field."

I move toward the passenger door. "But you're going to take that joyride."

"Most definitely," Mike says.

I slide into the passenger seat. Lars and Carol wedge themselves into the back. Lars's knees are up near his head. Carol tries to keep what distance she can from Lars. Mike turns the ignition and the car roars to life. Maybe it doesn't go all that fast, but it sounds like a powerhouse. Mike's hands glide over the wheel.

"A dream come true," he says, fairly purring.

Carol pokes her head between me and Mike. "At least one thing didn't disillusion you."

"Nothing to be disillusioned about," Mike says, "It's just a TV show. But I love it."

Mike throws the car into reverse and the Nightmobile shoots out of the parking spot. He reaches into his coat and pulls out a pair of shades.

"What do you think, pal?" he asks.

I brace myself against the dashboard. "Let's roll."

"Back to the Nightplex," he says, "and home."

Mike punches the gas pedal. The Nightmobile squeals toward the front entrance of the parking garage. We can't go on the freeway, but we can zip through the city streets. Sure, Carol will mock us, and Lars will offer some ridiculous suggestion. But Mike and I will ignore them. We'll be too deep in the fantasy to care.

Pretty much the story of our lives, no?

THE (LIVING) END…?

Randall J. Funk is the writer of the Joe Davis Mystery series. He is also an actor, director and playwright. His plays include *The Hound of the Baskervilles*, *The Mudslinger Party*, and *Bring Me The Head of Dominic Papatola*. He lives in St. Louis Park, MN, with his son Ben.